THE SEARCH

Also by Shelley Shepard Gray

Sisters of the Heart series
HIDDEN
WANTED
FORGIVEN
GRACE

Seasons of Sugarcreek series
WINTER'S AWAKENING
SPRING'S RENEWAL
AUTUMN'S PROMISE
CHRISTMAS IN SUGARCREEK

Families of Honor
THE CAREGIVER
THE PROTECTOR
THE SURVIVOR

The Secrets of Crittenden County
MISSING

THE SEARCH

The Secrets of Crittenden County

Book Two

SHELLEY SHEPARD GRAY

AVON

INSPIRE

An Imprint of HarperCollins*Publishers*

THE SEARCH. Copyright © 2012 by Shelley Shepard Gray. Excerpt from *Found* © 2012 by Shelley Shepard Gray. All rights reserved. Printed in the United States of America. No part of this book may be used or reproduced in any manner whatsoever without written permission except in the case of brief quotations embodied in critical articles and reviews. For information address HarperCollins Publishers, 10 East 53rd Street, New York, NY 10022.

HarperCollins books may be purchased for educational, business, or sales promotional use. For information please write: Special Markets Department, HarperCollins Publishers, 10 East 53rd Street, New York, NY 10022.

FIRST EDITION

Library of Congress Cataloging-in-Publication Data has been applied for.

ISBN 978–0–06–208972–4

12 13 14 15 16   OV/RRD   10 9 8 7 6 5 4 3 2 1

*To fellow Amish authors Amy Clipston and
Vannetta Chapman, the best touring buddies ever.
Thank you both for the laughs and the smiles and
the endless inspiration. I have so much to learn from
you both.*

I have learned, in whatsoever state I am, therewith to be content.

Philippians 4:11

Though no one can go back and make a brand new start, anyone can start from now and make a brand new end.

Amish Proverb

Prologue

"I'd love to say drugs are never a problem in Crittenden County. I'd love to say it, but it wouldn't be true."

MOSE KRAMER

December 31

Perry Borntrager had been taking drugs again.

Frannie Eicher had suspected it when she first spied his glazed expression, then had known it for sure when she heard his slurred words. Now, here she was, alone with him on the outskirts of the Millers' property. Not a soul knew where she was, or that once again she was meeting him in secret in a place where they weren't supposed to be at all.

Oh, she was sure he wouldn't hurt her. Perry wasn't dangerous. But knowing that they were completely alone, that no one would hear if she cried out for help, was unsettling.

Especially since at the moment Perry wasn't acting like himself.

The Perry she'd known all her life had been patient. Methodical. Years ago, he'd been slow to smile and even slower to frown. Everyone far and near had agreed that he was a good man. A man who was easy to get along with, a steady kind of man.

That was not the case anymore.

"Glad you finally made it." His voice was snide, clipped.

"I'm sorry I'm late," she said. "I had a terrible time getting out of the inn—everyone wanted 'just one more thing.'" Frannie smiled sheepishly. Then waited, half hoping he'd take her bait and ask about her cherished bed-and-breakfast.

He didn't.

"It didn't matter if you came on time or not. Nothing would change my feelings. I hate it here. I always have." A low laugh erupted from his chest. "But you knew that, right?" He was walking somewhat unsteadily. In a zigzag way. As if he was having trouble placing his feet just so on the uneven ground beneath them.

"You hate being here at the Millers' farm?" she joked as she struggled to keep up with his awkward pace.

He didn't realize she was kidding. *"Jah,"* he said over his shoulder as they approached the abandoned well on the edge of the property. "The Millers' farm, Marion, Crittenden County. Kentucky . . ." His voice grew louder. More hostile. "What's the difference, anyway? I hate it all."

She stopped a few feet away from him. Where it was safe. She did remind herself, though, that he would never hurt her. "If you don't like it here, what are you going to do?"

"Get away when I can."

She shouldn't have been shocked, but she was. "And go where?"

"I don't know. Anywhere. Someplace else." Slumping against the stacked rocks that surrounded the top of the well, he looked at her contemptuously. "What about you, Frannie? Don't you want to get away?" The cold air made his breath appear like little puffs in the sky. It also made her aware of how cold she was.

And how much colder their relationship had become.

She felt his gaze skim her whole body, as if he was looking at her from the top of her black bonnet covering her *kapp* to the toe of her black tennis shoes, and had found her wanting. "I've never thought about leaving here," she said hesitantly, trying to negotiate the conversation that made no sense at all. "Crittenden County is home. Besides, I just took over the Yellow Bird Inn." Unable to stop herself, she added, "I refinished the wood floors, you know, and it looks so pretty . . ."

Perry merely stared.

She swallowed. "Um. I . . . I could never leave it."

"You could never leave it." His blank stare turned deriding. "That inn ain't nothing special."

She'd spent the last month helping two men paint the outside a wonderful, buttery yellow. The yellow color went so much better with the name of the inn than the black-and-white paint ever did. The Yellow Bird Inn needed yellow paint, surely.

Because it was a special place. And very special to her. "One day it might be."

He spit on the ground. "It's not going to make any money. No one comes here unless they have to."

She fought to keep her expression neutral. To pretend he hadn't hurt her feelings. "My great aunt seemed to do all right with it. And some people have come to visit and stay." Lifting her chin, she said, "Why, just the other day an English couple all the way from Indianapolis said they'd tell their church friends about my B&B."

His voice turned darker. "The only reason the English come here is look at the Amish."

"They come for the scenery and the greenhouses, too." She bit her lip. "We are blessed to live in such a pretty place, you know. Why, we are surrounded by trees and hills and valleys."

He laughed softly. "Frannie, you need to get your head out of the clouds. The English come here to gawk. To take our pictures with their camera phones." His voice deepened. "You're not going to make any money. You ought to leave that place."

"And do what?"

His mouth opened, then shut again quickly. Like he was having difficulty forming his thoughts.

She waited. As she stood there, her toes began to burn from the cold ground. Her eyes watered from the brisk wind.

Oh, how she wished Perry would act like himself again. When they'd begun to court, she'd been well aware of his problems. But since they'd known each other all their lives, she'd been sure that she could change him back to how he used to be.

If he'd only try just a little bit.

"The guys I've been working with, they've promised me big things," Perry finally said, his voice strained tight with emotion. "You . . . you could come with me. If you changed."

If she changed? Frannie knew that the men he'd been working with were *Englischers*. *Englischers* of the worst sort. They weren't local. They only came to their area with the intent of causing trouble, of encouraging more people to take the drugs Perry was now so fond of.

"I don't want to be different, Perry." Feeling her way through the conversation, she looked beyond him, looked into the dense, lush woods on the outskirts of the Millers' property. "I like it here. And I like how I am."

And though she didn't want to be prideful, she felt disappointed that he didn't see her attributes. Most boys had found her pale blue-gray eyes and auburn hair pleasing. Most people found her effort to take over the bed-and-breakfast once her aunt got sick to be commendable.

It was obvious he did not.

"Let's be honest, Frannie. You are stuck in an old boardinghouse in the middle of a county down on its luck."

She gritted her teeth. "Perhaps." And smiled slightly, determined not to let him see how nervous she was becoming. "But I don't think it's so bad. I mean, I like to look on the bright side of things, for sure. I'm still the same Frannie I've always been."

For a moment, his gaze softened. Just like he, too, remembered how they'd once played tag in each other's yards after church. How they'd been friends before he'd ever courted Lydia. Before he'd finally looked her way with a new appreciation, as if she hadn't been there all along just waiting for him to notice.

But then he blinked. "You aren't the same. Just like me, you've changed over the years. Don't deny it. Change always happens. It can't be helped."

"People do change, that is true." She bit her lip. How much did she want to say when he was in this condition?

But she was tired of tiptoeing around him. Didn't her heart mean anything? Didn't her soul and desires count just as much as his feelings did?

"Perry, I don't want you to move away. And I don't like the men you've been keeping company with. I wish you'd move on—" She ached to tell him more, to beg him to seek help.

But his thunderous response stopped all that.

"What are you? My mother?"

"Of course not," she said quickly.

His gaze darkened. "I don't need another mother, Frannie. One nagging woman in my life is more than enough."

"I know. I mean, I know that, Perry. I'm only offering my opinion. That's all."

"Don't."

There was a new anger in his voice, and she knew she'd put it there. It was time to go. Perry had chosen his path and he certainly wasn't going to change it for her.

He wasn't going to tell those *Englischers* goodbye. Maybe the drugs weren't ever going to loosen their grip on him.

She stepped backward. "I'm going to go home now."

"Alone?"

"*Jah*. I . . . I think it's best. I mean, I don't think we have much more to say to each other."

He stared at her for a long moment, then held up his hand. "Hold on. I . . . I brought something for you." He fumbled in a pocket in his coat, then pulled out a pair of sunglasses. "These are for you."

Walking to his side, she took his gift. "You brought me sunglasses?" She couldn't imagine a more peculiar thing for him to give her. Especially on such a cloudy, wintery day.

"Yeah. They're nice, ain't so? Expensive, too. Cameron, one of my friends from Louisville, picked them up for me. He got two pairs." He threw off the comment, just as if she were no more important to him than an afterthought.

She was confused. He'd brought her men's sunglasses, given to him from one of his drug-dealing friends? Holding them up in front of her face, she turned them this way and that. "Whatever would I do with them?"

"Wear them, of course." His voice grew impatient. "Try them on, Frannie."

They were only sunglasses. Though it wasn't the norm for Amish to wear sunglasses, it wasn't unheard of, either.

But these sunglasses looked expensive. And worldly. These screamed English and were built for a man's face, not her own.

They seemed to stand for everything she was not.

And right then and there, she knew she couldn't accept them.

Every time she looked at them, they'd symbolize everything that was wrong with them. With her. With Perry.

"I don't want them."

"You're not even going to try them on? What's wrong, Frannie? Afraid you're going to get tainted?" His voice was loud now—loud enough to reverberate around them.

But there was no one to overhear.

She stepped farther back. "I just don't want them." Holding out her hands, she attempted to give them back. "You should keep them."

His eyes narrowed. Then, to her great surprise, he stepped back. "*Nee.*"

Oh, she hated when he acted like this! "Perry, please—"

"If you don't want them, get rid of them yourself."

She was so frustrated, so hurt, so mad at herself for continually thinking she could make a difference to him, she did what he suggested. In one swift motion, she tossed the glasses into the woods. Frannie followed their path with a lump in her throat. And immediately felt guilty.

"I'm sorry. I'll go fetch them. I shouldn't have done that."

He stopped her with a firm grip on her arm. "No, let them be. If you don't want them, I don't, either. We'll leave them for the Millers. Maybe their cows can use them." He grinned at his joke.

She shivered at his dark tone. Who had Perry become? With a jerk, she pulled her arm from his grasp. "I'm going to leave now."

"*Jah*. I think you should. Go, Frannie. Go on, now."

She stepped backward, relieved to be leaving him, but so disappointed about his troubles. "Maybe we can get you some help—"

"I don't need *help*, Frannie. And I don't need you. Just go. And let's hope we never see each other ever again."

She turned. And headed home.

And realized as she heard his laugh behind her that finally . . . finally they had something in common.

She, too, hoped she'd never see him again.

But of course, she doubted she would ever be that lucky.

Chapter 1

"Perry and I kissed one time. Once was enough."

FRANNIE EICHER

Three months later . . .

Frannie Eicher didn't sleep at night. Actually, she didn't sleep that much during the day, either.

It was becoming something of a problem.

She didn't try to stay awake on purpose; it was just that sometime over the last couple of weeks, it had become a habit. One night, she hadn't been tired and read for hours. Once she'd realized it was past two in the morning, Frannie turned off her light and closed her eyes.

Nothing happened. She didn't relax, didn't yawn. Didn't feel that comforting blanket of sleep begin to descend. Instead, guilt would creep slowly into the forefront of her mind.

And then while the red numbers on her battery-operated digital clock flickered and changed, she'd start to remember her transgressions.

Until the sun began its morning climb up to the horizon.

The following evening, the same thing happened.

By the fourth night, she'd almost begun to accept insomnia as part of her life. Kind of like praying during the morning sunrise and doing wash on Tuesdays.

The good news was that she now had a very small to-be-read pile of books on her bedside table. The bad news, of course, was that she felt permanently tired. Her muscles ached, her head pounded. She'd begun to have small, silly accidents.

Her concentration would waver.

None of these things were welcome. She was a single woman running her own business. When her bed-and-breakfast was filled with guests, she needed to be at her best in order for everything to get done.

Everything was not getting done.

Every so often, her brain would listen to her body and she'd instantly fall asleep, wherever she might be. Sometimes it would be at her desk; she'd awaken with a crick in her neck and a drool spot on the papers she was reading—and a fresh wave of embarrassment, too. No one wanted to be seen passed out in public with one's mouth open wide.

Other times Frannie would fall asleep on the couch when she was working on her mending. Right in plain sight of all her guests!

She'd wake up besieged by feelings of guilt warring with the delicious sensation of finally feeling refreshed.

All in all, her insomnia was becoming a difficult secret to keep.

Especially from her best friend, Beth.

"Frannie, maybe you should go to a chiropractor," she said as they pressed dough into tiny pastry molds for the mini quiches that Frannie liked to serve with fruit and muffins at breakfast.

"A chiropractor?" Frannie turned to her in surprise. She'd never thought of her friend as one who would be needing a chiropractor. To one and all, Beth was always happy and healthy. A joy to be around. "My back is just fine."

"I've heard chiropractors can do wonders with other parts of your body, too. And Dr. Collins is a *gut doktah*, for sure." As she smoothed more dough in her hands, she added, "You know, he helped Katie and Mary John with their stomach ailments. Cleansed their colons, it did."

Frannie privately thought a better diet would have helped Katie and Mary's stomach problems years ago. She almost blurted her thoughts, but held her tongue. Detective Reynolds's criticisms about her tendency to stick her nose into places it didn't belong still stung.

Beth seemed to take her silence as an invitation to talk some more. "If Dr. Collins can help Katie and Mary John, he could surely help you, too. Maybe even help your sleeping problems."

She knew what her problem was, and it wasn't likely to be solved by a doctor's visit. But of course, she couldn't tell Beth that. So she kept the conversation easy. "You think I have a sleeping problem?"

"Sure you do. No one should be as tired as you are, Frannie. You've got circles under your eyes like a raccoon."

Almost against her will, Frannie touched the tender skin under her eyes with some dismay. "I have circles?"

Never one to temper bad news, Beth nodded. "Dark ones."

Frannie cleared her throat. "If things don't get back to normal soon, maybe I'll talk to the *doktah*. But for now, I'll keep trying to rest when I can. I'm a busy innkeeper, you know."

"If things don't change, something bad's going to happen."

"Something bad has already happened. Perry's body was discovered in a well." Sheriff Kramer had called in Luke Reynolds, a city detective from Cincinnati, to investigate, and now the whole county was up in arms. He'd been staying at her B&B until he'd discovered she'd kept her relationship with Perry from him. He felt he could no longer stay there, as it was a conflict of interest.

Looking more and more distraught, Beth added, "I mean, something bad is going to happen to you." Beth made a show of looking Frannie up and down. "I know you've lost weight. And you seem far more tense than usual. If you're not careful, you're going to fall apart soon."

"I don't have a choice. This is my business and I have guests to take care of."

"But someone needs to take care of you." She snapped her fingers. "Maybe your *daed* could help out some?"

"You know my father wasn't happy with me taking this inn over from my aunt. I promised him I wouldn't bother him with the business. That is one promise I intend to keep."

"He is a good and kind man, Frannie. I bet he will change his mind once he knows what a time you're having."

"I don't intend for him to find out."

"He won't like that you're keeping secrets, Frannie."

Frannie loved her father very much. For all her life, she'd enjoyed a good and peaceful relationship with him. They'd gotten closer when her mother passed away after battling pancreatic cancer. After her sister got married and moved to Michigan, they'd become a little family of two, doing things together and helping each other with chores. Never had he openly disagreed with her.

Until she defied him by accepting her great aunt's gift. And though she felt bad for not abiding by her father's wishes, she felt the pull to step forward into her new venture even more. It felt like God had put the bed-and-breakfast opportunity in her hands, and that she needed to listen and follow His will.

Her father hadn't seen God's guiding hand in her new undertaking at all. Instead he'd wanted her to refuse the gift and continue to stay home, waiting to be married one day. Their few conversations about it hadn't ended well. And so, typical of them, they'd decided to agree to disagree. As long as Frannie wasn't expecting any help from him.

Since she'd taken over the inn, four months ago, she'd kept her promise.

"Beth, he's a shy man, and a man much more comfortable with sheep and cows than with people, especially English people. I cannot ask him for help."

"If you don't ask him, I hope you will allow someone to help you. No one can live on no sleep, you know. I read about sleep problems when I was sitting in the waiting room at the dentist the other day. Scientists have studied situations like this. Someone is going to get hurt. Probably you. Then what will happen to your inn?"

"Beth," she said with exaggerated patience. "It's not like I'm not trying to sleep. It's just that when I put my head down at night, my eyes pop open and my mind speeds up. Suddenly sleep is the last thing I can do."

After a long moment, Beth clucked her tongue. "You should talk to Micah about it."

Frannie jerked her head so fast, she was surprised it hadn't wrenched from her neck. "What does Micah have to do with anything?"

"He's sweet on you. Has been forever."

"Not forever. Not exactly."

"All right. He has been for almost forever. For most of your life."

Except when Perry had been courting her.

"I'm not ready to see Micah again."

"No? Well, all right, then." After finishing her pan of twelve, Beth sighed and grabbed another muffin tin and began filling more cups. "I can't believe we make sixty of these at a time," she grumbled.

"When I make sixty, I have enough pastries for a few days," she explained patiently. "I do appreciate your help."

"It's no trouble. I just wish we could figure out why you can't sleep. If we got to the root of the problem, I bet you'll get some rest again."

Frannie nodded, but she felt as if her insides were ripping apart.

Because, well, she knew exactly why she couldn't sleep. It was the same reason she couldn't see Micah. It was the reason she felt guilty and anxious. And why she looked at everything and everyone in the county in a new way.

All because of Perry Borntrager.

Her memories of the last time she saw him caused her to ache. So did his murder. And the investigation.

"I'll start putting the filling inside the pastry cups," she said briskly, picking up the antique glass bowl that her aunt had left to her as an "innkeeper gift."

"Frannie, be careful, that glass bowl is so old and fragile."

"You've become such a worrywart, Beth! I use this bowl all the time." She held it up to show how well she managed it.

Which was a foolish thing to do, for sure.

No sooner had she lifted the bowl to show off—

The bowl slipped out of her hands as if it had been coated with oil, crashing onto the hard tile countertop.

The old glass was thin. Thin and delicate. When it hit, the bowl shattered into a hundred—if not thousand pieces— each shard sharp and dangerous. And somehow, the majority of the glass bounced off the countertop and took aim at her. Flying right into her face.

All at once, a thousand needles pricked her skin and sent waves of pain throughout her body. Shock engulfed her.

She stood frozen, confused, dazed.

Immediately, her skin felt wet, and instinctively she knew it was from blood, not tears . . . because one of her eyes felt covered in glass.

The pain was unbearable.

Finally, her sluggish brain kicked in and reported the news to her mouth. She cried out, raised her hands up to her face— Too late!

Instead of creating a shield, her hands only served to embed some shards deeper.

It seemed so, anyway, because that was what she felt as the whole room turned dark. And whether it from the pain or the glass, she wasn't sure.

As she sank to the ground, she was only vaguely aware of Beth's cries for help.

And that, though she'd done her best to go on with her life with no sleep, perhaps Beth had been right.

A person without sleep could only last so long without consequences.

From the other side of their table at Mary King's, Mose Kramer glared hard and long at Luke. Then he spoke.

"Luke, if you want more hot water than I can provide, you should have never left Frannie's bed-and-breakfast."

"Mose, you need to take care of the basics," Luke said as he picked up his fork and took another bite of the roasted chicken on his plate. "You know . . . all you have to do is pay your bills. Electricity. Gas."

"Those are taken care of. And that old water heater worked just fine for one person." The look he sent Luke was priceless. It told, without a doubt, that he thought Luke was complaining far too much. "Settle down, eat, and then we'll go back to my place."

"Settle down?"

Mose lifted his chin. "Again, if you don't want my company, you should go back to Frannie's."

"You know I can't stay there any longer. She was one of the last people to see Perry alive. Because of that, she's a suspect, or at least a person of interest."

Mose rolled his eyes. "Miss Frannie's as much a suspect in Perry Borntrager's murder as you are."

"I'd say she's got more of a motive than I do, Mose. She was seeing him when he died."

"That don't mean much. Frannie sees just about everybody. That's her way." Primly folding his hands on the table between them, Mose added, "She's an innkeeper, you know."

"You, Mose, are a piece of work." Luke was sure he was going to strangle his old friend before he ever got out of Crittenden County.

Mose chuckled as he dug back into his own plate of food. As the minutes passed and their stomachs grew full, the investigation surfaced again.

"You should forget about Frannie Eicher."

"I can't, and you know that. She and Perry were courting." Luke put emphasis on *courting*, pushing away the thought that the antiquated word now seemed to be a viable part of his vocabulary.

"Courting don't mean everything you seem to think it does, English."

Luke bit back a caustic comment, afraid that with the way he was feeling about his friend he was going to make things worse between them. Already their friendship was becoming strained as he remained in Crittenden County much longer than planned. Plus now he was staying with Mose in his already cramped quarters.

He'd arrived in Marion a little over two weeks ago, intending to put his skills as a detective with the Cincinnati Police Department to good use while he recuperated from a bullet wound. His friend Mose had asked him to help uncover the secrets that surrounded the death of Perry Borntrager. Mose had felt he was too close to the community to get many honest answers, and adding to that was his inexperience dealing with homicides.

Luke, full of pride with his experience in Cincinnati, imagined the whole investigation would only take a few days at the most.

He'd been wrong.

It seemed there were more secrets about Perry than lightning bugs at night. The case was proving to be both frustrating and curiously humbling.

Until he'd found a pair of sunglasses at the crime scene. He shook his head, remembering that moment.

He'd returned to the Millers' land again, hoping that another walk in the field where Perry's body was found would reveal a new clue or, at the very least, clear his mind. The ground was dry for once, and as Luke crunched through the grass, a swarm of cicadas began to cry, their shrill humming piercing the air, growing in volume until a man could hardly think about anything else.

He walked on, finally taking a seat where Abby Anderson had said she'd smoked a cigarette and tried to fit in with the wrong crowd.

Closing his eyes, he tried to imagine what the scene had been like, back when someone had taken a young man's life, carted him across this field, and dumped him in a well.

He tried to imagine what the guys who'd done it had been thinking. Were they angry?

Just doing a job?

Looking off into the distance, he mentally traced a path from the woods, to the area where Mose had decided they'd carried him.

He started walking. Looking around for stones, trash, anything else that could provide enlightenment. Soon after, he tripped, wrenching his leg.

As he fell on his backside, he gasped and silently cursed, wishing his leg would finally work.

Getting up to his feet wasn't easy. He was going to be back on crutches and icing his knee all night to help with the swelling.

Well, this was probably no less than he deserved, out here by himself. Rolling to his side, he braced himself on his hands, trying to balance his weight so he could get up.

Doing all this, he almost missed the pair of black sunglasses just inches from his right hand. Scooting over, he grabbed a handkerchief from his back pocket, then picked them up.

Black Oakleys. Expensive. Maybe they wouldn't stand out somewhere like Boulder, Colorado, or Miami. But in a rural place like Crittenden County? . . . They would have stood out like a cop from Cincinnati.

It was his first real break, he was sure of it then. Though, he had no idea whose they were . . . not Frannie Eicher's, of course.

The glasses belonged to someone, but Luke wasn't holding his breath. Too much time had passed already. It was very likely that any number of people could have left a pair of expensive designer sunglasses behind. However, his gut had told him he was on to something.

He leaned back in his chair. "Any chance you've sent those sunglasses to the lab to be checked for fingerprints?"

Mose eyed him over his pair of reading glasses. "I told ya I did, Luke. Just like I told ya I went around and got finger-print samples of most everyone who'd ever talked to Perry in his lifetime."

Luke felt his neck heat up. He would've never asked his partner in Cincinnati if he'd actually done what he'd said he was going to. "Sorry. I just want to do things right."

"I do too, Luke." Mose took a breath, looking about to remind Luke that he wasn't a fool, when his cell phone went off.

After checking the screen, Mose answered, turning all business.

When Luke spied the look of concern on his old friend's features, he pushed aside his apology and got ready to lend assistance.

"You sure?" Mose asked after a moment. "They need help? All righty, then. Keep me posted." After he hung up, he leveled a glance Luke's way. "Well, speak of the devil."

"What happened?"

"That was Melissa, the dispatcher. Have you met her? Kind of a large woman. President of the PTA?"

Mose could talk a gnat's ear off, if gnats had ears. "What *happened*, Mose?"

"Melissa just heard from Jason Black. He's an ambulance driver, you know—"

"I don't know Jason or Melissa." Mose's slow way of talking, combined with his penchant for sharing stories about everyone and their brother was driving him crazy. "*What. Do. You. Know?*"

"Oh. Jason's driving Frannie Eicher to the hospital right now."

Immediately, Luke feared the worst. "Did someone hurt her? Does this have something to do with Perry's death?"

Mose shook his head. "Oh, no. She was involved in a kitchen accident. She owns the bed and breakfast, you know . . ."

"I know! Of course, I know! Is she okay?"

"That I do not know." Mose brushed a hand over his face. "Jason said she looks bad. Well, her face does."

"Why?"

"It seems that a glass or something shattered, and the pieces flew into her face. There was blood everywhere." He paused. "Jason said a couple of the shards got an eye real good. It might be nothing, but you never know, ain't so?"

Mose only used an Amish expression like that when he was rattled, which only heightened Luke's worry.

His stay at Frannie's Yellow Bird Inn had been frustrating. Frannie had been so eager and attentive, he'd felt stifled. They'd definitely butted heads a time or two. But when she'd admitted to dating Perry briefly, he'd moved out. It had been the right thing to do.

Yet, even though they'd had their differences, he couldn't ignore the many attractive things about her. She was inquisitive and caring, and would have been downright cover-model pretty if she'd been the type of woman to care about such things. Thinking about her beautiful face covered in cuts made his breath catch.

"I bet she's in a lot of pain. Does she have family? Did anyone go in the ambulance with her?"

"Family? Well now, let's see. She has an older sister who lives in Michigan, and her father is here in Marion. Jason said most likely Frannie will be in surgery after they admit her to the hospital. In a little while, I'll stop by her father's house and see if he wants a ride." He paused and looked at Luke. "Hey, you want to go with us?"

Luke knew he couldn't wait for Mose to finish his meal, talk to Frannie's father, and then meander to the hospital.

The panic that mixed in with the dismay that was bubbling forward was as much of a surprise as the news. "I need to go there now."

Mose waved a hand. "It wasn't a crime. Like I said, just an accident. There's no investigating needed. Guess Frannie was talking with Beth Byler when it happened. Hey, do you know Beth? Her real name is Elizabeth, but I'm sure I don't know anyone who calls her by that." He drummed his fingers on the table again. "Maybe her mother?"

Mose's rambling was going to send him over the edge. Luke stood up. "Which hospital?"

"Our only hospital, of course. Crittenden County Hospital. It's on West Gum." His face went slack as he caught sight of Luke's determined expression. "You're really going to go over there? Right this minute?"

Luke was already putting on his rain slicker. "I am. I've got to get over there as soon as possible."

"Why?"

Luke didn't know why. All he knew was that if Frannie Eicher was going into surgery, he didn't want her to be alone.

"I just do." While Mose continued to study him like he'd just presented him with another mystery, Luke turned and walked out the door.

Chapter 2

"Sure I knew that Frannie hoped Perry was the right man for her. But he wasn't. Never would he have been good enough for Frannie."

BETH BYLER

With her heart in her throat, Elizabeth Byler—Beth to her friends—watched the ambulance carry Frannie away. As the sirens blared and the bright blue and red lights flashed down Main Street, she stood on the front porch and prayed for both Frannie's well-being and the emergency workers' patience and abilities.

All of them would have to be at their best. Frannie was in a terrible way, for sure. Though the EMTs had checked her pulse and heartbeat and had started an IV drip, they had done little else.

Well, as far as Beth could tell.

After they'd very gingerly put Frannie on a stretcher, then carefully carried her to the ambulance, Beth asked why they hadn't done more for Frannie's hurt face.

"We can't take a chance on making things worse, miss," a

burly man in a crisp white shirt explained. "We want to wait for the surgeons at the hospital."

What he said made sense. But as she was standing off to the side while the EMTs efficiently packed up the ambulance, she heard them whisper. And with each technical word and warning, the knot in her stomach grew bigger.

She figured it wasn't going to take a surgeon to determine that things with Frannie's right eye were really bad. There was a good size cut on the outside of it and a whole lot of swelling, too.

After the siren's blare faded, and she said goodbye to the few neighbors who had run up to see what was the matter, she went back inside Frannie's little yellow bed-and-breakfast. When she closed the heavy oak door behind her, she sighed, strangely discomfited by the sudden silence. With Frannie, one never had to worry too much about things being quiet.

Frannie was a gregarious sort, to be sure. Pleasant to be around, ready with an easy smile and conversation. Perfect for the host of a B&B.

With some dismay, she was reminded of just how different Frannie's manner was from her own. With children, she felt always easy and free, full of laughter.

With adults, though, she'd always been far more reserved.

"Well, you don't need to be good at chatting with strangers to be good at cleaning," Beth chided herself. In the midst of the commotion, she'd promised she'd hold down the fort until Frannie could come back. She was determined to keep her promise even though she didn't have the first idea of what to do to keep things running.

A quick search located some kitchen gloves. After her hands were protected, she got to work picking up large pieces of glass, sweeping up shards, and wiping up the blood that seemed to have spattered everywhere.

Not wanting to risk the food, she threw all the mini quiches, cooked and uncooked, into the trash. Just thinking about making sixty pastry cups again made her exhausted.

"Well, there's no hope for that," she told herself reasonably as she put out more margarine to make a new batch. Of course, that brought forth a whole new nest of problems. She could cook just about anything . . . as long as she had a recipe.

Did Frannie even use a recipe book? From the time she and Frannie first met, her best friend had cooked well. Not once had Beth paid attention to how Frannie had known what to do. Beth had been as uninterested in Frannie's recipes as Frannie had been in Beth's many babysitting jobs.

But now she didn't have a choice.

Panic surged forward as she felt the Lord gently remind her that sometimes it wasn't the best idea to make promises that were difficult to keep. What was she going to do if she couldn't make those quiches? Or the muffins Frannie was so proud of?

Or the granola? Frannie was mighty proud of her inn's granola, and rightfully so. The granola was a crunchy mixture of brown sugar and oats, raisins, dried cranberries and dates, too. Sweat beaded her brow, showing Beth once again that blood and accidents and ambulances didn't affect her half as much as an empty bowl of granola.

"Hey . . . is everything all right?"

She looked over her shoulder at the English man who leaned against the doorway. He had crystal blue eyes that were peering at her curiously, and an arrogant-looking posture that was in direct contrast with his question. Instead of

looking like he wanted to help, he looked like he was count-
ing on her not being able to do anything.

His arms were crossed over a scruffy-looking T-shirt hanging over a pair of jeans that had a rip in one of the knees.
He was tan and fit and sure of himself. And all at once, he
seemed to symbolize everything that had gone wrong over
the last three hours. *"Nee,"* she finally replied. "I'm afraid
everything is not all right. Frannie had to go to the hospital."

"Frannie?"

"Frannie Eicher. She owns this place." Glaring at him, she
said, "You are a guest here, yes?"

"Oh. I am, but I never paid too much attention to the
woman's name."

"Well, the woman you never paid too much attention to
has gotten hurt."

He scowled. "Hey, I booked the room through the Internet, and got in late last night. We spoke with each other only
long enough for me to give her my credit card and for her
to hand me a key. I wasn't about to start making friends at
midnight."

"Oh. I'm sorry." Feeling rather shrewish, Beth forced herself to explain a little bit. "I'm Beth Byler. I'm a friend of
Frannie Eicher's. I don't know much about her guests." Or
running a bed-and-breakfast, for that matter.

Now that things were smoothed over a bit, he wandered
in, his heavy tan boots looking dusty, but luckily not tracking
any dirt on the freshly mopped floor. "So, is she hurt badly?"

Beth hesitated. What was appropriate to share? She realized that she'd never paid too much attention to how Frannie
dealt with her guests. "I'm afraid she's hurt bad. Some glass
got into her eye. An ambulance carried her away."

"I saw that." He looked around, taking an extra second

or two to stare at the lone stick of butter in the bowl. "So, do you need some help in here? This place looks like it was turned upside down. I can help you clean up, if you really need it."

Perhaps it was his confident tone and the way he said "really." Or because he was pointing out the obvious. Whatever the reason, his offer rubbed her the wrong way. "There's no need to help me clean. You're a guest."

"And you're not?"

"No. Like I said, I'm a friend of Frannie's." The moment she said the words, she wished she could have taken them right back. She sounded prissy and full of herself. As if she was someone's maiden aunt.

He leaned against the doorjamb, making Beth realize that he was a lot younger than she'd first thought. "So how does one become a friend of yours?"

If she hadn't been so stunned at the question she probably would have stood there with her mouth open. But instead, she glared. "What kind of question is that?"

"An honest one."

"Why? Are you looking for friends?"

"Maybe. I just got here. I could use a friend or two."

"As could we all."

"I hope you're not always this suspicious of newcomers. You know I might be here for a while. I'm thinking about moving here permanently."

"Why would you want to do that?"

"Seemed like a good idea," he said, sounding like he was taking great pains to keep purposely vague.

Which she did not appreciate. She was rattled and worried about her friend. And worried about her promise to Frannie. The last thing in the world she needed was a secretive guest who spoke in riddles! "I'm surprised you even found us on the map. We're pretty out of the way."

"You think so?"

"I know so. I mean nothing ever happens here."

"Short of that guy being murdered, huh?"

Her breath caught. No one she knew spoke of Perry—or the mystery surrounding his life and death—unless it was in whispered tones in private.

Or under duress. She shivered. "How do you even know about Perry?"

"Why do you sound so surprised that I brought him up? Is his death a secret?"

"It's just that no one likes to talk about what happened."

"Just want to pretend it didn't happen, do you?"

She couldn't lie. "Sometimes," she said shortly. Wondering selfishly why she'd ever decided to come to Frannie's on a day off, anyway.

Why she'd had to be the one to promise things that she couldn't deliver.

Why she had to be the person volleying words back and forth with a man who was so evasive, it was bordering on scary.

Something flickered in his face. "That's too bad."

"That I don't want to think about Perry's death all the time? I think it's a normal reaction . . . Mr.? . . . I'm sorry I don't know your name."

"That's because I didn't tell you," he replied, turning to leave. Then he paused, just as if he'd suddenly changed his mind. "What do you know about the quarry?"

She froze. "Not much."

"It looks pretty big."

"It's not a part of town that I get to much." But what she didn't say was that her brother spent a lot of time there. Near the entrance to the quarry was an old, abandoned trailer, and that was where Eli used to buy drugs from Perry Borntrager.

Until Perry had gone missing.

Now she didn't know where he bought drugs. He'd taken off to parts unknown and broken her heart.

"What are you not telling me?" His tone had become harder, his easy cadence now clipped.

Making her even more wary.

She hoped he was safe to be around. She wished she didn't feel so awkward and scared, standing alone with him in the kitchen.

"What is it?" he asked. "What is wrong?"

"Not a thing is wrong," she lied. After all, why would she tell this man things she'd never told anyone? "If you don't mind, I'd like you to move along. I have things to bake. Well, things to bake if I can find a recipe book. Dear Lord, please let Frannie have used a recipe book."

Only after he turned away and finally left did she realize that she'd never learned his name. She didn't even know how long he was staying at the inn.

The knot in her stomach hardened, threatening to overtake her. The fear that she'd tried to hold at bay rose as she realized that she didn't know how Frannie was, she couldn't cook very well, and she had no idea what to do next.

"Oh, please get better quick, Frannie," she whispered. "If you don't come back soon, I don't know what is going to happen."

Only after she said her prayers did she allow herself to fear for the worst.

She was now going to be living in the same building as this *Englischer* stranger, who seemed far too interested in things that weren't any of his business.

Chapter 3

"When Perry was twelve, he broke his collarbone jumping out of a hay loft. Until they found his body, I do believe that was the last time he'd been seen by a doctor."

ABRAHAM BORNTRAGER

They called it a corneal obstruction. Through her haze and pain, Frannie was coming to understand that the glass had scratched the surface of her cornea, which was the covering of her eyeball.

It was a painful thing, and an injury that would need to be looked after with care for a bit. But she wouldn't go blind.

The cuts around her eye, however, were another matter. A special eye surgeon was on his way to mend the torn skin at the corner of her right eye and to examine the abrasion on her lid.

Someone had already stitched up the other cuts on her face. Though no one would let her see a mirror, Frannie could feel that her whole face was covered in stitches and bandages. Her face had become a pincushion for those shards of glass.

All she wished for was a cooling ointment or cloth to cover

her face with. The sensations were as if a hundred bees had launched themselves at her face and angrily stung her.

As she held up her two hands, one with just two bandages and one completely covered in gauze, she sighed. Could she look any more terrible? How could one little bowl raise so much havoc?

"Hey, look at you!"

It was as if he had read her mind. Feeling like a puppet on too-stiff strings, she slowly turned her head so that her un-bandaged eye could see who was speaking. "Detective Reynolds? Luke?"

"That's me."

"Did you come to make fun of my bandages?"

"Maybe."

"Honestly, Detective—"

"Nope. You are not allowed to start calling me detective again . . . just now you called me Luke. Now we're on a first name basis."

Only this man seemed to be able to push away her anxiety and turn all the tumbling feelings into spunk. "Ha, ha. If you aren't here to tease me . . . why did you come?" Truly he hadn't thought her cuts were a crime?

"I came because I had some time. And because I heard through the grapevine that you got yourself into a mess."

"I didn't get myself into anything. A glass bowl fell and broke." Even though vanity was a sin, Frannie felt herself frown. "Now I'm a scratched-up mess."

"You sure are. You are scratched up something awful." Lowering his voice, he said, "Are you in a lot of pain? Do you want me to get you anything?"

"I'm all right."

"Okay, then." For some reason he took what she'd just said

as an invitation to stay a while. As he walked closer, she could feel his gaze settle on her. "You look like a prizefighter." And with that, he took a seat right next to her.

Even though he hadn't been invited.

The immediate flood of happiness that she'd felt by his sudden appearance slowly gave way to dismay. "What are you doing?"

"This is called sitting in a chair, Frannie."

Oh! "I mean, why are you here? Why, really?" Embarrassed about her warming feelings for him, she lashed out. "Detective, I am sorry. I cannot answer any questions from you right now."

He stilled. "Did you really think I'd come here right now to question you about the case? Do you really think I'm that cold?"

She didn't think he was cold at all.

But she also didn't know why else he would have come all the way to the hospital to see her. Though she might have had secret wishes where he was concerned, he certainly didn't need to know that. "I can't think of why else you would be here."

"You can't, huh?" The tender look that she'd thought she'd spied in his eyes vanished. "Well, I only came because I was worried that you'd be alone here. And it looks like you are. Or, are you waiting on someone else to visit?"

She'd been tempted to tell him that there was no one else. But then she remembered her conversation with Beth.

Which made her think of Micah. Would he come? Did she even want him to? "I'm not sure if anyone else is coming or not. It ain't easy to get here by buggy you know."

"It's easy enough to hire a driver, Frannie. Even I know that."

While she lay there, slightly embarrassed for being so snippy, Luke's voice turned gentle. "Where is your father?"

As usual, their topsy-turvy interactions made her mind spin. To buy herself some time, she said, "You're only asking about my *daed*?"

"I, uh, discovered your mother passed away a few years ago."

"Cancer," she murmured, remembering those awful months all over again. It had been so difficult to keep her mother's spirits up when the chemotherapy had made her so weak. "My *daed*, he is at home on the farm, I suppose."

"He didn't think he should come to the hospital and sit with you?"

"I don't know if anyone has told him about my accident yet." Or, for that matter, if the news would spur him to come.

Little by little, she felt the tension leave him. "I'm sorry. I remember now that Mose was going to pay a visit to your father and tell him the news and see if he wanted to come up here."

Imagining her father leaving the safety of their farm was like imagining the detective suddenly feeling at home in Crittenden County. "It would be best if he stayed home."

"Why? You don't think he'd accept a ride from Mose?"

Frannie struggled to describe her father's personality. "He's a cautious man. Shy, too. He wouldn't venture far unless he was truly needed."

"And he isn't needed right now?" His voice rose as he made no effort to conceal his confusion. "You're badly injured, Frannie. "

"I know."

"Who knows how many cuts and stitches you received."

The reminder made her face throb even worse. "I know," she said again.

"He should be here for you. You shouldn't be here alone."

But, yet . . . she wasn't. "Next time I see my father, I'll pass on your thoughts on the matter."

"I'm not trying to be critical."

"But you are." Her good eye saw him flinch. And immediately she felt bad. She didn't know the detective all that well, but she was certainly coming to understand that he was a man used to being in charge, and used to saying what he thought.

Maybe a little bit like herself?

"Luke, I'm sorry if I don't sound grateful for your concern. I thank you for that. And I thank you for coming here to check on me. It was kind of you."

"What are the doctors saying?"

"I don't know. Everything's been pretty fuzzy." She thought for a moment. "I think I remember them saying that they'd come back soon."

"When they do, would you like me to talk with them, too?"

Just the idea of someone taking over her worries and questions sounded wonderful. With the way her head was pounding and her cheeks and face stinging, she was having trouble even keeping her good eye open. "Thank you for that," she said quietly. "If you could get some information and hold on tight to it, I would be most grateful." She leaned her head back and closed her eyes.

"You don't need to thank me. I'll be glad to help." He paused. "I don't usually argue with people all that much, you know."

"I don't argue that much, either," she admitted. "I guess we bring out the worst in each other."

"I hope not. I don't want to always argue with you, Frannie."

She didn't know how to respond to that. Changing topics,

she opened her good eye again. "One doctor stitched up my face, and another doctor examined my cornea. But neither of them wanted to tackle the cuts on the side of my eye. I'm waiting for that eye doctor. When he gets here, he's going to fix the cuts on the side and lid of my eye. I might have to get operated on."

"And that worries you."

Her lip trembled. "I'm tryin' to be brave, but in truth I'm scared."

"You know what? You have every right to be, too." As tears leaked from her good eye, Luke grabbed a tissue, hovered it over her, then set it down. "Fran, I don't have a clue about how to wipe your tears away. Want some water? There's a straw."

"Okay."

When she attempted to sit up, he placed a hand behind her shoulders and clicked his tongue. "Easy now. Don't want you to hurt yourself. Just open your mouth like a baby robin and I'll give you the straw."

The image of the fierce-looking detective playing mama bird to her baby bird was so ludicrous that she opened her mouth without a complaint. And sure enough, a cool straw came filled with cooler water that tasted wonderful in her mouth.

Greedily, she swallowed, then swallowed again.

"Easy now. You'll choke if you're not careful."

Following his words, she swallowed more slowly, then released the straw and leaned back again.

"*Danke.*"

"You're welcome."

"If you'd like to leave, that's okay with me."

"I don't want to. I want to stay here and keep you company."

"You must know that I'm not the best of company right now."

He chuckled. "You must know that you're not the best of company a lot of the time."

By now she knew his words were only teasing.

"And?"

"And I don't feel like doing much at the moment. As a matter of fact, I think I'm going to sit here with you, and wait for the doctors with you."

"Don't expect me to be grateful." Because, of course, she was grateful. She hadn't liked sitting alone.

To her surprise, he chuckled again. "Don't worry, Frannie. I've come to discover that I shouldn't expect much from you. You have a tendency to surprise me."

Against her will . . . or maybe because of his frankness, she smiled.

Luke turned out to be an easy companion. He didn't say much. Instead, he encouraged her to close both eyes and relax. A nurse came in to take her blood pressure and to tell her that the plastic surgeon for eyes was on his way.

When they were alone again, he leaned closer. "You okay?"

"Truth?"

"Always."

"No. I'm frightened. I don't want to be blind, and I'm not too excited about getting stitches around my eye neither. And my face hurts."

"That's to be expected. Do you want me to see if they'll give you more medicine for the pain?"

"*Nee.* I need to be strong. I don't want to be in a greater daze than I am right now."

"That makes sense. I've always greeted doctors with a mix of anticipation and fear."

Just then two doctors and a nurse came into their little cubicle.

"Frannie? I'm Dr. Carlson and this is Dr. Arthur. We're going to look at your eye, okay?"

She nodded.

As they crowded around her, she did her best to lie still.

But she felt the shakes start, so much so that she knew everyone in the room was aware of it.

"Are you in pain?" Dr. Carlson asked.

"Some," she murmured. In truth, she was so stunned by the unexpected events, she wasn't completely sure how she felt.

"Do you want some more pain medicine?'

She didn't know. Weren't all medicines bad? But if the doctors asked her to take them, then she must need them, right? "I'm just afraid of what you're going to do," she said, hating that her voice was trembling.

Then, to her surprise, Luke took her hand. "It's okay, Frannie. You don't need to make any decisions right now at all. I'll stay right here with you."

And though it wasn't in her nature to accept help, Frannie found herself linking his fingers between hers and exhaling.

She needed someone to clutch and lean on. To calm her nerves. And Luke did seem more than willing to accept her burdens.

"I've got you, Frannie," he whispered.

And truly . . . right then and there, she felt like he did.

"Stay as still as you possibly can," Dr. Carlson ordered as he and the other physician bent close and peered into her eye.

The light felt blinding. Her vision blurred.

And she was so very glad that she couldn't see what was happening.

Chapter 4

"I never agreed with Mamm and Daed searching through the drawers and cabinets in our rooms. Everyone needs some privacy, I think. But Mamm said she only looked through my things because she'd gone through Perry's."

DEBORAH BORNTRAGER

Despite the rumors that were buzzing around their tight-knit community, Deborah Borntrager still loved her brother. Sure, Perry had made some bad decisions. He'd gotten mixed up with the wrong kind of people. Sometimes, too, he could be terribly mean, almost spiteful with his sharp words and temper.

Sometimes he'd even been that way with family members who cared about him.

But everyone made mistakes, right? Deborah knew she did. She knew she was still making mistakes.

She comforted herself with that thought every morning when she said her prayers. With each sunrise, she'd get down on her knees and reach out to the Lord. Then, in the quiet of her room, she'd talk to Jesus about Perry's good points. Even the ones that Perry had seemed to have forgotten about. Perry had never been one for self-reflection.

Next, she'd pray for the Lord to help everyone in their community to forgive Perry. He'd caused so much hurt by his lies and anger, and it was becoming mighty apparent that not too many people in the community were eager to simply forgive and forget. Especially since he had never admitted his sins or asked for forgiveness. With all her heart, she would pray people would remember that it had been the drugs that had made Perry do bad things. It wasn't his fault.

After she covered the community, she'd ask the Lord to forgive Perry for his transgressions. She'd pray that he had somehow repented before he'd died and was now in heaven with all the saints and angels. But always, as soon as she thought about his erratic behavior, about the terrible things he used to say to her, the way he'd lied and cheated and stole from them all . . . she'd open her eyes and get up off her knees.

And as her heart began to beat slower, she'd sigh and wonder how long she could blame the drugs for his selfishness. And the way he could be so cruel. After all, he might have been addicted. But he'd also made the choice to begin his drug use in the first place.

Not that she'd ever say any of those things out loud.

At first when Perry's body had been found and a thousand questions had buzzed through the community, her parents had sent her to Charm, Ohio. There, her grandparents had given her time to mourn. For two weeks she cried and prayed and slept. She helped her grandmother wash walls and move all the household goods from the basement to the main floor. The hard work, combined with her grandmother's sweet, quiet personality, had been the perfect medicine to her frayed nerves. Only in the middle of the night would she let the reality of Perry's death sink in.

Imagining the commotion that was surrounding the murder investigation, she'd feel guilty. It hadn't been right to escape to her grandparents' farm like she had, but her parents had encouraged the trip. They hadn't trusted the policeman from Cincinnati.

Actually, they hadn't trusted Sheriff Kramer, either.

"There's no reason for you to become entangled in the police investigation, Deborah," her mother had said. "After all, you knew nothing about Perry's habits. None of us did. I don't know how, but Perry pulled the wool over all of our eyes."

Deborah never said anything, but she privately thought that the reason Perry had been able to pull that wool so well was because they hadn't wanted to see what he was doing.

It had been easier to be ignorant.

But Deborah had known more than she'd ever let on about her brother's habits.

She'd simply chosen to do nothing about it.

Now, though, she was back and was determined to hold her head up high. Even if some people thought she should stay in hiding, ashamed of what her brother had become and what had happened to him.

After washing her face and getting dressed for the day, she did the dozen other things that were part of her normal morning routine.

Then prepared herself to finally go to Schrock's Variety.

Her mother wasn't happy about it. She'd been flitting around her like a hummingbird since breakfast, full of nervous energy and advice. "Deborah, perhaps you should stay home today," she said. "There is nothing we truly need at the store."

"I told you I'd buy you some fresh cottage cheese and buttermilk, Mamm. Mr. Schrock always carries fresh dairy on Tuesdays." Plus, she, at least, needed to begin her life again. Staying inside and sheltered from the rest of the community was becoming too easy.

If she kept it up, she'd soon never want to leave her house.

"But Perry used to work there." Her mother bit her lip. "And I'm afraid Mr. Schrock and Perry didn't part on the best of terms. For some reason, Mr. Schrock fired him."

Deborah fought back the urge to roll her eyes upward. Though not a bit of what they were talking about was humorous, her mother's penchant for turning Perry into a saint was hard to take. "Mamm, I know that. Of course I know that."

"Then you know there might be hard feelings . . . Some people might take out their anger toward Perry on you."

Deborah was sure they might. But she also knew things wouldn't get better until she made some changes in her life. She needed to move forward and find something to occupy her mind instead of grieving for her brother. "I'll be all right."

Her *mamm* wrung her hands. "But they might ask you questions."

"*Muddah*, Perry was murdered. People want to know what happened."

"But you shouldn't have to talk about him. You shouldn't have to dwell on things that make you upset."

"I already am upset, Mamm. He was my brother, of course I'm going to be sad that he's dead."

And before her mother could refute that, Deborah slipped on her black tennis shoes and began the trek to Schrock's Variety Store.

It wasn't a short walk. Easily three miles. But the day was sunny and the sky was blue—and the exercise would improve her spirits. Already, the plan to get out of the house for the day was lifting her spirits.

She grabbed a tote to carry the dairy products home and swung it a little at her side as she left the house. She was happy not to have to be fussing with a horse and buggy and all the headaches that came with driving a buggy through traffic on a Tuesday morning.

As she passed Stanton Park, she was reminded of the rumor that Lydia Plank liked to meet Walker Anderson there, and then she passed a pair of nurseries. Finally, after almost an hour, Deborah arrived at Schrock's.

Now, as she stood outside the door, all the doubts she'd tried so hard to keep at bay rushed forward. Perhaps she shouldn't be so bold?

Perhaps she should feel more dismay for Perry and more shame for her brother's actions.

Then the door opened with a jerk, making the decision for her. She hastily took two steps back.

"Careful in there," a man muttered before dashing out of the way. "Things are crazier than usual."

She stood at the stoop, watching him in confusion.

Mr. Schrock was known for outlandish schemes. It was part of his charm, really. Entering the store always made her think of the fun house she'd visited once when a carnival came through the area. You never knew what was going to pop out at Schrock's.

"You coming in or out?" a woman's voice rang out from the back. "Make a choice, and be quick about it."

Deborah felt her breath hitch at the harsh command. She hesitated, but only for a moment. Then she stepped in, fast. Before she could change her mind.

"Ach! Shut the door, wouldja?" the same harsh voice yelled.

Deborah shut it. Then wished she was still on the other side.

Four large gangly puppies were gallivanting her way, taking down everything in their path. Their paws were overlarge and their tongues wet and drippy.

"Dogs?" she yelped.

"Prepare yourself! They're a mite rambunctious right now. Real excited for sure." Mrs. Schrock was hustling in from the back with her warning.

She barely had time to brace herself as one let out a friendly *woof* and leapt.

Two paws landed on her thighs. Its littermate jumped right next to her.

When she bent to steady herself, two wet tongues whipped out and swabbed her cheeks. "Oh!" she squealed as a third puppy barreled her way, attacking from the side.

She fell on her bottom. With a few triumphant yips, the puppies gallivanted closer. In no time at all, she was soon covered with paws and fur and puppy slobber.

"*Woof!*" a fourth exclaimed, barking and licking with playful moves. She would have loved to play with them all. That is, if they weren't bounding on top of her lap with the force and energy of four tiny locomotives.

"Oh, you puppies!" Mrs. Schrock exclaimed as she scurried to Deborah's side and came to her rescue. With a gentle tug, the lady maneuvered the pups off and helped her to her feet. "All you all right, dear?"

Deborah was not. Her *kapp* and bonnet were skewed to one side, her pink dress and black apron were covered in dog fur, and one of her black stockings now had a quarter-sized hole at the knee.

But she pretended none of that mattered. "*Jah*. I am fine.

Never better." She smiled wanly. "Those puppies are sure frisky."

"Indeed." Still trying to corral the exuberant monster pups, Mrs. Schrock looked her over with a worried expression. "You're not hurt? Are you sure?"

"I am fine, Mrs. Schrock. Truly, I like dogs. They just caught me off guard, that's all. They are adorable puppies." More like overgrown horses, but still . . . their sweet brown eyes, pink tongues, and happy antics were terribly cute.

Mrs. Schrock chuckled as two of the puppies lay down, exhausted. "They don't usually greet newcomers quite so enthusiastically. They must like you."

"Lucky me."

Mrs. Schrock's eyes twinkled merrily. "Yes, indeed." Raising her voice, she opened the door to the storeroom and called out, "Walker? Where are you? I need your help, dear."

"Walker left, Mamm," a familiar voice replied, sending the last tiny bit of Deborah's composure out the window. "It's just me here."

Her arms full of puppy, Mrs. Schrock frowned. "I didn't see Walker leave."

"Daed sent him to go help with a delivery—I thought you knew?" Jacob called back.

Listening to the conversation, Deborah's spirits sank. Oh, but this visit to Schrock's had just gone from bad to worse.

Jacob Schrock was back in town.

Chapter 5

"Perry loved animals, for sure. He cried for days when his beagle died. It was a blessing we had a new puppy for him."

GLORIA SCHROCK

Deborah fought to keep her expression neutral. But it wasn't easy, because all she really wanted to do was leave the store and never return.

Ignoring Deborah, Mrs. Schrock shifted the puppy in her arms. "Well, what are you doing, son? Haven't you been hearing the commotion out here?"

"What do ya think I'm doing?" Through the open doorway, Jacob's voice held more than a touch of impatience. "I'm trying to fix this pen so the dogs stop escaping."

"It shouldn't be too difficult. Your father put it together last night."

"Daed put it together wrong. That's why the pups were running loose all night."

Mrs. Schrock glanced at the entrance to the storage room and winced. To Deborah, she whispered, "It was quite a mess back there this morning."

"Ah," Deborah said.

Raising her voice, Mrs. Schrock said, "I don't know what your *daed* could've done wrong, Jacob."

"There's no telling. Daed can hardly put a shoebox together, let alone a wire pen."

"Now, Jacob, that's not very charitable."

"You know I'm right."

Deborah couldn't help but smile at the interplay. It was so familiar. Well, how her family would have been if Perry hadn't . . . if everything hadn't fallen apart like it did.

As if she had suddenly remembered Deborah, Mrs. Schrock cleared her throat. "Jacob, I need your help right now. These puppies are running amuck. We can't go on like this much longer."

"Mamm, stop. I can't round up puppies and fix the cage at the same time."

Deborah gasped at his tone.

Mrs. Schrock, too, looked a bit disgruntled by his remark. However, she must have been used to it, because after a moment's pause, she glanced Deborah's way. "Do you have a problem with the puppies, dear?"

Deborah shook her head.

"*Gut.* You may make yourself useful. Go grab a puppy and help me carry them all to the kennel in the back."

Deborah's feet felt paralyzed. Out of all the things she would have imagined happening, being greeted by Mrs. Schrock and four oversized puppies was truly nothing she could have dreamt up.

But beyond all that was the terrible suspicion that she was the absolutely last person Jacob was going to want to see for any amount of time.

Resolutely, she refrained from looking at the door he was behind. "Mrs. Schrock, I'm happy to help you, but I'm not sure . . . Perhaps I could use your restroom and get cleaned up?"

"Later, for sure. But for now, go pick up a puppy and follow me."

The order, given in that no-nonsense way, finally spurred Deborah into action. "Here, puppy," she said gently. One chocolate brown nose nudged her hand and whined. As its tiny pink tongue slid out with a pant, Deborah couldn't resist a giggle. "Yes, that means you." She wrapped her fingers around its thin collar, then with a heft, lifted the overgrown pup into her arms.

The puppy shifted and cuddled close, not worrying at all about its chunky weight or squirmy body. "Come on," she whispered. "Let's go follow your mother."

"I'm most certainly not that puppy's *mamm*, Deborah," Mrs. Schrock protested while carrying a puppy of her own. "Only its owner. And a temporary one at that."

Luckily, the other two pups ran to their sides, completing their little line toward the storage room.

When Mrs. Schrock noticed that Deborah was right behind her, she smiled kindly. "Thank you for your help. I tell ya, my husband comes up with the strangest ideas sometimes. I didn't think anything could beat the guinea pig and snake incident, but these giant puppies might come close."

Deborah looked at the puppy padding by her side. "What kind of dogs are these?"

"Mastiff," Jacob said, then stilled as if he suddenly noticed who he was talking to. "You."

She froze. "Yes. Me."

His eyes narrowed. "What are you doing here? And what are you doing, wandering around our store like you own it?"

"I only came in for a few supplies," she said helplessly. "Cottage cheese."

"And out of every store in the county, you chose our store? I find that pretty hard to swallow."

Deborah knew he had reason to dislike her. But she wasn't her brother. And Jacob wasn't the only person Perry had taken advantage of or been cruel to. Perry had hurt her deeply a time or two as well.

Or twenty.

But out of respect for his mother, and for the simple reason that she had no desire to make trouble, Deborah kept her words light. "As I was saying, I only came in for a few things, but the puppies came rollicking forward, and one thing led to another."

"They almost attacked her, poor thing," his mother said. "Knocked her down!"

"But you weren't hurt."

Deborah winced. It almost sounded like Jacob was disappointed about that. She lifted her chin. "Your mother asked for my help. And so I said yes . . ." Her voice drifted off as his expression became cooler. Like ice.

Giving up, she handed over the puppy in her arms. "Here. Excuse me. I'll go now."

He took the dog, obviously trying his best to not touch her.

But by his side, his mother looked to be losing patience. "Jacob! You are being rude. You apologize."

"I will not." Jacob glared. "Don't ask me to pretend she's my friend, Mother."

"You used to be friends."

"That was a long time ago. Before—" He opened his mouth to say more, but must have changed his mind, because he cut himself off.

"Before what?" Mrs. Schrock's eyebrows rose, practically daring her son to continue.

But instead of continuing, he turned away.

Deborah's visit to the store had now gone from bad to worse, and she had no one to blame for the situation but herself. She should have listened to her mother and stayed away.

Because if anything was true, it was that she wasn't Jacob Schrock's friend at all. In fact, she could very well be his enemy. She'd known he felt like that, and once more, she couldn't say she blamed him.

Turning around, she mumbled to his mother, "Goodbye, Mrs. Schrock."

"But, didn't you want something? There must have been a reason you came in," Mrs. Schrock said.

"It wasn't anything important."

The lady's expression turned hesitant. "Do you still want to use the ladies' room and get cleaned up?"

"Let her leave, Mamm," Jacob said as the puppies started barking again. "The sooner she's out of our lives, the better."

Deborah tucked her chin and strode from the back room toward the front of the store, nearly running into Walker Anderson.

He held up his arms to keep her from knocking into him. "Hey, Deborah. When did you get back in town?" he asked with a smile that slowly vanished as he noticed her disheveled appearance. "Um . . . how are you?"

She'd just walked three miles to get humiliated by Jacob Schrock and was now covered with puppy prints and slime. Now she was going to have to walk back without getting what she'd come for.

So, she wasn't fine. She wasn't close to fine. But she

couldn't very well say that, now could she? "I'm all right." Trying to smile, she said, "You?"

His eyes narrowed. "Where is everyone?"

"Mrs. Schrock and Jacob are in the back room. With the puppies."

Walker's eyes suddenly looked as pained as she felt. "Those puppies are like miniature horses." He ran a hand through his short hair. "I tell you what, some days I'm sure this place is going to kill me." As if he'd suddenly noticed her hands were empty, he said, "Hey, do you need some help? You came here to shop, right?"

There was nothing she needed more than to get out of the store. "I don't need anything. I'll just be going."

"All right. Well, I'll be seeing you." Just as he turned away, she heard Walker groan in frustration. "These puppies have now left a present for me to pick up."

Walking quickly to the front door, she heard him grumble some more. He sounded so put upon, she would have normally found it funny.

But the tears were falling too fast. Much too fast for laughter.

As she began the long walk home, Deborah considered praying for Jacob. He was obviously in a lot of pain, but she so wished things would get better between them.

But unfortunately, she barely believed even the Lord could convince Jacob Schrock to ever forgive her.

After all, her brother had made his life miserable. And both she and Jacob knew it.

Chapter 6

"Perry was the type of man to give you the coat off his back. If he didn't need it, that is."

JACOB SCHROCK

"Frannie, can you hear me?" A pause. "Frannie? Frannie, try to wake up now."

She heard the voice clearly, and understood what he was asking. Part of her wanted to open her eyes and focus on the voice, but the rest of her far preferred to stay in the peaceful foggy slumber.

It had been a long and difficult night. After her surgery, she'd spent time in a recovery room, where she'd been poked and prodded by nurses who wouldn't tell her exactly how bad her wounds were.

Would she see out of her eye again?

She fought a rising panic and focused on what she did know. That she wanted to leave this place, if only to get some rest.

Hours had gone by before she was wheeled to a regular hospital room.

But it offered no rest, either.

Throughout the night, she was alternately awoken up by her roommate—a chatty, rather loud woman occupying the other side their room—or by nurses taking her blood pressure and temperature.

Only during the last few hours had the painkillers kicked in enough to drown out the noise, the visits, the ache around her eye, allowing her body to finally relax and drift into a peaceful slumber.

She stretched a leg. Then the other. Perhaps if she shifted just enough, she could drift right back into oblivion and ignore her visitor.

Ignore his summons.

"Frannie?"

Wearily, she gave up sleep's grip and allowed her attention to drift to the voice coming from the chair next to her bed.

A voice, which had risen yet again. "Frannie? Francis? Wake up."

There was only one man who said her name like that. With the speed of ice melting, she opened her left eye. "Micah."

"*Jah*." A satisfied smirk appeared.

"How long have you been here?"

"I've been sittin' here an hour. Watching you sleep."

Watching her sleep? In a snap, her grogginess disappeared. She hastily double-checked to make sure her sheet was pulled up to her chin, and wished he'd left her asleep. Why was he here? Why had he woken her up? "Seeing you—it is most unexpected," she mumbled, her throat dry and scratchy.

"Unexpected" was something of an understatement. For the last month or so, Micah had been making himself terribly scarce. She'd seen him only once or twice.

Under his straw hat, the man who'd courted her off and

on for most of her life stared right back. "My being here shouldn't be much of a surprise. I came as soon as I heard about your accident." He paused. "I wanted to be here when you woke up." His satisfied smile grew. "And I was."

Indeed, he was! . . . And, well, he had certainly done his best to make sure she woke up.

Over and over he'd said her name, loud and clear. Almost as if he'd been sitting across the room instead of right by her side. It had been the exact opposite of a certain *Englischer* detective's husky baritone.

She needed to remember what a good catch Micah was. After what happened with Perry, and her unfortunate attraction to the detective, she needed to remember where her attention should really be focused. She summoned a smile. "That's very kind of you."

"Someone needed to be here, don'tcha think? Can't have you sitting here alone."

His words were everything she should want to hear. But they felt the same as hearing recorded messages played at regular intervals around the hospital halls. Canned, monotone, meaningless, insincere. "Hmmm."

Micah reached for her hand, saw the bandages wrapped around her palms, then awkwardly folded his hands together on his lap. After a moment, he exhaled.

He was waiting for her to make the next move.

That was how it had always been. Frannie was the leader in their relationship. When they were courting, he never approached her until she smiled his way. He didn't take her walking or driving unless she mentioned that she wanted to. He didn't call on her without an invitation. And he rarely conversed on any topic that she hadn't initiated.

So now, here they were.

If there was ever a time she needed him to step up, to take control, this was it. She was scared, worried, hurt.

It shouldn't be up to her to ask him to comfort her. He should want to comfort her.

And him, sitting here exhaling? Well, it didn't comfort her one bit.

And though he had taken the initiative to visit, he wasn't prepared to offer her anything else.

Same as always.

As covertly as she dared, she glanced his way. He continued to stare at her, his light brown eyes full of want and expectation. Much like a well-trained spaniel awaiting the next command.

Being with Micah was terribly exhausting.

On the other side of the room, her roommate flicked channels on the television set. A nurse came in and spoke to her. A cell phone rang.

Frannie and Micah sat in silence.

"Tell me about the farm," she said at last, unable to take the tense silence. Unable to bear the weight of his expectations. "What is new?"

He relaxed. "Well, wouldn't you know it? Gretta had her kids."

"Your goat had babies?" She had a special fondness for Gretta. "I bet they are *wunderbaar!*"

"Indeed, they are. I reckon they are the cutest kids in the county," he pronounced, sounding like a proud papa. "Frannie, when you get out of here, I'll have to take you to our barn to see them." He scratched his head. "That is, if you would care to visit."

Finally! He had finally asked her somewhere. "I would enjoy that. How many babies did Gretta have? And what color?"

"Three, white and tan."

She waited for more details. Waited some more. Then realized he was again expecting her to lead the conversation. But though she liked goats just fine, Frannie couldn't think of another thing to ask. Her head was throbbing, and the eye that wasn't bandaged was watering terribly. All she wanted was to sink back into oblivion.

But Micah was now leaning forward in that eager way of his.

His short visit now felt like the longest journey imaginable.

"Um, anything else new?" she asked, grasping at straws.

He frowned, obviously thinking. "*Nee,*" he finally said.

"Ah."

As they once again lapsed into silence, she let her thoughts wander. It was no wonder, actually, why she'd been tempted to explore what Perry had to offer when he'd shown the slightest bit of interest in her. Sometimes a woman didn't want to be in control, at least she didn't. She had no need to always have her way.

Her parents' relationship had been more of a partnership, full of a constant push and pull. What she could remember, anyway. Closing her eyes, she let her mind drift toward the past, back to when her mother was still cancer-free and vibrant. Frannie recalled her mother busily bossing her father around the kitchen, and then his teasing whenever she tried to reorganize the cellar.

They'd playfully argue about all sorts of things. Their marriage had been noisy and full of life.

She wanted that. That give and take. A man who was a match, not a man who only wanted to do as she bid. But she also knew that what she wanted wasn't necessarily what she needed.

A union with Micah would never be full of fiery arguments, or even much teasing laughter. That wasn't Micah's way.

But she would feel catered to and cared for. And she had no doubt that if they both tried, they would have a happy marriage. Perhaps even years of compatible living.

What else could she possibly want, really?

Who else?

It was a fine question. Because there was no one else sitting beside her bed. Only Micah. Who patiently sat. Even though they had little to talk about, he never questioned her or did anything other than make her feel like she was the best part of his life.

He was so terribly loyal.

Surely, there were worse things to start a marriage with? . . .

"Frannie, are you back asleep?" he whispered. "Frannie, I thought maybe we could talk about our future some. You know . . . me and you?" He cleared his throat. Leaned so close she could smell the lingering scent of horse on his clothes. "I care for you, Frannie, though I expect you know that."

Here he was. Finally initiating a conversation. But perversely, she now didn't want anything to do with it. Like the coward she was, she kept her body still.

"I think you've always known how much I care for you," he continued. "I think we would have a wonderful-*gut* union. For sure."

A union? Was he talking about their relationship now? While she was wrapped up in a hospital sheet, had a tube stuck in her hand, a bandaged eye, and was pretending to sleep?

But if she opened her eye and turned to him, he would

expect her to talk. To ask him more questions. To make the plans for their future together. To tell him what to do, what to say.

And at the moment, she didn't think she could do anything more than just lie there. She tightly held her eyes closed and let him continue to think she was sleeping.

Go away, she silently pleaded.

What felt like hours later, he stood up and walked out—leaving her feeling slightly guilty but relieved, too. She heard the curtain part and him as he stepped across the linoleum with sure, even steps, and then the door open and close.

He was gone.

She sighed.

"That man is an eager one, huh?" said the voice from the other side of the curtain.

With a flood of embarrassment, Frannie realized the voice was the other patient . . . and that she'd heard every single word that had been said.

Feeling awkward, she went ahead and answered. "Yes. He is."

"In my day, the men didn't propose at the hospital. Wasn't seemly."

"He didn't propose."

"Sounded like he was about to!"

No, she thought. He'd been waiting for her to suggest it. But there was no use in explaining that to a stranger. "Perhaps."

"Hope you'll weigh your decision carefully. I'm not at all sure he's the man for you."

Intrigued, Frannie said, "Why do you say so?"

"He's too weak-willed. A woman needs a strong man to hold her up from time to time. Just like a strong man needs a strong woman to allow him to show weakness once in a while."

Was Frannie strong? Yes, she supposed she was. Suddenly, she was feeling a little better. "If he asks," she said, "I'll be sure to think about my answer."

"Good, good."

The woman coughed a bit, then picked up her phone when it rang. She began to talk about her sheepdog and her boss's terrible habits.

She talked so much, and in such a speedy, friendly-sounding way, the words began to blend together. Before long, Frannie closed her eyes and let the woman's voice wash over her, lulling her to sleep.

Where she was thankful to drift back into the warm comfort of her dreams.

"Frannie?"

Her name was being called yet again. Oh, couldn't anyone here simply leave her alone? The words felt like needles to her brain, prickly and stinging.

"Stop," she mumbled.

But it still continued. "Frannie? Frannie, wake up."

Slowly, her eye opened. Immediately, she felt the pain. The ache of her wounds throbbing around her eye, her cheeks, her jaw.

Wincing, she tried to focus on her newest visitor, wondering if Micah had returned—and what she would say to him if he asked her to marry him.

But instead of Micah, she saw that Luke now sat by her side.

"Hello, Luke," she whispered. Her throat was still scratchy, strained.

Without her having to ask, he reached for the pitcher on the side table and poured her a cup of water. Placing a straw in the cup, he smiled as he held it to her lips. "Sip," he said.

She sipped, and stared in wonder as he set the cup back on the nightstand. "Thank you."

"Do you need more pain medication? I'll talk to the nurse . . ."

She was going to try to be brave, strong, but realized it was foolish. With the way pain was tapping a steady drumbeat behind her eye, she wouldn't be able to focus on a word he had to say. Slowly, she nodded.

"I'll be right back."

Purposely, he strode out of the room. While he was gone, she made sure she was tucked in, and even tried to tidy her hair a bit. A lost cause.

When he finally came back in and sat down, she said, "Are you here to ask me more questions?"

"Ah, no." He settled into the plastic chair beside the bed. "I rarely question women in hospital rooms. I had some extra time so I thought I'd stop by to see how you're doing."

"Ah." She wanted to tease him about caring for her, but she was afraid of his answer.

Afraid he was here out of duty. Out of friendship. Nothing more.

But of course she couldn't ask, and she shouldn't even think about it. To him, she was merely another suspect in his murder investigation.

And his former innkeeper, merely an acquaintance.

So instead of saying anything, she tried to relax against the pillows.

She was amazed that with him, there was no awkward silence. And when he smiled at her, his grin did more to comfort her than a hundred visits from Micah ever would.

She didn't know what to think of that.

"So," he said, "I used my considerable charm and coaxed some information from the hospital staff. They said you had a rough night of it. But . . . the word is out that the doctors think you're going to be just fine."

She'd heard that, too. But it didn't hurt to be sure. "My eyesight?" she asked.

"As far as I've heard"—he paused before continuing—"that's just fine, too. The doctor will be here in a while to tell you all about it." Tossing another smile her way, he said, "I tell you what, Frannie Eicher, you gave me a scare."

Now that she was fully awake, she noticed the beige walls and the beige shade covering the window. The television continued to hum next to her, as did the woman's one-sided conversation on her cell phone.

"You, scared?" She smiled weakly. "You're not scared of anything."

The nurse hurried in and injected something into her IV. She gave Frannie a friendly smile and bustled right back out.

Within seconds, the pain in Frannie's face started to ebb.

"As much as I appreciate you thinking so, when I heard about all that blood . . ."

Before she could apologize for scaring him, he added, "But that's in the past. You're going to be fine. Just need a few days' rest. You'll be good as new and making horrible pies before you know it."

"Oh, how you flatter," she said, yawning. "Do you think I can go home today?"

"I hope so. If not today, then early tomorrow. Though, if I

were you, I'd try to stay as long as possible. You have guests staying at your inn. So no rest there."

"But that's my job, Detective. I can't keep depending on Beth to take care of them."

"Now, now, no you don't. I was 'Luke' just moments ago. I'm Luke now, too."

She smiled weakly. Enjoying their shared moment. Enjoying the way that they weren't arguing, weren't talking about Perry's death.

They were having a conversation—well, as good as they could have when it was obvious that he was being on his best behavior.

"You are a *gut* man, Luke. Some of the time."

"I know," he said with a smile. "And maybe I can be your friend, too?"

"I would like that," she said after a moment's pause. She wasn't too familiar with the concept of having a man as a friend, but they'd come too far to pretend they weren't bound to be close.

She was enjoying the quiet between them, the knowledge that they had formed some sort of truce, when she heard the door to the room creak open.

"Frannie? Frannie?"

Her father.

"Excuse me," her roommate called out. "I'm on the phone."

"I am not," her father said crisply. "I am looking for my daughter."

"Daed, I'm here. On the other side of the curtain."

Frannie's mood lifted at her father's terse tone. He was introverted but not timid. Never had been.

She was sharing a smile with Luke when the curtains parted.

Seeing him in his usual blue shirt, black pants, and wary expression made her smile broaden. "Daed, it is so good to see you."

"I wish I could say it was *gut* to see you, but it ain't. You look terrible."

"*Danke.*"

He paused, then smiled. "Sorry, but it's true, you know." He was walking with a limp, as was his way, since he'd gotten on the wrong end of a cow decades ago and was too stubborn to get his injury checked out.

"You didn't have to come to the hospital," she said.

"Why would you think I wouldn't want to be here? You're my daughter. My only one here in town. Why wouldn't I want to see how you are faring?"

Now she was embarrassed. "No reason." She'd gotten so used to not asking for much from him, she supposed she had forgotten that he still loved her. Even if he had no desire to help out at her inn.

As she watched him silently, Luke stood up. "Here you go, sir. Take my chair."

Her father took it with a grateful sigh. "*Danke.* This leg of mine don't seem to want to give me a moment's peace."

Luke patted his brace with a smile. "I know the feeling."

Her *daed* looked at Luke with a bit more interest, now that they had something in common. "Now, who might you be?"

"Luke Reynolds, sir."

"You are English?"

"Yes."

When it was becoming obvious that her father was trying to piece together the information, Frannie hastened to explain. "He's a detective from Cincinnati, Daed."

Her father frowned. "Why are you here?"

"We met because of Perry."

He shook his head. "No, I'm not wondering about why you are here in Crittenden County. I'm curious as to why you are here in my daughter's hospital room?"

"I didn't want Frannie to be alone."

"And you think she wants your company?" Her father's voice was full of indignation and concern. "I would think even the best of detectives would understand that she is in no condition to be questioned."

"He's not questioning me, Daed."

"Then?"

Luke supplied that answer. "We're friends. When I heard she had been injured, I was worried about her."

But that explanation only seemed to confuse her father more. And made Frannie realize that she'd made a mistake when she'd decided to keep most of the investigation out of her father's hearing.

"I thought she might need someone." When her father's gaze sharpened, Luke continued back-pedaling. "I mean . . . the surgeries and doctors can be tough to handle by yourself. Especially if you're not used to hospitals and everything."

"And you are used to them?"

"I've had my share of days in one." He touched his leg. "I've been recovering from a gunshot wound."

Frannie coughed loudly, letting Luke know that he had just made a fatal error in the "trust me, I'm basically harmless" department.

"Is she in trouble?" her father asked. "Is that why you're sticking to her like glue?"

"Trouble? Oh no. I just thought . . . well . . . it's not like I have a lot of other commitments right now. I simply thought

I'd stay here a while. You know, so Frannie wouldn't be alone."

"Is that what you want, Frannie?"

As she pondered his question, she looked at Luke. He seemed like someone she could count on. Their friendship was based on the short time he'd spent at her inn, and the questioning he did relating to Perry's death. Though she knew deep down that she felt the beginnings of a real attraction for him, she was enough of a realist to know that they had no future.

But instead of that making her suspicious of him, it only made her trust him more.

Luke was her perfect companion. "Yes, it is what I want," she said quietly. Then she closed her one good eye so she wouldn't have to see what everyone thought of that.

The nurse cleared her throat. "You all really do need to leave now."

The two of them filed out past the curtain, leaving Frannie alone with the nurse.

And very curious about what Luke and her father would say to each other next.

Chapter 7

"Perry Borntrager was the type of boy to race buggies in the middle of the night. Though I've done my share of foolish things, I ain't never done anything so foolhardy. I told him that, too."

JOHN PAUL EICHER

"Detective, maybe now you could tell me the truth about you and my daughter," Mr. Eicher announced once the two of them were standing out in the hall. The look he sent Luke's way reminded him of picking up his prom date back in high school and meeting her father for the first time.

And just like those days, he began to feel self-conscious. What was it about dads and daughters that never failed to change?

"Mr. Eicher, I promise, Frannie and I are just friends."

"Friends?" One graying eyebrow rose so high it was removed from view under the brim of his black felt hat. "My daughter has a great many friends. And those are girlfriends. You are not like them."

"Ah—"

"Now, she also has Micah."

Almost against his will, Luke snapped to attention. "Micah?"

Bushy eyebrows furrowed together. "You've never heard Frannie speak of him?"

"If she has, I don't remember." Which was a lie, of a sort. If Frannie had spoken of a man in her life, he would have paid close attention. "Are they courting?"

This time, Mr. Eicher looked a little uncomfortable. "Sometimes they are . . . sometimes not." When Luke stared at him, waiting for more of an explanation, he said, "Micah has been around Frannie for most of her life. He's always had a sweet spot for her. Nothing would make him happier than for them to marry."

Luke noticed Mr. Eicher didn't say that it would make Frannie happier. Or him, for that matter.

"Do you think they will marry?"

"I don't know. Perhaps they will get more serious now that Perry is gone." He winced. "I'm sorry, that don't sound right, does it? I just meant that Frannie had been caught in a whirlwind by Perry."

"You don't owe me an explanation," he said, though he filed away the information about Perry to revisit later.

"That is true," Mr. Eicher said smartly. "However, you still owe me one. Is there something special between you and my daughter?"

"No." That was another lie, of course. He had become very fond of Frannie. There was something about her that was special to him—and he had a feeling that Frannie felt the same way about him. Even if neither of them had spoken a word about it.

"There can be nothing between you two, you know. You are English. You live far away, in Cincinnati. And, of course, you are a police officer."

Mr. Eicher said "police officer" the way most people would say "child molester."

"I realize that." Because, after all, what else could he say? He was also starting to bristle. He knew the man was probably worried about his daughter and lashing out at him because he was a stranger, but he didn't have to be so gruff.

"We are just friends. I used to rent a room from her. Nothing more, nothing less."

Someone guffawed. Luke glanced down the hallway and wasn't the least surprised to see that it was Mose. He'd texted that he was bringing Frannie's father to the hospital. This soap opera of a visit was going to be ammunition for Mose's jokes for years to come.

Luke couldn't believe the situation he was in. He was almost thirty years old. He'd dated his share of women. Never before had he been treated to the steely-eyed intense glare of a concerned Amish father.

Before Mr. Eicher could think up more questions to ask, Luke decided to ask some questions of his own. "Are you uncomfortable with me being here at the hospital? If so, I could leave."

Immediately, the man's expression eased. *"Gut."*

Ready to make good on his promise, he paused. "If I leave, are you planning to sit with her the rest of the day? Because I think we both know that she shouldn't be alone."

The older man averted his eyes. "I'm afraid I canna do that. I have to get back to my animals."

"So you'd rather she sit by herself than with me?" He looked around. "Or is this Micah here? I would have thought you'd want the man who intends to marry your daughter to be a little more concerned."

"I do not know what else he had planned for his day. I couldn't begin to imagine." But a healthy sheen of red floated up through his cheeks.

Now that he'd been able to make his point, Luke retreated a bit. Softening his voice, he said, "Mr. Eicher, listen. All I'm trying to do is help Frannie in any way I can. And right now, that's not leaving her alone. Hospitals can be very lonely places."

"You aren't intending to court my Frannie? Because if you are, I'd like to know. I'd rather hear bad news instead of lies. I don't care for liars."

As prickly as Frannie's father was, Luke was discovering that the more they talked, the better he liked him. "I don't care for liars, either."

"Then?"

All of a sudden, Luke felt tongue-tied. But then he remembered just how unsuitable they were for each other. And he couldn't afford to let any romantic feelings color the investigation.

In addition, as her father had pointed out, she was Amish. Granted, she was new order Amish, and allowed a lot of modern conveniences that the more conservative sects did not.

But even so, a life with a Cincinnati detective who made his living investigating crimes and murders in the most violent neighborhoods of the city was not the right type of man for a woman whose teachings and beliefs were centered on peace and nonviolence.

"I don't plan to court Frannie."

Pale blue-gray eyes the same color as Frannie's regarded him intently before he nodded, and then, without another word, started walking toward Mose.

As Luke watched him walk away, he felt slightly guilty. He hadn't promised that he would *never* court her. Just that he didn't *plan* to. He'd chosen his words with care. Hmm. Who was he trying to fool now?

Mr. Eicher's voice rang through the hall. "Mose, are you ready now? Because it's close to feeding time and no one will do the work if I don't."

"I'm ready. But give me a second, John Paul," Mose replied. "I need to speak with Luke for a moment."

"Can't it wait? I just spoke with him."

"It won't take long. It's about police business," Mose said easily.

With a grumble, Mr. Eicher said, "I'll go downstairs, then. Where I'll be waiting."

After they watched Frannie's father deliberately ignore the elevator and walk down the steps, Mose grinned. "He's a piece of work, isn't he?"

"He's something. Is he always so taciturn?"

"Pretty much. If you want to know the truth, this is a good day for John Paul. Usually he substitutes conversation with glares and sighs."

"He was getting on my last nerve."

"Oh, he does that with most all of us," Mose said dryly. "He's never been one for conversation."

"Or smiles."

Mose laughed with his usual ease. "That, too. Most folks think Frannie's bed-and-breakfast would do a far sight worse if her father took a mind to spend more time there. He could run off a bull with a cold, he's so ornery."

"I bet." Luke figured the bull-with-a-cold comment meant something in Mose's mind, but he was too tired to figure it out. "Well, good luck getting him home."

"I'll take that luck," Mose said with a slight grin. "Now, you ready for some news?"

He'd been so rattled by the grilling, he'd almost forgotten that Mose said he had information for him. "I am."

"Jacob Schrock is back in town. So is Deborah Borntrager."

Immediately, all thoughts of overprotective fathers fled. "It's about time." Both he and Mose had interviewed the Schrocks, the owners of the general store where Perry had worked, several times.

Their son, who was about Perry's age, had been mysteriously absent. Deborah, Perry's sister, had also been out of town. For them both to be called out of town right when Perry's body had been found seemed a little too coincidental. But, of course, neither Luke nor Mose had had any cause to be suspicious of them.

But everything in his experience told him that there was more to the coincidence. "Have you questioned them?" he asked in a rush. "What did they say?"

"I haven't spoken with either of them."

"Why not?"

"Because I thought you might like to do the honors tomorrow, that's why."

"But the questioning should be done today. While the news is still fresh."

"Ach, Luke. We both know none of the news about Perry's death is still fresh! It's all old, and interwoven with suppositions and secrets."

"But what if they start talking to their families?" Luke felt bad about even mentioning it. After all, Mose wasn't a green rookie cop; he'd been on the job as long as Luke had.

But of course, he hadn't been investigating murders in Cincinnati like Luke had. Most of Mose's detective work had concerned domestic disputes and a few petty thefts.

"Settle down, Luke. Deborah and Jacob will still be in town tomorrow. I checked on that. You stay here at the hospital with Frannie. She seems happy to share your company."

Sitting with her made him feel good, too. But Luke didn't like putting off the investigation for personal reasons. "Mose—"

His buddy held up a hand. "We've waited this long, we can wait a little longer."

"Look, you need to know that just because I'm here with Frannie, it doesn't mean I've gotten sidetracked." But even as he said the words, he started to worry. Since when had he ever worked on an investigation where his complete focus wasn't on the case twenty-four-seven?

Mose chuckled. "Oh, Luke, I know you haven't gotten sidetracked! All that's happened is you're getting settled into Crittenden County."

"What's that supposed to mean?"

"It means that you're starting to learn how we do things. We take things slow and steady, and think them through. And," he added with a smile, "we remember that there's a whole lot more to life than solving somebody's death. Now, I'd best get on downstairs before John Paul starts calling for me. And he will!"

While Mose trotted downstairs, Luke pressed the button on the elevator and went up to the third floor to where the small snack bar and coffee shop was located.

"What can I get you?" a Mennonite woman in a flowered dress at the counter asked.

"Coffee fresh?"

"Yep. And so are the Danishes. We've got cherry and lemon today. You should try one, they're worth the calories, I promise."

He laughed. "If they're that good, I know I won't want to pass them up. I'll take a cup of coffee and a cherry Danish."

"Room for cream?"

"Nope."

After he paid, she noticed his brace. "You go take a seat. I'll bring both out to you."

With a grateful smile, Luke followed her directions and took a chair at one of the five tables. Just minutes later, the woman brought him his Danish and coffee.

Both were outstanding. Hit the spot.

And that's when he started thinking that maybe Mose was right. He was starting to get used to things here. When someone offered to do him a favor, he didn't think it was a sign of weakness to accept.

He was even coming to expect that the food and coffee offered at the hospital would be delicious.

And though he was still having trouble coming to terms with the fact that he was putting off the interviews until another day, he had to admit that what Mose said was true.

It wouldn't make much of a difference to talk to the two new suspects tomorrow.

He really was changing in spite of himself.

"Mister, how about a refill? Free of charge."

"I'd love one, thanks." And instead of standing up, he merely gave the woman a grateful smile when she approached.

Yep, he was definitely getting used to things here. So used to things, it made him wonder how he was going to handle things back in Cincinnati. Back in his real world.

Chapter 8

"Perry and I never had much to say to each other. I didn't care for the way he treated Lydia or Frannie. He didn't care for my opinion."

BETH BYLER

The man with the ice blue eyes was back. During the last twenty-four hours, Beth Byler had been too busy with cooking and cleaning, answering the phone, and greeting concerned neighbors to even look up his name.

She should have been too busy to even realize he hadn't been around. But she'd felt his absence in the back of her mind, part of her continually wondering when he would show up again.

And why he hadn't returned.

"Hey," he said.

"Hey, yourself," she replied, and made sure that she didn't spare him more than the briefest of glances as she kneaded bread dough.

But as he leaned against the doorway and slowly looked her over, she could feel his gaze as sharply as if he'd reached out and touched skin.

She really should have been infuriated at this blatant inspection. Instead, she only felt that crisp sense of awareness
that had caught her off guard the last time he'd come to the
kitchen. She darted another look his way.

He lifted an eyebrow. "So, how are you doing in here?
Everything going okay?"

She knew he was teasing. She obviously wasn't doing very
well at all. Bowls and ingredients littered every surface. A
dusting of flour coated the floor. Actually, she felt like she
was covered with flour from head to toe. Making cinnamon
rolls from scratch was not for the fainthearted!

And though Frannie enjoyed baking, it was becoming very
apparent to Beth that she did not enjoy it. At all. Not that
Mr. Blue Eyes needed to know that. "I am doing just fine,
thank you very much."

"You don't look fine," he murmured. "You look like you're
in a competition to see how much flour you can wear."

"I am in no such thing."

"I'm just teasing, Beth. You know, if you try to clean your
area every so often, the mess is more manageable."

"Thank you for the tip," she said sarcastically. She was
about to ask him what he needed when, to her surprise, he
took his sweatshirt off and tossed it on a nearby chair. Then,
just as if he hadn't taken off part of his clothes in Frannie's
kitchen, he turned to the sink and turned on the faucet.

Now clad in nothing but another light blue T-shirt that
made his chest and arms seem even more muscular, he
grabbed a plate.

Embarrassed about her staring, and embarrassed about
the mess, she snapped at him. "What do you think you're
doing?"

He paused. "This is called washing dishes. I know you may

be unfamiliar with that task, but it involves turning on the water, washing things with soap, rinsing them, drying them with a clean dishtowel"—he stopped, raised an eyebrow—"and then putting them away." With a wink, he added, "If you are good, I'll give you some tips."

So, he could give as good as he got! For some reason, that made her thaw a little bit. "I know how to wash dishes. It may not look like it, but I do. I meant, why are you helping me?"

"Because it looks like you need it. You do, don't you? Or is someone stopping by to clean everything up?"

There was no one. No way was she going to ask either her mother or her sisters to help her at Frannie's. Oh, they wouldn't mind. They'd scurry over in a heartbeat, for sure. But they'd also have a jolly good time teasing her about her messy kitchen and her lack of baking skills.

She'd never live it down.

As she looked at Mr. Blue Eyes, and saw that his willingness to help was genuine, she came to a decision. There was pride, and then there was being smart enough to know when a kitchen had her beat.

And this kitchen had gotten the best of her from the first moment she'd stepped inside it. "I do not have anyone coming to help. And . . . and, I'd be much obliged if you would lend me a hand."

"Was that so hard?" He turned back on the water and grabbed the bottle of dish soap from under the sink. With a few squirts, the sink began to fill with hot, soapy water.

"Yes."

He smiled as he swished around the water with one hand, making the suds multiply.

"Oh! Wait a sec, would you . . . ?"

"What is wrong now?"

"I don't even know your name."

He turned to her as he turned off the faucet. "And why does that bother you?"

Was he really still not going to tell her his name? With a little vinegar in her voice, she replied, "For your information, I only let people I know on a first-name basis clean up after me."

Their eyes met. He slowly smiled, turning an already attractive face into something truly handsome. "My name is Chris."

It suited him. "Chris is a nice name." Of course, the moment she said the words, she wished she could take them back. Were any names not "nice"?

His smile deepened. "Thanks. I'm kind of partial to it." Then, like there was no need for further conversation, he turned again and plunged a bowl into the soapy water.

Beth watched him for a moment. Tried to imagine her brothers washing the dishes without a whole lot of prodding, but couldn't do it. Her brothers never would have done something so thoughtful without a good reason.

As he continued to scrub, she turned her focus back to the task at hand: kneading dough. Moments later, she rolled it out for the cinnamon rolls. When it was the right thickness, she sprinkled the sugar and pecan mixture she'd already made. Next, it was time to carefully roll the dough into a neat cylinder, and finally slice off the end of the log into neat one-inch sections.

After about the third slice, she found a good rhythm. She sliced and placed the circles into the greased pans by her side. It was a *gut* feeling to finally be doing something right for Frannie.

In no time at all, she was finished—just as Chris was finishing up his third bowl and the last of the thick blue stoneware plates that Frannie was so proud of.

"The cinnamon rolls look good."

"You know what, I think they might even turn out, when they rise some. I'm not much of a baker." Feeling her cheeks heat, she said, "Though, of course, I guess you have realized that."

"I've only been teasing you. I didn't come in here to judge, Beth."

She nodded, taking his words to heart.

Looking at the pans filled with rising sweet dough inside, he murmured, "So, are you planning to bake any of these today?"

She grinned, because Chris wasn't even trying to hide his anticipation of a taste testing. "I'll bake half today, and the rest tomorrow morning."

"Maybe I'll stick around, then."

She didn't know why that made her so happy all of a sudden.

Looking for something to say, she stammered, "S-s-so, did you come here for a job?"

"I did."

Stung by his lack of explanation, she faltered, desperate for another avenue of conversation. She knew from babysitting a great many children that most men loved to talk about their work. Trying to be friendly . . . and yes, because she was a little bit nosy, too, she said, "And . . . do you think you're going to like this job?"

"I hope so." He eyed her again, looked like he wasn't sure whether he wanted to reveal more of himself or not.

"Is it near the quarry?" she pressed, remembering his early question about the quarry.

"Close enough."

Oh, brother. She was just about to tell him that he could move on with his non-conversation when he said, "Listen, I know I sound pretty secretive. I don't mean to be. It's just that I don't want to jinx anything."

"Jinx?"

"I've been out of work for a while. So getting hired in Marion was a real relief. For right now, it doesn't matter if I like my boss or my job. Quite frankly, I'm going to like being employed. Good jobs are hard to come by, you know?"

"Oh, I know that," she said in a rush, now realizing why he hadn't been more forthcoming. "My *daed* was laid off for three months last year. Him being without a job was scary."

For the first time, his expression softened. "But he found something?"

She nodded. "He got on with one of the greenhouses in the area. Everyone needs help in the spring and summer. It was tough because he got laid off in October. No one wanted to hire anyone new before winter."

"So he had no job during Christmas?"

"Yep," Beth said, wondering how this man—this Chris—was managing to control the conversation again. He was telling her no information and she was practically telling him her whole life story! " Now, about you . . . do you know what you'll be doing?"

"I do. But it is sure to bore you."

"I'm sure it will not." Was he keeping his life a secret on purpose? "I find most things interesting."

His lips quirked. "Have you heard any news from your friend Frannie?"

"I got a phone call from the sheriff. I guess they're going to keep Frannie overnight again. But she will recover just fine."

He looked wary. "Why would the sheriff tell you that?"

"What do you mean?"

"I mean, why is the sheriff calling you with updates for the woman's injury?"

She relaxed. "Oh, you don't understand how things work in Crittenden County. The sheriff is Mose Kramer. Everyone knows him. He's more of a gossip than the sewing circle at the library. Plus, he knows it would be difficult for me to visit there. I have no car, of course."

"Hmm." Chris didn't look very impressed, and she supposed he wouldn't be. Describing Mose was a difficult thing, and she wasn't doing a very good job of it.

"Anyway," she said, feeling her way around, now that he seemed so discomfited, "Mose said that Frannie's eye is bandaged, but she should be just fine, and will probably be healed up by tomorrow. She's only staying another night because the doctor didn't think she would rest here."

Chris looked at her with a steady gaze, his lips pursed, the muscle in his cheek tense. "I hope and pray that is what happens, then."

Hearing the word *pray* set her at ease. "Are you a praying man, Chris?"

Just like that, his expression shuttered. "I am. At least, I used to be."

"But not anymore?" She shouldn't have asked such a thing. It was rude and none of her business.

"No. I've learned that prayer doesn't always help."

His honesty shook her hard. She, too, used to feel more of a connection with the Lord. But like going for daily walks or eating three servings of vegetables, her good habit had drifted to the side. Now praying to give thanks seemed like a lot of bother, as well as a futile exercise.

And now she seemed to only pray when she wanted something. Or needed something. Or was afraid.

"I notice that you aren't correcting me."

"I don't know you well enough to correct you," she said primly.

Something shuttered in his eyes and suddenly, he became more distant than ever. "You're right." Rapping his knuckles on the wooden counter, he said, "I should probably get going."

Yes, she supposed he did need to go. To prepare for a job he wouldn't describe, so he could go to a place he wouldn't disclose. As he looked ready to run out of the kitchen, she blurted, "I thank you for your help. It was mighty considerate of you to give me your time."

But all she got was a hand raised. It was a half-wave, a half-goodbye.

She did the same, half teasing him, just to see how he'd react.

But she never found out because he never turned back around.

Chapter 9

"Of course I began to hate Perry—he stole from my parents. But that don't mean I killed him."

JACOB SCHROCK

Deborah still couldn't believe she'd had the misfortune to see Jacob Schrock at his parents' store. What luck! No one had even mentioned that he was back in town. If she'd known that there was a chance of seeing him, she definitely would have listened to her mother and avoided the Schrock's Variety at all costs.

Now that they'd spoken and it was evident that he hoped to never see her again, Deborah was even more determined to stay away from the market for good. It would be a nuisance of course. Schrock's wasn't the only store in town, but it was the only Amish market of its kind. There was no other store in walking distance where it was possible to buy fabric, kerosene, homemade rolls, and farm-fresh eggs.

But talking to Jacob brought back too many emotions she didn't want to feel. Embarrassment about her brother's actions. Pain that stemmed from lost opportunities. Then there was her childish crush that never seemed to vanish.

After all this time, she'd thought she'd become used to other people's accusing looks and pointing fingers. She'd thought she'd finally pushed aside the shame about her brother. But her conversation with Jacob proved that she'd been hopelessly naïve. No matter what she did, for the rest of her life, Deborah was going to be known as the drug dealer's sister. There was little chance of redeeming herself in people's eyes.

To some members of her community, she was going to always be in Perry's dark shadow. It cast a long shadow, too—terribly hard to step out of.

It was beyond ironic that Jacob Schrock—the man she'd always secretly hoped would be her husband—couldn't seem to stand the sight of her.

Perry would no doubt find that amusing.

Armed with her tote that she'd hoped to fill with fresh dairy products but which now remained empty because she'd been so anxious to leave the market, she started on home. As always, the three miles it took to get home was calming.

As difficult as it was, she was glad to be back in Crittenden County, surrounded by the things she knew so well. The lush scenery, with the creeks and valleys and dense foliage, looked so different than the acres of farmland that covered almost every inch of Charm. There was a sense of coziness to Crittenden County. The narrow rural streets, the abundant greenery. All of it gave one the sense of closeness, of being cushioned in security. So different than Ohio's wide-open spaces.

So, though she'd been charmed by Charm and relieved to get away from the scrutiny here, she was glad to be back in her comfortable surroundings. As she continued walking, she looked with longing at the entrance to the Millers' farm. Before everything had happened, she would've been tempted to trespass and cross through the middle of it. The Millers didn't care for people walking through their fields, but most people went through, anyway. Their land was vast and underutilized. The Millers were older and just couldn't keep up with their large property like they used to. But instead of selling it to one of the many young Amish couples desperate for farming land, they'd selfishly clung to their property.

As if giving it away would diminish their importance.

Instead, their intent to keep it for themselves had made everyone feel like it was fair game. And because of that, no one had really been surprised to hear that those English girls had decided to smoke in the middle of it.

The Millers' land had lately become something of a spot to do things in private.

She'd even heard that Perry and Frannie had met there more than once.

Remembering when he'd come home from one of their meetings so angry, she flinched . . . sensing his anger and feeling it all over again.

"Perry, what happened?" she'd asked when he'd stormed up their driveway.

To her surprise, her brother had answered immediately. "Frannie Eicher . . . she left me."

Left? Warily, she said, "You mean that she doesn't want to see you anymore?"

With a jerk, he shook his head. "She said I changed."

He had. "What did you say?"

"I said if I changed, that was good. And she should want to change, too."

Everyone knew Frannie to be one of the most easygoing

women in the area. "I'm sure if you go visit her and explain that you were tired . . ."

"Tired? I'm not tired."

Ah. So his red eyes and antsy moves didn't stem from lack of sleep. Once again, she chided herself for being so childish and naïve. Like her parents, she'd been happy to see only what she wanted to be true.

"If you aren't tired, then what is wrong with you?" she blurted, finally ready to hear the truth. "Why are your eyes so red and glassy?"

"I'm fine. My eyes are fine." His voice turned hard. "Deborah." When she'd been little, she'd truly hated her name. She had thought it far too big and old-sounding for a girl her age.

When she'd told Perry that, he'd promptly called her "D"—rarely ever addressing her by her first name.

But now, he had a new edge to his voice. She should've heeded it. "You are not fine," she'd pushed. "You're acting so harsh. Nothing like the Perry we know and love."

He'd frozen, then looked at her like she'd just said the best thing in the world. "*Gut*. The last thing in the world I want to be is the Perry you knew. I'd rather die than be the way I used to be. If I'm acting harsh, then that means I've stopped letting others take advantage of me. That's something, ain't so?"

He'd pushed by her then, walking into the house, past their questioning mother. He'd closed his door and hadn't come out until late the next day.

At first, her parents had blamed his disappearance on her. On something like sibling rivalry. Later, they were sure she'd known more than she was letting on. Of course she had. She remembered feeling so trapped, so torn. But if she told everything she knew, then she'd be betraying someone who trusted her.

Still walking, still fretting, Deborah scanned the area,

hoping to see anything to take her mind off the dark memories. About a block from her house, she saw Abby Anderson, the girl who had found Perry's body. Because she was Walker's sister, Deborah had seen her from time to time. But they'd never had the occasion to talk.

Maybe they could now?

As the girl unabashedly stared right back, Deborah realized that Abby was probably thinking the same thing.

Eager to continue to face things instead of avoiding them, she stopped. "Hello. You're Abby, right?"

"Yeah. It's been a while since we've seen each other." Perhaps thinking of the funeral, when a few *Englischers* had stayed to the back of the crowd, she bit her lip. "I mean, it's been a while since we've talked."

Amazing how even recalling the funeral could still make her choke up. "How are you?"

Abby looked at her feet. "I don't know. Still shaken up. Would you be upset if I said that I'm sorry I found Perry?"

"I wouldn't be upset." Actually, she was so tired of talking around her problems, talking around the circumstances of Perry's death, it was a relief that someone mentioned him outright. She almost smiled.

Noticing the way her features relaxed, Abby frowned. "I said the wrong thing, didn't I?"

"*Nee.* It's just that I started realizing that of course you wouldn't have wanted to find my brother the way you did. It wasn't your fault."

"I don't know why I found him. No matter how hard I've tried, I haven't been able to understand why God led me to that spot." Her voice lowered. "It was so scary."

For the first time, she saw the event through Abby's eyes. "I imagine you were terribly frightened."

"Frightened and afraid." Still not looking her way, Abby added, "And so alone. I don't know if I've ever felt so alone."

Deborah thought that was curious, for sure. She'd heard that Abby had been with two friends. Had they abandoned her? Though she'd just been feeling alone herself, she dug deep and tried to offer solace. "I've come to realize that some things are God's will and that it isn't up to us to wonder why we are put in difficult situations. Or wonderful-*gut* ones. Sometimes all we need to know is that it is His will."

"And you believe that?"

"I have to. If God isn't involved in our lives, then we are completely alone, and we can't have that."

Finally, Abby stared at her. "I suppose."

"I suppose that, too." Deborah smiled and felt a warmth spread inside her when Abby returned the smile. Impulsively, she spoke. "You know what? I'm on my way home, but would you like to go to Mary King Yoder's instead? A slice of pie sounds like a good idea."

After a moment's pause, Abby nodded. "I'd like that." When they started walking in the direction of the restaurant housed in a somewhat rough-looking trailer, Abby spoke. "Deborah, this is nice."

"What is?"

"Meeting you out of the blue. Having you not hate me."

"I would never hate you for finding my brother's body." She paused, thinking about what Abby had said, wondering why she had to be the one to find her brother's body.

"You know, I've wondered time and again why the Lord picked my brother to take the path he went on. I've been angry and hurt and I've prayed." Deborah thought about continuing, but she didn't have any more to add. She had done all those things—but so far, they hadn't seemed to make much of a difference.

"Did you get answers?" Hope shone in Abby's eyes. "Did God talk to you?"

Deborah considered lying. It would be the kinder thing, surely, to offer Abby some sort of hope in an almost hopeless situation. But she was so tired of lying. And keeping secrets. She just didn't think she was capable of covering up one more. "Truthfully? No."

"Oh."

"But that doesn't mean He won't," she declared. If she'd learned one thing since hearing about Perry's death—and then discovering what was in his room—it was that sometimes hope was the only thing a person was able to cling to.

Chapter 10

"Some say a fool can't be trusted. I prefer to say that a fool can't be trusted twice."

AARON SCHROCK

Frannie Eicher was bored. She had now been in her beige hospital room for twenty-four hours, and that was twenty-three hours too long. There was truly no reason to still be trapped there. She felt fine now. Almost good.

Okay, *good* was stretching things a bit. Her face was bruised and swollen, and there were too many cuts on her face to count. Above all that, her eye ached. She was more tired than she could ever remember being, and her brain felt a little fuzzy.

But all that aside, she was definitely well enough to be released from her side of the beige, sterile room. After Luke left, the walls seemed to close in on her, making her feel like she was trapped in a closet.

More than anything, she ached to open a window and have the fresh air fan her face and cool her worries. But the nurse had told her that the windows were not made to be opened.

As her roommate's voice grew louder on the phone—truly

the woman had more friends and problems than a whole congregation—Frannie gritted her teeth.

Which is how the doctor found her.

"You're looking pretty upset, Frannie," he said after checking her pulse and reading her chart. "Is the pain worse?"

"*Nee.* I just don't like being here."

His worried expression eased. "You'd be surprised how many people tell me that. No one likes being in the hospital."

"The windows won't open and my roommate is chatty. Don'tcha think I could leave now?"

Dr. Carlson looked up from the notes he was taking. "You're really chomping at the bit. Are you sure you feel ready to be on your way?"

Hope filled her tone. "Oh, yes. My eye will soon be better, right?"

"It's healing, and the pain should lessen every day." He looked at her chart again. "I see here that you're only taking Ibuprofen now. That seems to be taking care of the pain?"

"*Jah.*" She'd take the dull pain that remained over the feeling of being trapped.

He glanced at her chart again. "The stitches can come out in a week. You can come back for that, or perhaps you have someone who could remove them for you?"

"Yes. We have a local midwife who's had some medical training. She's given children stitches. Perhaps she could take them out, too?"

"Most likely."

All that news sounded hopeful. "So you will let me leave? Soon?" She was proud of herself for not saying *immediately*.

His lips twitched. "I didn't say that."

"What are you saying?" She felt crestfallen. "What are you waiting for?"

To her irritation, his half-smile turned into a broad grin. "You are an impatient patient, aren't you?" he asked, making a little joke. "Frannie, before I sign your release form, I'd like to know what you're planning to do when you get home."

The question caught her off guard. "What I'm planning to do?"

"Yes." He looked at her steadily. "I want to know what you intend to do for the next few days."

It sounded like a trick question, but she didn't see how it could be. "Well, I run a bed-and-breakfast, you see. It's called The Yellow Bird Inn. It was once my aunt's." Though she knew her mouth was running, she couldn't seem to stop. "The Yellow Bird is not too big of a place. There's only six bedrooms. But it keeps me plenty busy, with cooking and cleaning, and organizing things."

He shifted. "Cooking and cleaning and organizing?"

Though she could have sworn she heard a note of dismay in his voice she got so excited about getting back to the inn, that her mouth just kept moving. "Oh, *jah*. I have become a pretty good innkeeper. And I even have guests, now." The good Lord knew that wasn't always the case.

"How many guests?"

"Three rooms are full up."

He gazed at her once again, then scanned her chart. "Your inn sounds very nice."

"Oh, it is! You should come one day and stay for the night. Each bedroom has its own bathroom. All the furniture is Amish made, and Amish sewn quilts are on every bed. Outside, we have a nice garden and some walking paths. I just painted the outside yellow."

"You did?"

"Well, me and a pair of painters. The men did the high spots, but I painted much of the trim a shiny bright white."

"When did you have time to paint?"

"Oh, I made time. I'm not much for sitting around."

A line formed between his brows. "It doesn't sound like it."

"It's impossible, you see, because there really is a lot to do. I'm a *gut* cook too. Every morning, I make eggs and bacon for the guests. Along with granola and fresh muffins and little quiches."

"My mouth is watering. I'll have to tell my wife about it."

"I hope you do."

"And who runs it with you?"

She paused. "No one."

"Ah."

Ah? Suddenly, he wasn't sounding all that excited. "I'm a mighty good innkeeper, *Doctah*. I work hard to keep the place looking nice and clean."

"I'm sure you do a very good job. I bet your inn is exceptional." He wrote something down. "When you get home, will you, by chance, still have guests?"

"I hope so." She bit her lip. "If they haven't left by now. My friend Beth was going to try to stay and help out a bit. But you never know . . . It takes a lot of work to keep things running right. And she doesn't cook all that well."

"So she's not much help?"

"She is, but Beth has her own job, you see. She's a babysitter for some women in the area."

"So you won't have Beth's help."

"No." As soon as she said the word, she wished she could take it back. Saying she intended to do a lot of work might not have been the best way to assure him she was ready to leave . . .

He crossed his arms over his chest. "So you're saying that as soon as I release you, you're going to go right back to work." He took a breath. "Then, when you do go to work, it's going to strenuous and you have no help."

She couldn't lie. Though she wanted to. "Yes."

He looked at her steadily. "I see."

She smiled. "I'm glad we discussed this."

"You're staying another night."

All happiness vanished like a blink of her one eye. "What? But I'm better!"

"You're better, but you're far from being healed. I think another twenty-four hours of rest and relaxation will help you."

Frannie closed her eyes in frustration. She was just about to argue, to do anything she could do get herself out of her half of that beige prison . . . when she realized he'd already gone through the curtains.

"*Doktah?*" she murmured.

"Oh, he's long gone, honey," said the lady from the other side. "You sure dug yourself a deep hole, though. Really fast, too."

Frannie wanted to ignore her. She really did.

But she was so lonely and depressed, she found herself responding. "What do you mean?"

"I mean that if you want to get out of here, you have to tell everyone that you aren't going to do anything but sit and rest when you get home. That you won't hardly lift a finger."

"But that's not true."

"That's why they invented the word *lying*, dear. So you can make stuff up and pretend it's true." She chuckled again, her laugh sounding so warm and full of mirth that they could have been close friends. How strange, since Frannie had never actually even seen the woman.

"I guess I shouldn't have told him I was going to be so busy," she admitted. "Next time I see him, I'll follow your advice. *Danke*."

"You're welcome, dear."

Then something occurred to her. "Ma'am, if you know what to say, why haven't you said any of that? Why are you still here?"

"That's easy, dear. Unlike you, I don't want to leave."

"Oh," she murmured, just as the lady's phone rang and she answered.

What did it mean to be more comfortable with a hospital room than in your own home?

Pushing aside her worries, Frannie focused on the lady sharing her room. Had the woman been so distressed that she could only find comfort in her constant phone conversations? Could she never find peace by herself . . . knowing that the Lord was beside her always?

Though Frannie knew there were times in her life where she was sad, frustrated, and confused, she always knew where to turn when she felt alone. How thankful she was for God's presence in her life.

Frannie was still sitting and trying to be thankful despite the doctor's orders when she heard the door open. It was followed by a shuffling from the other side of the curtain.

Since her roommate's noisy relatives seemed to enter at all hours of the day and night, Frannie half listened. Hoped an orderly or nurse was making plans to wheel her roommate out for a bit.

Getting a break from the noisy woman would be welcome, for sure. When she heard nothing, she found herself leaning a little bit closer to the curtain, listening for a clue of who had just arrived. If the woman was due for more company, perhaps at the very least they would talk about something interesting. For the last hour, the only thing the lady had talked about were her friend's children, who sounded like the worst sort of hellions. Frannie didn't understand how telling children "no" could be such a difficult thing.

The steps pattered closer.

Wary, she looked at the curtain. Saw it flutter.

Oh, surely another nurse wasn't coming in with a needle? She was so tired of getting her blood drawn.

The curtain parted, and she blinked in surprise. "Micah!"

"Yes, it is me. Hello, Frannie."

"It's *gut* to see you again," she said, smiling.

"I am happy to see you, too." Pausing with his back brushing the curtains, he looked her over with frank appreciation. "I do like your smile, Frannie. You must be doing better."

"Some, but not much. The *doktah* is making me stay another day."

"That is a shame. But if the doctor says you must stay here, then I suppose you should. He is in charge."

That was Micah. Nothing if not practical.

To her surprise, he walked closer and sat right down without being asked. And then, to her further surprise, he reached for her hand despite the bandages—and clasped it gently between his own. Immediately, she felt his warmth.

"What is going on?" She didn't mind his hand-holding. Not really. It was just that it was terribly unlike him to show affection.

"Nothing. I decided to take some time off and spend it here with you."

Uncertainty threaded through her. First the hand-holding, now he'd taken time off from the farm? In all the years she'd known him, he'd never willingly done either. "I'm grateful that you stopped by," she said cautiously.

Why was he here? Why was he *really* here? She was sure it wasn't just to spend time with her. No, he seemed like a man on a mission.

Which made her mighty uncomfortable.

"You should be grateful. I had a lot of other chores that I had to push aside in order to pay you a call today."

She *should* be grateful? Carefully, she looked for any sign that he might be joking. But no, he was perfectly serious.

Now she was no longer uncomfortable. Not the slightest bit nervous, either.

She was now angry.

"I've also been waiting for you to notice me. To notice how serious my regard for you is," he added, holding her hand tighter. Sounding vaguely disapproving.

She glanced his way. Surely he really was joking?

If he'd shown her any attention, it was because she had asked for it. He'd never offered anything on his own.

She looked at his hand, holding hers. Suddenly, he'd taken a keen interest in her and her attention.

With a wince, she realized he was gripping it so tightly she could feel the slick moisture of his palm.

Studying the set of his strong jaw, Frannie realized he was nervous. Whatever had brought him here had made him uneasy.

In a blink, she turned nervous again.

"I've always been grateful for your friendship," she said. "What is wrong, Micah? Why are you acting so strangely?"

"Friendship?" His brows rose under the black brim of his hat. "I think you know that there's more than that between us. Quite a bit more."

Was there? At one time she'd hoped that was the case. But since all that had happened with Perry, and her reaction to Luke, she began to realize that Micah was just . . . convenient. But perhaps he had viewed their disjointed relationship far differently? "More?"

"Our relationship is not like the one you have with the detective," he said tightly.

"Luke?"

He nodded with a jerk of his head.

Ah. Now she understood. This visit was about Luke. Micah obviously hadn't taken her friendship with the *Englischer* in stride.

"Indeed, you are right. It isn't," she said, unsure what else to say. She didn't want to talk about Luke with Micah. Didn't want to explore feelings she shouldn't have. Didn't want to think about a future that was impossible.

Her reality was sitting by her bedside. She needed to remember that.

After a final, gentle squeeze, Micah released her hand and braced both his palms on his knees. Then leaned forward and spoke. "I did something important. I talked to my mother about us, Frannie."

"You did?" She swallowed hard. She had never particularly cared for Micah's mother. She was a bossy woman who rarely wanted to listen to Frannie's opinions. "And what did you say?"

"I told her that I intend for us to marry soon."

"You told her what?" Oh, surely he was not intending to propose marriage to her here, after all?

And if he was going to, what would she say?

Her earlier conversation with her roommate played through her head. Frannie needed time to think about all this. Micah's sudden, smothering attention. His intentions.

This was not the right time. Or place. But how could she possibly tell him so, especially with the earnest look he wore? After all, it was the man who took charge of things like this.

"It is time I set things in motion, don'tcha think? I believe a small wedding would be best."

Or . . . perhaps he didn't feel the need to propose at all? Was he simply assuming her answer would be a yes and the formality wasn't necessary?

Oh!

If she hadn't been stuck in the hospital bed, tethered by tubes and electronic cords, she would have kicked him out.

Suspiciously aware of how thin that curtain was between her and her roommate, she sputtered a reply. "Micah, I'm not altogether sure we should be discussing this now."

"Why not? Mamm said talking to you in the hospital is as good a spot as any." He grinned. Then winked! "Here, you can't run away."

Oh, but this was terrible. Terrible and awkward, too. She had to stop him. Somehow. Some way.

She lowered her voice. "We don't have much privacy here."

He puffed up his chest. "We don't need much privacy. I mean, I do not. There is nothing on my mind that would embarrass me if it became known."

Who was this . . . this eager man sitting by her bedside? It was as if someone had taken the Micah she'd always known and put this man in his place. "Micah, I'm glad you want to talk about our relationship but I'd rather not discuss it here. Perhaps when I get back home?" That is, if she ever got back home . . .

She had a sickening feeling that the only reason he was here was because he'd heard of Luke's visit. Because Micah felt that Frannie's attention might have strayed. Even worse, she suspected he cared little about Frannie's feelings, that he simply didn't want the embarrassment of an *Englischer* stealing her away. Not after she'd shown so much interest in Perry as well.

Her temper rose. The right thing to do would probably be to admit that there was nothing going on between her and Luke, and there never would be.

But as she stared at him, at his sudden eagerness, all she could do was bite her lip and listen.

"I disagree." Softening his tone, he continued. "So, Frannie, you are ready for us to move forward, yes? Because you cannot expect me to always wait quietly by while you make up your mind."

Her hands fisted around the hospital sheet. "I've been running my inn, not sitting by the door, thinking of ways to make you wait." The truth was, she had been waiting to feel something more for him. To feel able to overlook his flaws and their differences . . . and feel certain that they could have a happy life together.

However, now was the not the time to point out any of that. She was too angry and would surely say something she might regret. "Perry died, don't you forget. That has been hard."

"Only to people who will miss him," he said piously.

Though in her opinion, he wasn't saying anything particularly Christian at all. "Micah, I am starting to get a headache. It might be best if you come back later."

"Truly?" He looked perplexed, as if he'd expected her to leap out of the hospital bed and jump for joy that he'd finally, finally decided to talk about their future.

She cleared her throat and patted his hand. "It is time you left."

"I see." He stood up.

"Thank you for stopping by." She managed a smile.

Right before her eyes, he suddenly became a completely different man. His soft edges became hard, his almost guileless expression turned sharp.

"You may have gotten your way in the past, and you may get your way right now, but I won't be pushed away when you are my *frau*, Frannie. When you are my wife, I will be in charge of the household."

After treating her to one more frightful look—one that validated her earlier nervousness—he tipped his head, turned, and shoved the curtains aside.

As he walked away, he didn't look back.

Frannie closed her eyes. Before, she'd yearned for him to have more of a backbone. She'd always looked forward to her husband being in charge of their family.

But this conversation with Micah made her reconsider all of that.

When at last she heard the door close, she breathed a sigh of relief.

And then heard a cackle next door to her. "You better watch that one, Missy," the voice in the bed next to hers called out. "He's got secrets that aren't all good. You mark my words about that."

With a sense of doom, Frannie found herself agreeing. There was definitely much more to Micah than she'd ever imagined.

Much more than she'd ever guessed.

"I used to really like him," she said.

"Come, now. Did you really? He seems a little whiney to me. Were you that desperate for a man?"

Had she been? *"Nee,"* she said softly, and knew the truth

of her words. "I've been desperate for love," she murmured, half to herself.

It was why she'd been swayed by Perry's attentions.

It was why she'd kept things open and undecided so long with Micah.

The woman tsked. "Aren't we all, child. Aren't we all. But my advice is to keep on looking. That boy isn't the one for you."

Frannie rolled onto her side and looked out the window at the darkening sky . . . . desperately doing her best to push both her doubts and the sudden image of Luke's face from her mind.

She dozed for a while, and when she awoke, it was dark and all was blessedly quiet. As she lay there, adjusting her eye to the light, she realized Luke's image had been completely banished during her nap.

But it had been replaced with the memory of Micah's determined expression . . . and Perry's laughing scorn.

She realized then that she was more nervous about the future than ever before.

It was too bad that she didn't know why.

Chapter 11

"When Perry was twelve, he broke his collarbone jumping out of a hayloft on a dare. I could be wrong, but I do believe that's the last time he was seen by the doctor. Until he died, of course."

SHERIFF MOSE KRAMER

"Beth, dear, you don't look too well."

Leave it to her mother to be brutally honest. That was okay, though. Beth loved her mother's honesty. "As a matter of fact, I'm not feeling too well. My legs are sore, my shoulders have knots in them, and I'm so, so tired. Being an innkeeper is not for me, Mamm."

"Poor Beth. Perhaps we should find you some help. Who do you think could lend you a hand at Frannie's inn?"

"There is no one else. I would never betray my promise to Frannie by passing on this job."

"Do you want me to come help you?"

"No, Mamm. I want you to stay here and take care of yourself." Her mother had been diagnosed with MS years ago. For most of her life, it had lain dormant, with only minor flare-ups. But lately, she'd been showing more and more signs of being tired and having blurry vision.

Beth alternated between pretending that nothing was wrong and trying to convince her beautiful mother to do less.

"I'm feeling pretty good this week."

"Then we should celebrate that instead of making you work harder. I'll be fine. I just miss being around the *kinner*, that's all."

"I'm glad you enjoy babysitting, but you need to have some *kinner* of your own one day." What went unsaid was that she wanted Beth to be happily married with a home and family before her health got worse.

But even thinking about that day made her sad. How had this conversation gone from innkeeping to her lack of children? "You know there's no one special in my life."

"There could be if you would be more open-minded. Beth, you should give the men in our community another chance."

This was a common bit of advice that her mother brought up with surprising regularity. "Love doesn't work that way. I have to feel something special for the man in my life."

"How do you know if you will, if you don't give any one a chance?"

"I will, one day. In its own time, Mamm. Don't push."

Immediately, her sweet-tempered mother backed off. "I'm sorry. It's just that looking around again worked for Frannie. One day she and Perry decided they wanted to be closer." Beth knew her mother had found Frannie and Perry's brief relationship a great matter of interest. It didn't seem to matter to her that Perry had turned out to be a terrifically bad person to fall in love with.

"I'll find the right man for me one day, Mamm. And in the meantime, I have a *gut* job helping to take care of other people's children. They need help and I enjoy getting paid for something that I'm good at."

"You're right, of course. I just can't help but wonder . . ." Her mother stopped herself with a sad look in her eyes and changed the subject. Looking her over, she added, "So, how many guests are at the Yellow Bird Inn right now?"

"There were three, but now we're down to just one."

"Only one? Well, perhaps that won't be too hard." Leaning forward, her mother's face lit up. "Now, you know how much I enjoy hearing about your days. Where is the guest from? Is she nice?"

"Oh, it's not a woman, it's a man. An *Englischer.*" She smiled softly, because just thinking about him made her tingly.

The expectant look faded. "The guest is a man? Dear, is it safe for you to be alone with him?"

"Very safe. He's a nice man." She paused, then divulged her secret, just because she knew it would make her mother smile. "He's mighty handsome, too."

"Oh." She paused. "Oh?"

"He has light blue eyes, the color of the winter sky. And somewhat shaggy blond hair that is the color of wheat."

Her mother's eyes narrowed. "Winter sky eyes? Wheat-colored hair? He sounds mighty nature-like. And you two have talked?"

"Oh, *jah*. We've talked a bit. He's come to the kitchen while I've been cooking."

Her mother's lips curved into a wry smile. "Visiting you in the kitchen, hmm? He must be a mighty brave man."

"Ha, ha." Sobering, she said, "I am having a fearful time cooking. But I'm doing my best."

"That's all anyone can ask for, Beth." Clucking her tongue a bit, she turned the conversation back to the man. "There's nothing wrong with looking at a handsome man. Or even chatting with him from time to time. But don't get your head turned. You need to find a man interested in sharing your life with you . . . not taking you away from everything you know and love."

"I hear you, Mother."

"Now, you promise there isn't anything I can help you with there?"

"No, Mamm. You need to stay home. I hate to think of you worrying yourself on my account."

"Oh, I'm glad for the excuse to leave the house. Besides, worrying about daughters is what mothers do. One day you'll realize that. If, you know, you ever find yourself a man. An Amish man. Who lives here. That is the man for you."

"Yes, Mamm. I hear you."

And she certainly did hear her. And she agreed with everything her mother said, too. Finding a man who was Amish who wanted to live nearby and have a household of children sounded like a good plan.

It just wasn't that easy to do. Especially since no matter how hard she tried, she couldn't stop thinking about Chris.

Frannie had barely recovered from Micah's visit when Sheriff Kramer poked his head through the curtain.

It was somewhat disconcerting to see him peer at her without a word.

She nodded her head slightly and felt the tug of the bandages around her eye. For a moment there, lost in the haze of the medication, she'd forgotten her injury. "Hello, Sheriff Kramer."

The sheriff's sun-weathered face creased into a smile. "I am glad you are awake. The nurses weren't sure if you would be up to talking with me." He looked her over. "Are you?"

"I can talk with you, for sure." But even as she said the words, she felt her body fill with dread. Sheriff Kramer had come to the hospital for a reason.

The sheriff sauntered closer and took the seat next to her bedside. "Did you know you're frowning? That's not good. We need to turn your frown upside down, Frannie Eicher."

"I'm afraid I don't feel like smiling much at the moment. Dr. Carlson said I have to stay another day. He feared I would do too much when I got home." Then, of course, there had been Micah's disturbing visit. Every time she tried to relax, his words kept replaying in her mind.

"I can see you being disappointed that you're not at your inn. You always have been a hard worker." Making himself comfortable in the chair next to her bed, he kicked his legs out and crossed his ankles. Smiling, he said, "To tell you the truth, I never liked being stuck in hospitals, either." Looking around her room, he added, "These rooms have always reminded me of old oatmeal, so cold and boring."

As usual, the sheriff could outtalk a preacher and charm a rattle from a rattler. On a normal day, Frannie would've made a quip right back. Teased him about how he shouldn't be lurking around hospital rooms, anyway.

But she wasn't up for joking.

And though he was good at making conversation, she knew he wasn't there just to make her smile.

"Are you here to discuss the investigation?"

"Actually, ah, there are some things we need to discuss."

"All right."

As if she wasn't lying beside him, struggling to breathe, the sheriff shuffled in the pockets of his jacket for a pen and reading glasses. Then he rummaged around for a small spiral notebook. After slipping on his glasses and flipping through several sheets, he took the cap off his pen and looked at her again.

Frannie held her breath as a dozen questions filled her head. She wondered why Luke hadn't come to give her any breaking news. She wondered what the sheriff could have found that had made him stop by and visit her here in the hospital room. He'd already been there this morning with her father.

He took a breath. "Frannie, it's come to my attention that you and Perry went walking at the Millers' farm a time or two. Henry Miller saw you there himself . . . as did a few other people."

Scrambling to keep her emotions in check, she replied, "Yes. We did. Perry liked to go on walks. I . . . I know we were trespassing." Against her will, images of being with Perry filled her head. Reminding her of how little she'd known him. And how flighty she'd been, so happy that a man like him had turned to her after Lydia Plank had broken his heart. How she'd been so sure she could draw him back to his roots.

She'd been a fool.

"When you went to the farm . . . where did you go?"

Frannie closed the one eye that wasn't bandaged, mainly in an attempt to buy herself some time. She knew exactly where they went. But could she tell the sheriff? That seemed foolhardy.

"Oh, we only walked around," she murmured. "The Millers' property is big, and not used much anymore."

"It is big. And what you say is true. Much of their fields are fallow. So where did you and Perry walk to?"

Though it was no excuse, she couldn't help adding, "A lot of people cut through the land. It's in the center of town."

"I'm aware other people walk through." His voice was sharper now. Gone was his usual gossipy nature, when his words were slow and his voice was tinged with humor.

Now his tone echoed Luke's. The difference was unsettling.

"Sheriff, I haven't walked through the Millers' land since. Since, you know . . . when Perry and I were still courting."

"When you two walked, when you were still courting . . . where did you walk?"

"I'm not sure I remember, exactly."

"Frannie, some honesty would be mighty appreciated about now. I've asked you the same question several times and you've done your best to not answer. I'd like you to answer me."

His voice was as stern as she'd ever heard it. "Yes, sir."

"Let's begin, then. Where, exactly, did you two go, when you went walking on the Millers' land?"

"Sometimes, we . . . we, uh, walked in the woods near the highway." Remembering how secretive Perry had been, how emotional and tumultuous his moods had been, she added, "Perry liked to walk there, because it was hidden."

"And?"

"And sometimes we would kiss." She felt her cheeks flush. Here she was, twenty years old, practically covered in bandages. But still blushing.

"I want to know other places you walked on Millers' farm, Frannie. Did you two go anywhere else?"

One image flashed forward as clear as day. Even though she'd tried so very hard to forget, it seemed determined to never go away. "Yes . . ."

He crossed one leg over the other and stared at her.

And that's when she knew he knew the truth.

"Sometimes we walked in the Millers' west field." She looked at Sheriff Kramer. "Do you know the one I mean? It's the field that begins right across from the high school."

"The one with the well?" he asked softly.

"*Jah.*" She swallowed hard and told herself to speak clearly. To force back the worst images and concentrate on the facts. "The last time Perry and I went walking on the Millers' farm together, we were in that field near the high school."

"When was this?"

She swallowed hard. "December."

"When in December?"

"The thirty-first."

His gaze sharpened. "On New Year's Eve. So you saw him right before he went missing."

She nodded, feeling the dark emotions that had cloaked her while she'd been in Perry's company return. "That last time we were together, it was near twilight. We were walking alone." She paused for a moment as the memory sharpened. "Well, Perry was walking quickly and I was struggling to keep up."

"Why do you think he was in such a hurry?"

"I don't know. Back then I could never guess how he would act. Or the reasons."

"Then what happened?"

"When I caught up with him, I knew he wasn't safe to be around."

"And why was that?"

"His eyes were glassy." Though it hurt to do so, she wrinkled her nose. "It had become obvious that he'd been taking drugs again."

He started scribbling in his notebook.

Hoping to finish the interview quickly, she said, "Anyway, we stopped, and I told him I was going to go home. We got in a terrible fight."

"What was the fight about?"

It had been about a great many things, she thought. But mainly it had been about the fact that she didn't want anything to do with him anymore. "We fought because neither of us was going to change." Before she lost her nerve, she shared the rest of the story. "Sheriff Kramer, we were fighting where he was found."

"Where exactly?"

She was confused by his question. They all knew the place where Perry's body had been discovered. "You know. Right by the well." Oh, but she felt sick at heart now. When she'd left Perry, she'd been so disappointed by how things had ended up between them that she'd never spared a thought of what might happen to him out alone on the Millers' land in his state.

Maybe his killer had been lurking there, just waiting for his chance to attack Perry?

She looked at Sheriff Kramer and couldn't take it any longer. "Do you think I had something to do with his death? Is that what you are worried about? Is that why you came here to the hospital?"

"I didn't say that."

He was speaking so . . . so differently, not in his usual way. He was frightening her. "Mose, I mean, Sheriff, I promise you this, I did not kill Perry. I would never have killed him. We might have had our differences, but that didn't mean I wanted him dead. You know that. Right?"

With some dismay, she realized her hands were shaking.

She could never have imagined anyone would think she was capable of doing such a thing.

She paused, half waiting for him to rush to her defense. Half waiting for him to tell her that of course no one would ever think she could harm another person. After all, she was a nurturing sort.

But the sheriff didn't respond. Only continued to scribble on his notepad.

Panic engulfed her. "Sheriff Kramer, you believe me, don'tcha?" Tension infused her voice as she rushed on. "You agree that I could never harm Perry. You agree that I'm not capable of hurting him. Right?"

Instead of nodding he looked directly at her. "Besides you wanting to go home . . . what did you and Perry talk about? Do you remember?"

Unfortunately, she remembered every bit of their conversation so clearly it could have been stamped into her head. "Perry, he wanted me to change. And to think about moving."

Sheriff Kramer, busy writing, stopped. "Change, how?"

"He wanted me to leave the order. He wanted me to change who I was," she explained in a rush. "Perry wanted me to become English and follow him to wherever he wanted to go." Of course, she'd realized that those things were just the beginning. She knew that if she couldn't change to suit his new life, she'd lose him.

"And what did you say when he asked you to change? To leave Crittenden County?"

"I told him I didn't want to leave. And that I didn't want to become English," she confessed. "I said that I liked who I was, and that I had thought he'd liked me, too."

Though she was talking to the sheriff and not a girlfriend, she finally voiced the private worries she'd been harboring.

"Why did he ask me to court him if he didn't like who I was in the first place? It makes no sense."

Sheriff Kramer crossed his legs.

She knew he was waiting. "I told Perry that I couldn't move. I told him that I loved my bed-and-breakfast and was hoping it would become a success."

"And Perry, did he understand your reasons?"

She shook her head slowly. Even now his dismissal of everything that was important to her stung like a slap in the face. "Not at all. He said it was destined for failure. That no tourists would come to Crittenden County."

"Ah."

Frannie watched him pull the cap off the pen and scribble more on his paper. And the butterflies got worse in her stomach. She didn't want to remember any more. She wanted to pretend that the rest of what had happened could be erased.

As she continued to hesitate, he eyed her. "And then what happened, Frannie? After he asked you to change, after you told him you wanted to leave . . . what happened?"

He wanted answers. She knew she had two choices. She could either tell the complete truth—tell Sheriff Kramer about the sunglasses that Perry gave her, tell how she'd tossed them into the woods because she'd been hurt and confused.

Or she could tell only half of the truth. Say that she ran.

If she told the full story, it would undoubtedly bring more questions. Questions about where he got the sunglasses, about the *Englischers* he was spending time with who she knew nothing about. If she never mentioned throwing the sunglasses or running into Jacob Schrock . . . if she said she just went home, perhaps Sheriff Kramer would be satisfied and leave. Leave her in peace. Maybe then she wouldn't have to think about the whole incident anymore.

Maybe then she could finally move on. And not have a smidge of guilt.

There really wasn't a choice.

"Then what happened?" she repeated, attempting to smile. "Oh, nothing much. After I told him I wouldn't change and wouldn't move, he was angry and upset. So I turned away and ran."

He leaned forward. "And what did he do? Did he follow?"

"I don't know what he did, Sheriff. I never looked back." Her voice had been even and calm. It almost sounded truthful, even to her ears.

He looked at her sharply. "You are sure that is everything that happened?"

"Yes, Sheriff. That is all," she lied. No longer caring if she was going to get into trouble later for lying. No longer caring what Sheriff Kramer thought of her anymore.

All that mattered right that minute was that she find a way to get the sheriff to leave her room. Even sitting by herself in a beige hospital room would be better than remembering the look on Perry's face when she'd tossed those sunglasses into the woods.

Two minutes later, he fulfilled her wish and got to his feet. "If you happen to remember anything else, use that card I gave you and call me. Or you could tell Luke, too." Without waiting for her response, he shuffled out, his manner looking exhausted.

He didn't even say goodbye.

It left her unsettled and anxious, worse than she'd felt after Micah had left earlier.

Oh, how she just wanted to go home and return to her regular routine. She wanted to wait on guests at the inn and pretend that nothing mattered except cleaning rooms, making coffee, organizing the linen closets.

Five minutes after the curtains parted and his footsteps faded away, Frannie could still feel the sting of unshed tears in her eyes, her nose. A puddle welled in her good eye, and she absently wondered if crying would hurt her injured one. She didn't care—there was nothing she could to stop the tears from spilling over.

She cried softly, hoping all the while that the patient on the other side of the curtain had been asleep and hadn't heard her conversation with Mose. Or at the very least, wouldn't comment on it if she had.

Chapter 12

"This would be a better world if everyone were as good as he wished his neighbor was."

AARON SCHROCK

"I was beginning to think you were determined to stay a stranger. Staying away ain't no way to get to know people," Mr. Schrock chided when Luke wandered into the family store just minutes before closing.

The comment was said in jest, but the words caught Luke off guard. His first days in Crittenden County had been difficult. No one had spoken to him—in fact most had gone out of their way to avoid him. But little by little, folks were starting to warm up. Now it even seemed that some folks were determined for him to become a part of the community, at least for a little while.

"I never wanted to be a stranger here," Luke said. "I just thought it would be a good idea if I waited a while in between visits."

"And why is that?"

"Because," he quipped, looking around the store, "I have

learned that you never know what will pop out from the ceiling or run across my feet when I visit your store!"

"Come now, things aren't that bad."

"You've got more going on in this place than an amusement park. I needed to give myself some time for my heart to recover." He gave an exaggerated wince. "A man can only take so much, you know."

Rocking back on his heels, Mr. Schrock chuckled. "I guess some men are more able to handle an exciting life than others."

"Without a doubt." Thinking about what the other men on his squad would think about his efforts to fit in, Luke shook his head. He'd only been in Marion three weeks, but he'd noticed changes in his habits and demeanor. He was listening more to his heart and his internal clock. Rising earlier without the need for an alarm, and ending his days earlier. When the sky darkened and the streets turned still, he found himself looking forward to a stretch of peace and quiet.

He was making friends, too—or at least the first steps of friendship—in the most unlikely places. Never would he have imagined he'd feel so relaxed around an Amish owner of the most unusual general store in the state.

He wasn't sure how he should feel about these changes. He didn't belong here—his life was in the city. But it felt oddly like he was laying down roots. It was unsettling, but only because he didn't seem to mind.

"So, how are the guinea pigs doing? Any more of them on the loose?"

"They're all sold, though no thanks to them. One of 'em in particular seemed determined to remain hidden. Every time we tried to catch the fellow, he'd dart away. Finally had to move one of the shelves, then chase the rascal until Walker could grab him."

Luke could only imagine what the man had thought of that chore. "Good thing it worked."

"Oh, for sure." He grunted. "Wife was getting right tired of that critter, I'll tell you that."

"I can't say I blame the little guy all that much. Being free does have a certain appeal, I suppose."

"So does having a home," Mr. Schrock replied. "Those little pigs should have realized that they were going to good homes. If they'd been calmer and less pesky, they could have lived like kings." A line formed between his brows. "You know what they say? . . . 'Don't grumble because you don't have what you want, be thankful you don't get what you deserve.' "

Amused by both Mr. Schrock's latest bit of Amish wisdom, and the idea of a wayward guinea pig living like a king, Luke said, "How was the little guy when you finally caught up with him?"

"Hungry as a boar. He 'bout bit Walker's finger off when he captured him. That boy needed a good-sized bandage." Mr. Schrock grimaced at the memory as he rested his elbows on the counter. "Now, what can I help you with? Need some cottage cheese, by chance?"

Cottage cheese? "No. Uh, not today. Actually, I was hoping I might have a word with Jacob."

Mr. Schrock straightened, all traces of amusement and congeniality vanishing in a heartbeat. "My son?"

"Yes," Luke said smoothly. "Is he here? I heard he returned from his trip."

"*Jah. Jah* . . . he's back."

Though he got his answer, Luke noticed he wasn't getting much else. The warm bond that had been floating between them dissipated like a cold wind. Now Mr. Schrock was in full protective-parent mode.

It didn't matter if a man's child was six, twenty-six, or forty-six. If a detective was asking about him, men clammed up. Right before Luke's eyes, Mr. Schrock straightened and turned statuelike. Instead of offering more information, he eyed Luke apprehensively.

Pushing aside a momentary punch of hurt, Luke reminded himself that he'd been foolish to think that he'd made a real connection with the man. With this town.

So he pulled out years of experience and mirrored the older man's expression. Becoming still, pretending he didn't notice what had just happened between them.

"So, where's Jacob been? I'm afraid I never did hear that."

"He was just out working," Mr. Schrock said quickly. "He was doing some work in Lexington. Important work."

"Important?"

Mr. Schrock's chin raised. "Store business."

"Ah. Right." Luke smiled tightly as he realized that he'd just been fed a line. "Where is he now?"

"This minute?"

"Yes, sir. This minute."

"He's in the back." After a pause, Mr. Schrock said, "Would you like to talk with him up here? Or out in the parking lot like you did with Walker?" His eyes brightened. "Or how about I just tell him that you want to see him later on. Maybe tomorrow?"

A sixth sense told Luke that he had better not give the man any time to speak privately with his son. "If you don't mind, I'll follow you to the back and ask Jacob where he'd like to talk."

"That's not necessary."

"I'm afraid it is." Stepping forward, Luke motioned Mr. Schrock on with a wave of his hand. "Go on, Mr. Schrock. I'll follow you." He kept his voice pleasant. But he'd had enough of secrecy and half-truths.

He had a job to do and a promise to keep to Mose. Therefore, he stood unwavering as Mr. Schrock reluctantly started walking toward the back.

They passed through rows of shelves jam-packed with candies and cans and handmade clocks and baskets, through a brightly painted white door, and into a jumbled storeroom loaded with so much merchandise that it made the front of the store look almost empty.

In the midst of the clutter were two desks and three or four old Adirondack chairs in various stages of disrepair.

A young man who looked to be about twenty years old was sitting in one of them. He looked up from the catalog he was reading when they entered.

His father walked to his side. "Jacob, this here is Detective Reynolds. He's in town to help figure out who killed Perry. He wants to speak with you."

Jacob stood up. "All right."

Luke's first impression of the young man was that he looked nothing like his father. Neither his eyes, his jaw, or even his manner mirrored his dad. Where Aaron Schrock reminded one slightly of an elf, Jacob was taller and his shoulders broader. He had dark hair and dark, heavily lashed eyes. In addition, he seemed to have a strong confidence that far surpassed his father's.

With a look of interest, not wariness, he walked forward.

Luke put out a hand. "Nice to meet you, Jacob. I'm Luke Reynolds."

"He's from the city," Mr. Schrock interjected. "From Cincinnati."

Jacob shook Luke's hand. "I've heard you were in town. So, you're here investigating Perry's death?"

Luke nodded. "That's right. I'd like to talk to you for a bit, Jacob."

"All right."

Mr. Schrock moved closer to his son. "Detective, I think it would be better if Jacob came to see you tomorrow. He's just in now, you know. Tired, too. Tomorrow, he'll be more rested."

Jacob's cheeks flushed red. "I'm fine. I can meet with you now, Detective. It's no trouble at all."

Mr. Schrock frowned. "But Jacob—"

"No sense in waitin', it won't be easier tomorrow." Pointing to a narrow corridor with a steel door at the end of it, he said to Luke, "We've got a pen of puppies outside in the shade. I need to feed them and give them a little exercise. Do you mind if we talk there?"

Puppies on the loose sounded like a prescription for distraction. The last thing he needed was to have Jacob's attention diverted now that he finally was able to meet with him face-to-face. "Will you be able to talk outside?"

"Yeah." With a meaningful look at his father, Jacob headed toward the door. "I promise, out here it will be just the two of us. And the puppies are no trouble." He smiled for a moment. "Only a little rambunctious."

Still in protective mode, Mr. Schrock stepped forward as if to block Luke's way. "Jacob—"

Jacob turned around. "Daed, I'm not a child. I've got things handled. Now, go on up to the front before someone comes in and thinks no one works here."

Only when his father turned and walked back to the front of the store did Jacob continue on his way.

Chapter 13

"I've often wondered if Perry ever counted the number of people he lied to. But I suppose it doesn't really matter. He doesn't have enough fingers or toes to do the job justice."

BETH BYLER

Making beds was easier than making sixty mini quiches, Beth decided. With a flick of her wrist, she spread fresh crisp white sheets over Frannie's twin bed and smoothed the fabric tight. As she neatly tucked the corners under the mattress, she smiled with satisfaction. Frannie would have a fresh bed to lie down on when she returned.

Beth could hardly believe that her forty-eight hours as an innkeeper were about to come to a close just as she'd gotten the hang of things.

At first the time had gone by so painfully slow, she'd wished she'd been the one in the hospital with an injury. It was a difficult thing, attempting to do the best she could in an area in which she was terribly unfamiliar.

Tomorrow, she would be home again, then in no time, she'd be back to work with the infants and toddlers she loved so much. Instead of kneading dough, she'd be pushing swings at the park and changing diapers in her makeshift nursery. Instead of answering Frannie's phone and making reservations, she'd be holding chubby hands and cuddling sleepy babies.

She could hardly wait.

Beth had no desire to cover for Frannie ever again. It was a lot of responsibility, being an innkeeper, and far more nerve-racking than she'd ever imagined. Adults on vacation were harder to manage than toddlers, and that was a fact.

Before putting the quilt back on Frannie's bed, Beth sat down for a quick minute . . . to enjoy the fresh scent of clean sheets and carefully polished wood. It smelled perfect. Inviting.

However, there was still more to do.

As she bustled down the stairs, she took special care to step carefully by Chris-with-no-last-name's door. He'd left yesterday morning and hadn't returned until almost midnight.

She knew this because she'd made the mistake of waiting up for him, just like he was her wayward teenager and what he did was any of her business.

As the hours passed, she'd gone from sitting in bed, half listening for the door, to camping out in the back corner of Frannie's parlor. There, she watched the door, going from being aggravated that he was costing her sleep to concerned that he might have been hurt to angry for being so thoughtless to stay out so late.

By the time the clock's hands neared midnight, she'd been very ready to give him a piece of her mind. Either that, or use Frannie's business phone and call the police.

Then the door had opened quietly.

For a brief second, she'd considered greeting him like they

were true friends—perhaps see if he wanted some hot tea. Or ask if he was all right. Then reality had set back in. He was only a guest . . . and she was only helping out for a few days. They were nothing to each other. Not really. She'd curled back further into the fluffy confines of the couch.

And that was when she saw him carefully climb the stairs, looking like the weight of the world was resting on his shoulders.

Not long after, she'd gone to sleep, then had awoken early, eager to talk to him. But so far, he hadn't made an appearance.

She'd just stopped in the doorway to the never-ending messy kitchen when the doorbell rang. Wiping her hands on her apron, she rushed to answer it. Anything would be better than attempting to clean the counters. Again.

But as she saw who was on the other side of the doorway, she felt a tremor go through her. Three rather large men were staring right back, and not a one of them looked friendly.

The trio did not look like they were there to book rooms. In fact, they looked a little surprised to be greeted by an Amish woman.

Doing her best to keep her voice tremor-free, she said, "May I help you?"

The tallest man in the middle spoke. "We're looking for Chris Ellis."

Ellis? That was his last name? "Yes?"

The man's eyebrows edged closer together. "Is he here?"

Beth had no idea if she was supposed to keep the guest list a secret or not. But there wasn't time to figure that out, and for that matter she was wary enough of the three men to not give them the information they were asking for. "Well . . ."

"We know he's staying here. All we want to know is if he is here right now."

She was no match for the men. "He is."

As the other two men beside him shifted, looking like they were about to barge right past her, the trio's spokesperson remained frigidly, stoically polite. "May we come in, then?" he asked, in a low, smooth voice. "It's fairly important."

She gripped the door. Everything inside her wanted to refuse them entry.

One of the other men reached out and grabbed the edge of the door. Preventing her from pulling it shut. "We really would like to come in." He paused. Curved his lips up in a parody of a smile. "It's pretty damp out here. Rained all last night."

"It is wet."

"So of course we need come in now." Again, his voice was polite but firm.

Beth knew she had no real reason to stop them from entering. She stepped backward, now feeling even more wary. There was something dark and disturbing in the strangers' eyes that made her want to protect Chris.

Which was silly. The few conversations they'd shared had been fraught with tension. He would not appreciate her getting involved in his business. And who knew? He could have been with these men all last night!

The three men, each at least six feet tall and weighing over two hundred pounds, filled the foyer. Each wore a blazer and slacks and looked around the inn like they were searching for clues. Finally the same man spoke. "Where is he?"

She was afraid. But surely she was letting her imagination get carried away? Reminding herself that she wasn't Chris's friend, only his substitute innkeeper, she said, "Mr. Ellis is in Room 1A."

"Room 1A, huh?" The tallest man looked over his shoulder, met one of the other's eyes for a moment, then turned back to her with another insincere smile. "Thanks. Got it."

Just as they started for the stairs, a rumble of footsteps on the floor above them drew everyone's attention upward.

The men froze.

Chris was standing near the top of the flight of stairs, wearing his usual T-shirt and jeans, but now with a flannel shirt as well. His blond hair was sticking up all over the top of his head . . . and his expression was ominous. "Stratton," he said quietly. "There was no reason for you to come here." Looking at the two other men, standing like silent sentries, his gaze hardened. "You didn't need to bring reinforcements either."

"Come, now," the man said softly. "Besides, it's all for your protection."

"I don't need it."

"You might." He paused, then raised a brow. "After all, we found you. If we did, others could, too."

"I told you to call if you needed me."

"What we need to speak to you about can't be shared on the phone. So, stopping by was no problem. This young lady was extremely helpful." The first hint of a genuine smile played across his lips. "Very helpful."

Beth felt a hard chill race along her back. Something that almost sounded like a growl erupted from Chris as he glared at her. "You shouldn't have come here," he said again to the men.

"I had my reasons."

Confused by his anger and scared by the situation, Beth stepped backward.

If the men noticed her efforts to blend into the paint, they didn't make note of it. Instead, the tallest man smirked. "You're looking . . . fit. Work must be agreeing with you."

"Work is good. I told you that."

Beth was confused. Work? He had been working?

Had he been lying to her . . . or was he lying to the men right now? A hundred questions filled her head, making it spin. And making her feel even more distressed.

"Chris?" she murmured, not even sure what she was going to say. Offer him support?

Ask him why he'd chosen to keep so much from her?

Chris ignored her. Instead, he walked right by, not sparing her the briefest of glances. Instead, all his attention remained steady on the three men now standing in the foyer.

"Let's leave. Now," he added firmly. "I'll speak with you outside."

One of the men who'd been quiet finally spoke. "There's no reason for us to go outside, Chris. This lady here just invited us to your room. Room 1A." He smiled. "Why don't we all go there? We can have a nice chat." He turned to her with an ice-cold stare. "You wouldn't mind us staying a while. Would you?"

She was so afraid she didn't know what to say. With a jerk, she shook her head.

As the men smiled, Chris glared at Beth like she'd done something terrible. "That's not going to happen," he snapped. "We're going. Now."

"You sure that's what you want?"

Before her eyes, Chris transformed into a man she hardly recognized. His easy, relaxed posture vanished, his eyes turned even cooler. Suddenly he looked as dangerous as the other men in the room.

And maybe even more frightening . . . because she'd been fooled by his lies. She stepped backward until her shoulder blades met the wall.

If anything, Chris's expression became more thunderous. He pushed his way through the trio of men and grabbed the door handle. "Let's go. Now. None of you should have come here. There was no need, I told you that."

"You missed your check-in."

"I did not. I told you I would be late, and that I'd call you within four hours. I'm still within that window. There was no reason to look for me. I would have met you wherever you wanted."

One of the men gripped the door, preventing Chris from opening it farther. "Don't make this into a problem," he ordered. "All we want is to know how you are coming along with your assignment. You know, in case you needed help?"

Chris grimaced. "I don't."

"And we needed to see where you were staying." He smiled darkly. "In case we ever needed you."

Even to Beth's ears, the words sounded dark and threatening. She shivered from the veiled threats.

Chris's posture had changed again from tense to stoic. "You won't," he bit out. Then, with a show of muscle, he pulled open the door, overpowering the other man's guard. "It's time to go. Now."

He motioned them all back through the doorway. Slowly, each one departed without another word or another glance her way. He was last.

Beth was torn between relief that they were leaving the premises and fear for Chris. The men looked ruthless, and he was outnumbered. Her heart started hammering as she realized she was unable to help him. Were those men about to hurt Chris?

Or were they simply men that Chris associated with?

Then, just as the screen door snapped in place and she was

standing on the other side, watching him, Chris paused on the stoop as the other men walked forward.

For a split second, their gazes met. His expression was filled with a kindness and tender concern that took her breath away. It was as if suddenly all his layers were stripped away and she saw him for what he was—the good man she'd been starting to care for.

"Chris, are you in danger?" she whispered, her voice so frantic it wavered. "Do you need me to call the police or something?" She was scared to death but more than determined to help in any way she could.

Then, just as quickly, the covering was back. "I'm fine. Don't do a thing, Beth. Don't say a word about this to anyone." The planes of his face became hard again, his expression fierce.

He closed the main door with a snap, leaving her standing in front of it, staring at wood—and fearing what was happening on the other side.

Tears pricked her eyes. "Lord, what should I do?" she asked as she started to pace. A few seconds later, she followed her heart. She couldn't cower in a corner. Instead, she peeked through one of the windows near the door. Just to make sure everything was all right. She was finding out that knowing the worst was better than knowing nothing at all.

The four men were standing next to a black truck.

Unable to help herself, she peered closer, and saw Chris scowl at the men, then wave a hand. Two of the other men replied to him. One even went so far as to touch Chris's shoulder, but he shrugged it off.

Beth was about to turn away when she spied him glancing at the window. When he saw her, he scowled, then turned abruptly and jerked open one of the doors of the truck. In a fluid motion, he slid into the dark vehicle.

Removing himself from her sight. Eventually, the other three got in the truck. As soon as all the doors were shut, the black vehicle drove away.

Only when it was long gone did Beth realize she was gripping the edge of her apron in one of her fists. As questions and fear bubbled to the surface, she felt herself gasping.

Chris was obviously in trouble. It was also obvious that he didn't want her involved. Probably the right thing to do would be to go back to cleaning the house.

Not worry about things she had no control over. Yes, she should give her worries over to the Lord and know that He would care for Chris.

But what if He'd put Beth there for the whole purpose of helping Chris? After all, someone needed to help him!

There was no way Beth could stand still and do nothing. Just like she'd been willing to help run a B&B with little to no inkling of a plan, she was ready to go out on a ledge to help Chris. Deep inside she knew that she needed to help him. She needed to do this as much as she'd needed to help Frannie. But she had no knowledge of who he really was—or who the men who'd come to the inn really were either.

Frannie! Frannie was going to be home soon, and she had no idea what was happening with one of her guests! Beth couldn't leave now. If she left, she'd be leaving Frannie alone with a great many questions. And possibly even in danger.

Feeling her knees start to shake, Beth stumbled to the couch. What could she say, anyway? That her guest had scary friends?

But, of course, that wasn't the right thing to do.

No, what she was going to have to do was go upstairs and

let herself into Chris Ellis's room. She was going to have to search to find out more about him in order for Frannie to be safe.

All she was certain of was that if Chris found out she'd been looking through his things, she could very well be in danger, too.

Feeling like she was in someone else's body, she calmly walked to Frannie's office, pulled the main ring of keys out of her desk drawer, then made her way upstairs to Room 1A.

Chapter 14

"Once Perry and I snuck down to the quarry. The No Tres-
passing signs made no difference to him."

JACOB SCHROCK

Luke's first impression of Jacob Schrock was that he would
be a popular man whether in a large corporation in New
York City, in the middle of a college campus, or here in the
Amish community.

He was a handsome kid and seemed sure of himself.

Too sure and popular to get sucked down into the abyss
that Perry Borntrager had fallen into.

"So you were in Louisville?" he asked, purposely naming
the wrong city.

"Lexington," Jacob corrected. "I like going to the horse
auctions."

"But aren't those auctions just for racehorses?"

"Not all of them. Some breeders bring stock that they're
hoping to get off their hands. Every once in a while you can
find some horses perfect for buggies or working the farm."

"I'm surprised you'd spend two weeks going to auctions.
Your parents' store is always busy. Weren't you needed here?"

"It's not much of a surprise." Looking vaguely amused by Luke's ignorance, he said, "I like horses. If my parents didn't have this store, I probably would've done something with breeding or doctoring them. Besides, I work every day. It was as good a time as any to take a break."

Again, his manner was matter-of-fact, but Luke still had a feeling he wasn't getting the whole story. "I find it a coincidence that you left to go to the auction the same day that Perry's body was found."

Jacob shrugged. "I don't know what to tell you. I don't plan the auctions, I just go to them."

Luke didn't appreciate the flippant remark. Something about the boy's story didn't ring true to him. "I heard that you were once good friends with Perry. Why don't you tell me what you knew of him."

Jacob's eyebrows rose. "So, I guess we're done with pretending you're here for anything other than Perry's death, huh?"

"We both know there's no other reason for me to be in Crittenden County." With effort, Luke pushed away all thoughts of Frannie Eicher. It didn't matter that she seemed to be on his mind all the time. There was only one reason for him to still be in Kentucky, and that was to do a job. "So," he asked again, "tell me about Perry."

Jacob stretched out his legs and crossed his feet at his ankles. "Perry and I grew up together. A few years ago, he started working here."

"So you were good friends."

"We were friends most of the time. But we were close because of proximity, not by choice." His gaze turned shadowed. "For years, Perry and Deborah and I walked to school together."

"Deborah is Perry's sister?"

"*Jah.*" With a shrug, Jacob said, "There ain't much to tell you, Detective."

"Really? I would've thought Perry being fired from the store was a big deal."

Jacob swallowed. "It was a big deal. My *daed* was upset about Perry stealing. He felt bad for firing him, too. Mr. and Mrs. Borntrager thought my father was being too harsh."

Luke wasn't surprised to hear that. He'd come to learn that Perry's parents had made multiple excuses for his behavior over the years. "So how did you feel about your father firing Perry? Were you upset?"

"I was upset that he stole from my family's store," Jacob corrected. "I was upset that he was shifty and had seemed to think that neither my father nor I would notice money missing from the cashbox." He paused. "If you want to know the truth, when he was fired, I was glad."

"I see."

"Do you?" Jacob's voice now held a slice of bitterness. "Even when my *daed* confronted him, he acted so smug. I honestly think he was shocked that my father told him to leave."

"Why do you think Perry was so surprised?"

"Because he didn't think my father was smart. By now, you've probably had at least one run-in with my father and one of his schemes for the store."

"Like the guinea pigs?"

A slow smile lit his face as Jacob shook his head. "I'm so glad I missed those guinea pigs."

"The snakes were worse."

"I bet they were," he said with a laugh. Sobering, he said, "Here's the thing, Detective. My father is a good man, and though he comes up with fanciful ideas, the store has made a profit every single week it's been open. Not many businesses can say that."

"I don't think many could," Luke replied honestly.

"My *daed* runs a good business. But it takes a lot of patience. And some experience with keeping your mouth shut. Perry . . . he never learned to do that."

"Walker Anderson . . . has he?"

"Walker?" Jacob looked caught off guard by Luke mentioning him. "I don't think Walker cares one way or the other what plot my father has concocted, as long as he gets paid. But Perry, he took my father for a fool and started stealing from us almost from the beginning."

Luke noticed that Jacob was referring to the store as *theirs*. It was becoming obvious that his relationship with his father was strong on several levels. It was also obvious that the business was a family business, and that Jacob felt as much a part of its success or failure as his father did.

"So . . . how did your father find out about Perry stealing?"

Jacob's eyes darted to the left, looking like he was debating whether or not to answer the question. Finally, he said, "Walker told me."

"Maybe Walker was stealing, too?"

"No," he said quickly. "He wouldn't have done that." He cleared his throat. "After Walker told me, I noticed money was missing from the cashbox several times a week. There was only one way for it to be missing. Perry."

"What did you do then? Tell your dad?"

Jacob shook his head. "No. Not at first."

"Well, then?"

"I took care of it myself." As he heard his words, his lips pursed and he held up a hand. "No, that's not quite right. At first I thought I was going to be able to take care of it myself. Then Walker quit, and Perry didn't listen."

"You didn't want to just go tell your father? That seems to be the most reasonable solution."

Jacob folded his arms across his broad chest. "You think I'd go tattle to my father like a child? *Nee*, I didn't do that. Besides, knowing Perry was stealing from him would have broken his heart. My father has a kind heart toward all things . . . even liars and thieves."

"And hens."

The quip did as he'd hoped. Slowly, Jacob's shoulders eased. "Yeah, even hens."

"So, why did Walker quit?"

"He knew what was happening and got fed up."

"You sound like you resent that."

"Not really," he said slowly. "I can't say I wouldn't have done the same in his position. I mean, the store doesn't mean as much to Walker as it does to me. For him, it was just a job. And Perry was trouble."

"So, what did happen when you confronted Perry?"

Jacob angled his body so he could clearly see the door that opened into the main store. "What happened was I hit him, Detective."

Luke hadn't thought he could be any more surprised by the turn of events but he was. "You hit him? I don't want to sound rude, but I thought the Amish didn't believe in violence."

"We don't. I don't. But when there's a kid set on intentionally hurting your father, well, that's different. When your father's honor is on the line, when family is involved, everything that you know to be right doesn't matter. Don't you think?" He glanced Luke's way, his open gaze revealing nothing.

"I understand what it's like to feel betrayed," Luke hedged.

Seemingly satisfied that Luke was on his side, Jacob continued. "I promise you this. At first I only talked to Perry. Told him I knew that he was taking money from the cashbox and that it needed to stop."

It needed to stop. "And how did he respond to that?"

"Respond?" He laughed. "Not well. He told me I was a liar. And then he said I could never prove it."

"And so what did you do?"

"I slugged him in the stomach." Jacob's eyes warmed. "He doubled right over. It was a real sight, I tell you."

With effort, Luke kept his face impassive. "Then what happened?"

"Then?" Jacob blinked, as if he was surprised by the question. "Then he straightened and told me he was going to tell my father that I hit him."

"And you said . . ."

"I gave him the same words right back. I told him I'd like to see him prove it." He took a breath. "And before you start asking what happened next, I'll save you the time, Detective. I turned around and left. I knew if he smirked at me again, I was going to slam my right fist into his chin."

"Did he stop stealing?"

"You and I both know the answer to that, Detective. He was using the money to buy drugs. He didn't stop."

"How did you find out about the drugs?"

"It wasn't hard to figure out. There were rumors. He started acting like a totally different guy."

"What do you mean by 'different'?"

"His temper was quicker, his moods more erratic. He lied

more and more. And sometimes he never showed up for work." His gaze hardened. "He stole more money. Eventually, I had no choice. I had to tell my *daed*."

"And?"

Jacob looked sheepish. "Turns out he already knew. Like I said, my father is no fool." Crossing his arms over his chest, he spoke again. "So there you go, Detective. He stole from us, I hit him, he didn't stop, and my *daed* fired him. It's not a terribly pleasant story, but it's the truth."

"And did you ever see him again?"

"From a distance, sure."

"Did he ever offer you drugs? Pills?"

"Me?" Jacob's smile widened. "No. He wouldn't have ever asked me about such things, Detective."

"Why not?"

"Because I would've slugged him again. I don't do drugs."

Luke gingerly got to his feet, realizing that his leg had betrayed him again. It had stiffened up. "I have to say, I'm a little surprised you've shared so much."

"Punching a jerk is a whole lot different than killing a man, don't you think?"

"Perhaps. Perhaps not."

"Detective Reynolds, believe me or not . . . my life is a good one. I had no feelings for Perry Borntrager other than I didn't want him stealing from my parents. I didn't want him dead, I just wanted him out of my life."

"Well, he is now, isn't he?" Luke said before leaving through the back door.

He was more troubled by the conversation with Jacob Schrock than he'd been by an interrogation in some time.

He only wondered if it was because he found fault with

the way Jacob had dealt with everything . . . or if it was because he didn't believe everything that the guy had said.

Room 1A was dark when Beth carefully unlocked the door
and entered. After turning on the gas lamp beside the bed,
she scanned the area.

And almost immediately felt a feeling of dismay. She
wasn't quite sure what she'd expected to find . . . but nothing seemed out of sorts. His bed, though not exactly neatly
made, had the quilts pulled up and the sheets straight underneath. On the desk were a laptop computer and a leather
satchel.

One of the T-shirts she'd seen Chris wear lay on the back
of a chair. A portable alarm clock and an iPod was on his
bedside table. As was a hardcover book.

Beth was tempted to turn right back around. But then her
loyalty to Frannie took over. Beth had promised Frannie to
take care of things to the best of her ability in her absence.

And though of course Beth had never imagined that she'd
be worried about dangerous people coming to the inn, Frannie was going to need to know what had happened, and it
wasn't going to help anyone if Beth was only full of guesses
and innuendos.

Afraid someone was going to be lurking in the hall and
would see her sneaking around in the room, she shut the
door tightly behind her. Then locked it.

"You can do this," she muttered. "You can do this."

With that rather foolish encouragement, she strode forward and carefully opened the leather satchel. Looking for
what, she didn't know. All she wanted was to find proof that
she hadn't imagined the danger.

Inside the satchel was a series of folders. Inside were computer disks and papers, notes about Crittenden County.

Hands shaking, she skimmed the pages. Nothing looked familiar. Strange initials like DEA and ATF littered a few of the pages.

And then she saw Perry Borntrager's name.

She dropped the file like it was on fire as she tried to put the pieces together. Was Chris there to solve Perry's murder? Or had he had something to do with it?

With care, she slipped the papers back into the pouch and opened the desk's drawers. They were all empty.

Crossing to the armoire, she glanced inside, but only saw a few more T-shirts and a jacket.

Crossing to the bedside table, she picked up the book, and saw it was a historical novel set during WWII. Underneath it was a well-worn leather Bible.

Though she knew she was perhaps being naïve, she felt a little reassured. If Chris was traveling with a Bible, he had to be on the good side.

The door was beckoning her so strongly, she felt as if it was calling to her. Anxious to heed its call, she stepped forward. But then forced herself to finish her inspection. Carefully, she opened the single drawer in the bedside table. Saw a pair of glasses, a pencil.

And a black gun.

With a gasp, she shut the drawer and raced to the door. One quick motion unfastened the lock. She threw open the door, practically leapt through the doorway, then turned to lock the door behind her.

As soon as it was secured, she leaned against the wall, feeling a cold sweat transform her brow. She was panting so hard, it felt like she had run three miles.

She bit her bottom lip as it trembled.

And tried to figure out why she was so afraid. Was it because Chris had brought a gun with him . . . or that he'd left without it?

Then none of that mattered as she heard a brief knock and the front door open again.

"Hello?" a deep man's voice called out. "Is anyone here?"

More than anything in the world, Beth wished she wasn't.

Chapter 15

"I never understood what Frannie saw in Perry. After all, there is only so much a smile and sense of adventure can do for a person. Ain't so?"

MICAH OVERHOLT

After spending yet another rough night staring at the blank walls and listening to the soft snores of her roommate, Frannie had been overjoyed to see the sunrise. When the nurses came to take her blood pressure, she hadn't been able to refrain from chatting with them.

She'd visited with the attendant who'd delivered her breakfast, and had even shared a "good morning" with one of her doctors.

But when she saw Luke Reynolds walk through the beige curtain and toward her side of the room, she couldn't contain her happiness. She was so happy to have a visitor.

"Luke, you came back!"

He grinned. "I did."

"Sorry about my exuberance. It's just that I'm mighty happy to have a visitor." And, she privately acknowledged, happy to see him in particular.

"I couldn't stay away," he teased. "Plus, I thought you might like a ride home. Mose was going to come out here, but he thought maybe you'd be more comfortable in my car instead."

The reminder of Sheriff Kramer and her conversation with him darkened her mood.

But no matter what, Frannie knew that she would, indeed, be more comfortable with Luke. The last thing she wanted was to be trapped in a vehicle with Sheriff Kramer while being hammered with questions. "Coming here, volunteering to take me home . . . that was kind of you."

"Kind?" His eyebrows rose. "You must really not be feeling too well. I've never known you to speak so meekly."

"I don't spar with everyone, Luke. Only you."

"I guess I should feel privileged, then."

"Privileged or unfortunate!"

Taking the chair by her bed, he gestured to her arms, where only bandages decorated her hands and arms. "Looks like you got disconnected."

"I was thankful to have the IV out, for sure. Now I only have to wait for the doctor to give me permission to leave." Realizing he probably had a lot to do besides wait with her, she warned, "It might be a while. Nothing here seems to happen very quickly."

"I can wait." Lowering his voice, he said, "So, how is your neighbor? Anything new with her?"

Frannie had an idea the patient on the other side of the curtain had most likely gotten a real earful during the sheriff's visit. But though she'd been worried about being overheard last night, she'd forgotten all about her roommate this morning. "Is she still there? The television has been off for hours."

"I think she was asleep when I walked in."

"She's been a tiresome roommate. She doesn't sleep much and is restless. She also speaks too loudly, has lots of company, and tends to spout off her opinions about most everything." But even as Frannie mentioned her roommate's flaws, she also realized she would miss her, too. The woman had been a burst of color in an otherwise dreary room.

"I imagine she has been a trial." He rubbed his leg. "Being in the hospital gets old quick, that's for sure. When I was in the hospital with my leg, I thought they'd never let me leave."

"I'm sorry, Luke. Here I am, acting like I'm the only person to ever have a hospital stay. How long were you in the hospital?"

His eyes darkened. "Five days."

"That is all? I would have thought longer."

He sighed, as if even talking about his injury made it ache. "Like you, I wasn't a very good patient. Because I'd been shot, my buddies took turns standing guard over my room. I felt guilty for making them do that."

She knew nothing about standing guard, but she did understand loyalty. "I'm sure helping you made them feel *gut*."

Surprise flared in his eyes, then dimmed to a wry acknowledgment. "Perhaps it did." He sighed. "Anyway, I was anxious to get out of the hospital as quickly as possible. But even though I got out relatively quickly, I still had to go to rehab for weeks after that."

"What did they do there?"

"They helped me walk. I'm afraid that's when I became a difficult patient." He'd been frustrated with both his stamina and the pain that had rarely seemed to ebb. "Since then, I've had a long recovery at home." He frowned as he straightened his leg. "It's still not completely back to normal. That's why

I was able to come out here. Mose needed help, and I wasn't given permission to get back to work in the field."

"Will your leg ever be completely healed?" She blurted the question, realizing almost immediately that she was prying too much. "Sorry. It's none of my business . . ."

Luke reached out and pressed his palm on the back of her hand. His touch, so warm and sure, stilled her worries.

Just for a moment.

"Don't ever apologize for being concerned, Frannie," he said softly. Then, as if their contact had never happened, he removed his hand and spoke. "Actually, your question is one hardly anyone ever wants to ask." He rubbed his head, the short hair sticking up as he did. "They're afraid of the answer, I guess."

"Is there an answer?"

He nodded. "The short answer is that it will probably never be completely back to how it was."

"And the long answer?"

"The long one? It's that I'll be able to go back to work. Eventually, I'll learn to adjust. I won't be the same, but maybe I don't need it to be, you know?"

He was right. Life was all about learning to adjust, to make do with less or more.

He continued. "Being injured like this taught me to be more accepting of my faults. Going through rehab, when I could only do five or seven reps of an exercise at a time, it was easy to pretend that I used to be strong."

"I'm sure you were."

He grinned. "I might have been able to do twenty repetitions of a weight. Not fifty. Sometimes, I would kid myself." Looking sheepish again, he said, "For a while there, you would have thought that I could run a three-minute mile.

The fact was, I never was a great runner, but I did take my leg for granted. Being in a wheelchair and on crutches for weeks and weeks made me realize that my leg is a great tool to get me from one place to the next. And if it's scarred and sore and not quite what it was, it's okay."

"Sounds like life," she murmured.

"Like life?" His brow quirked.

"You know," she explained. "How we're all born perfect but then things happen. You get cut in the kitchen . . ."

"Or shot in the leg," he finished. "I never thought about it like that, but yeah, maybe you're right. Things do happen."

"Even when we don't want them to."

"It's tempting to paint the past as perfect. But I don't think it ever was."

Frannie was struck by his words, more than he probably could ever imagine. Because what he'd said was how she'd felt about Perry and his death.

Somehow, she'd started pretending that things before he'd gone missing were wonderful.

They hadn't been.

She'd been scared. In fact, once he was gone, she'd thought he'd made good on his promise to move away. She'd been relieved he was out of her life.

"Is every investigation like this, Luke?"

"Is every investigation like what?"

"Painful and scary? Raw? Sometimes, it feels as if you've taken my skin and peeled it back."

"To an extent, I think pain occurs every time peoples' lives are studied with a fine-tooth comb. However, in my experience, no two investigations are ever the same. There are motives behind every crime—and usually all motivations are personal."

"I know revealing secrets is painful."

His eyes flashed, and right then and there, she saw everything he was thinking—well, what he'd let her see.

"I don't know," he finally said. "Some murders didn't take much detective work. Pretty much everyone had seen it coming. Or we had an eyewitness."

"Ah."

"But what I'm trying to say is that most times, I've found the killer, cuffed him, and sent him to jail. I did the paperwork, and let the prosecutors take over. The only time they needed me was on the witness stand. And then I'd give my testimony, feeling like I was doing something good—putting someone dangerous off the streets. But I never really thought about what the murder had done to the community."

"Why not?"

"I had too much to do. There's a lot of violence in Cincinnati. If I spent as long on every case as I have on this one, nothing would get done."

"Ah."

"But there's more to it than that." He leaned forward, looking at Frannie intently, like he was practically begging for her to understand. "I also didn't want to feel. Feeling everyone's pain hurts."

She saw the guilt in his eyes. And though she knew little about the things he was speaking of, she ached to reassure him. "Perhaps that's what police officers need to do, *jah*? If you dwell too much on the hurt, you can't do your job."

"But is that doing my job?" His expression was doubtful.

"Someone has to. And it seems like you are the right man to do it. Otherwise you wouldn't be a detective, right?"

"I guess you have a point. Hey, how did you get so smart?"

"I'm not smart."

"I'd beg to differ."

Beg to differ. It was an unusual phrase, but it had a certain ring to it, she thought. "Luke," she asked. "Do you know who killed Perry yet?"

"You know I can't answer that."

"Ah," she murmured, just as the curtain moved and a nurse walked through.

"Frannie Eicher, I've heard you want to leave us," the woman who was her father's age said with a mock look of hurt. "Is that true?"

"I am afraid it is." She, too, pretended to feel something different than she was, but unlike the nurse, Frannie knew she wasn't fooling anyone, not even for a second. She was more than ready to say goodbye to her beige room.

The nurse smiled broadly. "If you're ready, then it is time for us to take care of things. We've got a couple of paper-work issues to deal with." She turned to Luke. "And you're going to take her home, sir?" When Luke nodded, the nurse showed them both forms and discussed pain relievers and follow-up appointments.

And Frannie felt her mind drift. She thought of all the information she'd shared. And about what she hadn't shared.

Did Luke know who killed Perry? Would the questioning ever end so the town could finally get back to normal?

Chapter 16

"The folks who visit my inn are sure nothing exciting ever happens in Crittenden County. I do my best to let them think that. It's better for business, you know."

FRANNIE EICHER

"Miss? Is anyone here?"

"I'm here! Hold on!" Beth fairly flew down the stairs.

But instead of a lone man, a couple in their mid-forties stood waiting for her.

Beth practically hugged them, they looked so nice and unintimidating. "I'm sorry, I was just cleaning a room." She definitely didn't want to share that she was snooping!

"It's okay, dear," the lady said. "We wondered if you had any vacancies tonight."

"Oh, certainly," she said. "For just one evening?"

"That's all we have time for." She pulled out a new map that the visitors' bureau of Marion had started passing out. "But I'm hoping we'll still have time to visit some of the Amish stores and nurseries in the area."

Still feeling like her heart was beating so fast it was going to jump out of her chest, Beth breathed deep and smiled.

"Oh, for sure. Tomorrow, go out in the morning and you'll see lots of farms and businesses."

"But not at night?"

"Most of the businesses close at sundown."

"I suppose that's just as well. We drove a few of the winding roads but turned around before *we* got turned around. I mean, it gets really dark out here. Who knows what could happen?"

"Only God knows, for sure," Beth said. After she got them settled into their rooms, another visitor appeared at the door—Lydia Plank.

"Lydia, hi. You don't need a room, do you?" she joked.

Lydia grinned. "I do not. Instead, I thought I'd stop by and see if you needed any help with the inn."

Almost afraid to accept, Beth tentatively said, "Help?"

With a wink, Lydia explained. "With the cooking and baking. And the dishes . . ."

"You, too, know I'm terrible at those things?"

"I know they're not your strongpoint," she clarified.

There was a time to have pride, and there was a time to know when pride was overrated. "I'd love the help."

"I'm so glad," Lydia said as she walked straight back to Frannie's kitchen. When she saw Beth's pile of dishes in the sink and stack of recipes on the counter, she raised her brows.

"I need a lot of help."

Rolling up her sleeves, Lydia said, "I'll make raspberry filled muffins. How's that?"

"Good. Ah, what would you like me to do?"

Turning serious, Lydia said, "Lend an ear? I need a friend to listen to me do some thinking about Walker."

"You two are in a hard place, ain't so?"

"Neither of us wants to completely give up our lives. But

so far, the compromises don't seem to be working too well, either."

Beth smiled. It was nice to have some companionship. She headed to the overflowing sink. "Lydia, you bake and talk, I'll wash dishes and listen. Sound like a plan?"

"It sounds *wunderbaar.*"

When Lydia walked over to turn on the oven and started talking a mile a minute, Beth found herself relaxing. Perhaps the inn would continue to run just fine for a little bit longer.

Since the last time she and Abby Anderson had spoken Deborah had thought about having hope and God answering prayers almost constantly. Looking back, she wondered if He had been answering her prayers but she just hadn't seen things that way.

After all, almost every night she had prayed for Perry's drug abuse to end. She'd asked for relief for her family, for there to be an ending to the stress his problems had brought both to herself and her parents.

And then he had died.

Had she brought that on? Or was she supposed to be giving thanks that she had gotten an end to the drug abuse and the stress?

It was starting to seem to her that the Lord had put Abby back into her life just to ponder that very subject. When their paths had crossed, Abby had asked if she could walk with her for a bit.

"Why are you looking for a job?" Abby asked when they entered Mary King Yoder's restaurant for another much-needed afternoon snack.

Deborah paused. "Pardon me?"

Abby had the grace to blush. "I'm sorry. I guess that didn't come out right. What I meant was that I thought Amish women didn't work outside of their home. I thought they stayed home and took care of their house."

As they stopped in front of the hostess's station, Abby bit her lip. "Don't you want to stay home and take care of things? It sounds like a great way to spend your days."

Deborah couldn't help it, she laughed. From the moment she'd met Abby on the sidewalk, the younger woman had been peppering her with one question after another.

They were as varied as could be, too. Sometimes Abby asked about prayers and church services. Other times, the questions seemed almost peculiar. But no matter what, Deborah was learning that Abby was certainly not shy about asking for information!

To buy herself some time, she murmured, "Abby, you are an Amish student, that's for sure."

"And?"

Deborah waited until the hostess greeted them, grabbed two menus, and started walking them to their table. "And I'm not so sure that you need to know everything there is to know about me. Not all at once, at least."

"I'm not trying to pry."

This time she couldn't hide her amusement. "Sure you are."

"I'm sorry." Abby's cheeks flushed as they were walked to their table. "I didn't realize you had so many secrets."

"I don't. Not really." Had things always been like this? she wondered. Had she always been afraid of someone getting too close or asking something too personal?

Or had it only been since Perry started doing things she was ashamed of?

"We all have secrets of one sort or another, Abby. Don't you think?"

"I suppose." But there was something in Abby's eyes that betrayed pure pain.

Making Deborah remember that there was a whole lot more to Abby than just what most people saw. She wasn't just a pretty English teenager about to finish high school. No, instead she was a girl struggling to find her place in the world after going through a very troubling circumstance.

"I don't know if I have all that many secrets," she said slowly, "but I do know that every person is different whether they are Amish or English. We all have our own likes and dislikes."

"Deborah, all I asked was why you didn't want to stay home and take care of things. If you didn't want to tell me, you could have just said that."

Deborah chided herself as she picked up the menu and studied it. Abby was exactly right. The question hadn't been all that prying. It had only been her reaction to it that had made it feel that way.

But that said, there was a limit to how much she wanted to talk about herself. "What looks good to you, Abby?"

She sighed. "I don't know. I don't see much low-calorie food here."

Deborah smiled. Most Amish women she knew kept busy lives, with a lot of labor around the house. There was no need for low-calorie foods. "Of course not! If we had wanted low-calorie, we wouldn't have come here to eat. Instead we need to work on feeding our souls."

A light entered her brown eyes. "Well, if we're not watching our waistlines, then my soul says it wants coconut cream pie."

"Mine does, too! And a cup of coffee." When the waitress came over, they both ordered the same thing.

Deborah was glad their paths had crossed. Looking for a job but only getting refusals was taking a toll on her confidence. Abby's smiles and unending questions were doing a great job of taking her mind off her problems.

She also knew that Abby was waiting for her to answer her question. And though she wasn't sure how to answer it, she gave it a try.

"Abby, the reason I'm not planning to sit at home and take care of things is because there's not much left. Now's not the right time, either. It's just my parents and me now. And to be truthful, we're a sad sort of trio."

"I'm sorry. I can't seem to stop bringing up bad subjects."

"We'd be that way whether you brought up memories or not, Abby." She hesitated, then deciding that talking about her family and Perry with someone who didn't really know him helped clear her head. "See, we're mourning his loss, but my parents and I are dealing with the things we're finding out about his life, too."

Abby averted her eyes. "Walker said Perry was . . . difficult."

Deborah was surprised Walker had been that diplomatic. Her brother hadn't been shy about complaining about Walker breaking off their friendship. "Perry made a lot of things difficult," she said, feeling like she was being honest about her brother for the first time in her life. "He was a mess and he was loud. He could be lazy and mean, too." Though it hurt, she pushed herself to say the rest. "Then, he was angry."

"But someone told me he'd been nice to her."

Deborah wondered if she was talking about Frannie Eicher or Lydia Plank. "Perry did have some good qualities," she allowed. "For most of his life, he was perfectly nice. But then he became someone no one recognized."

He'd also become someone she'd begun to fear. Afraid that Abby would sense her betrayal, she swallowed back a whole host of regrets and disappointments. "Perry had begun to take drugs, and then sell them, too. But I guess you knew that."

Abby looked at her for a long moment. It was obvious now that she had something on her mind that she was hesitant to ask.

Deborah braced herself. "Do you have another question about my brother?"

"Yes. No." She bit her lip.

"Go ahead and ask. If I don't want to answer, I won't."

"All right. Remember when we were talking about God's plan?"

"I do."

"Out of all the people in Crittenden County, why do you think He decided that I should be the one to discover Perry?"

Deborah had wondered why it had been her brother who'd become a drug dealer. Why her brother had been the one to go missing.

Why it had to have been her brother in the well.

Then, suddenly, she had the answer. Just as if God had decided to whisper into her ear in the booth of Mary King Yoder's restaurant. "Because you can handle it," she replied.

Their pie came then, and Deborah dug into her piece with gusto. Her mind was racing too much to talk to Abby.

The memories had come back, when she'd been sure Perry had run off to the city. She would sit by the window and stare blankly out. Wishing for a sign that he was on his way home.

Wishing that he would return and miraculously be the boy they'd always loved instead of the man he'd turned into.

But of course he never came home.

When Mose had appeared on their doorstep, hat in hand, and had told her parents the news, it had truly been one of the darkest moments in her life.

But now she realized that there had been some sense of relief, too. She and her parents had imagined Perry being homeless and hungry.

Or doing unlawful things. Or being hurt and unable to ask for help.

Deborah had learned that her mind could be a terrible foe in the middle of the night. At three in the morning, her worst fears about Perry surfaced . . . and those fears had been too frightening to ever share in the morning's light.

"I don't know how well I'm handling things, but I'm glad you think I am." When Deborah smiled, Abby continued. "My grandmother told me it's not a good idea to try to guess why God does the things He does. His plans are far bigger than ours could ever be."

"Well said, Abby," she said softly. "What your grandmother said is *gut* advice, for sure. It's human to doubt, though. Our mind plays tricks on us. Makes us doubt what our parents taught us. Or what the Bible says. Sometimes that's the hardest thing not to do."

Abby's gaze was piercing. "When I was following my girlfriends on that field, everything inside of me was saying that it was the wrong thing to do. That I should stop and turn around. I really wish I had listened."

"I'm sure you did."

"Deborah, do . . . do you think that voice was God?"

"I do not know." And that was the truth.

"If I would have listened to that voice, I wouldn't have been in the field. And someone else would have discovered . . . your brother. Maybe Jessica and Emily. Maybe somebody else . . ." Her voice trailed off with a shrug.

Deborah understood her confusion. What would have happened if Abby hadn't discovered Perry's body when she did? Would things be better for her parents if they still held a grain of hope?

Or would they all have delved into a darker place by now, not only sitting in silence in the evenings, but letting the doubts and worries and blame take hold of them. Turning what was already a terrible situation into something far worse?

She weighed her words carefully, then realized that there were no "right" words. What was in her heart counted. "That might be true. But perhaps other people might have been so disturbed by what they saw that they wouldn't have told anyone. Or perhaps they would have been too afraid to know what to do. But what's done is done. And please know that I don't blame you, Abby. I never have."

"Who have you blamed, then?"

Ah, so Abby was smart enough to know that Deborah wasn't strong enough to not blame anyone.

That no matter how easy it was to hope and pray for forgiveness, it was a far different thing to realize that instant forgiveness was almost impossible to do.

"I blame everyone and no one."

As Abby's eyes widened, she continued. "The truth is that I blame Perry and the detective and myself and my parents." She paused as the waitress refilled their mugs of coffee. "I blame Walker and Lydia and the drugs— And . . ."

"And?"

Unable to say the truth, unable to mention the letter she'd found in Perry's bedside table, Deborah shrugged and lied yet again. "And then? And then I try my best to blame no one at all."

Seemingly satisfied, Abby forked another piece of pie.

And Deborah wondered if she was becoming more and more like her brother with every day.

Chapter 17

"I used to know the name of just about every person in Crittenden County . . . until Perry started hanging around those men from the city. Then I was glad some folks were strangers."

WALKER ANDERSON

There was something wrong with Beth.

From the moment Frannie had walked in and had taken a good look at her friend's expression, she'd known something was off. Beth's expression was distant, and her questions and comments awkward.

It was if they were strangers—or as if Beth was walking through a dark cloud.

Whatever the problem was, Frannie was determined to get to the bottom of it.

But first, she needed rest. Her eyes were so tired that she was struggling to keep them open. As soon as she had made a wonderful cup of hot tea, she went to bed and lay down. Moments later her eyes drifted closed and she was settled into the bed for a quick nap.

It happened to last for two hours.

When she woke up, Frannie went in search of her friend.

She discovered Beth sitting in one of the uncomfortable ladder-back chairs lining the front parlor's walls. Beth was sitting perfectly still, staring hard at the front door. So intently, in fact, that she jumped when Frannie entered the room.

"Bethy, are you okay?" she asked.

"I'm fine. Why do you ask?"

Beth still hadn't moved a muscle. "For starters, you're sitting in front of the door like a beagle needing to be let out," she teased.

Beth rolled her eyes. "I wasn't staring at the door."

Still attempting to discover the source of her discomfort, Frannie said, "It's okay with me if you were . . . are you waiting on someone?"

"Not at all," she said quickly. "Who would I be looking for, anyway?"

"I'm not sure," she said slowly. "But I've never seen you look so tense or worried, Beth." Racking her brain, she said, "Did something go wrong with the inn that you're worried about telling me?"

Beth bit her lip. For a moment, Frannie was sure she was going to come clean, to tell her that a sink was clogged, or she'd messed up a bill, or had forgotten a reservation. But instead, Beth stoically remained silent.

"Beth," she said kindly, "Just so you know . . . if something did happen, I would never get upset. I've made a lot of mistakes myself—so many, that I've learned that nothing is so bad that it can't be fixed."

"I haven't done anything wrong, Frannie."

Well, that settled it. The inn might be running smoothly, but everything was certainly not all right. Frannie knew it in her bones as surely as she knew she'd always have a scar near her eye.

However, it looked like Beth was intent on keeping whatever was bothering her a secret, too. And though Frannie couldn't understand why, and because she owed Beth so much, she attempted to be a little more joyful and carefree than she felt. "Do you know where my hand mirror is?"

"Why?"

"Because I want to see my face, of course."

Something clicked in Beth's expression and she stood up abruptly. "I don't think seeing your face would be a good idea."

"No one at the hospital would let me see just how bad the damage is. It's time, I think. Go find me a mirror, would you?"

She hesitated, glancing at the door again warily. Like she was afraid it was about to blow open or something.

"Please, Beth?"

"Oh, *jah*. Sure." Moments later, she returned with the mirror and with obvious reluctance, handed it to Frannie.

She held it up and gasped—all her worries and concerns about Beth and her secrets vanishing the moment she saw the great many bandages and black stitches covering her face. And the bruises from the surgery.

"I look like a pincushion!" Frannie exclaimed, unable to temper herself. "A giant pincushion with scary black thread sticking out of it." She hated to sound so sad and sorry for herself, but the reality was worse than her imaginings.

She hated to feel so vain, but she now was certain that she would never look like her old self again. Forever, she would be marked with red lines—a constant reminder of a silly accident that could have been prevented.

Oh, but she couldn't believe that Luke had never once told her how ugly she was!

Feelings for him warred. She felt grateful that he'd been so thoughtful to not say a word about her wounds, but dismayed that he'd been able to hide the damage so well.

Or . . . maybe he'd never thought she was pretty in the first place? If that had been the case, then perhaps he hadn't even seen her cuts as anything to be concerned about.

"Come, now, " Beth said with a smile. "You look nothing like a pincushion. More like a scary doll that's been mended too many times."

Leave it to Beth to pull her out of her pity party and coax a smile! Tilting her head from one side to the other, she had to agree with the doll comparison. Her face did indeed look like it had been chewed on and then hastily repaired. "I suppose I do kind of look like a torn-up doll destined for the rag bin," she grudgingly said. Casting a look Beth's way, she felt a small measure of relief. At least her little outburst had shaken off Beth's worries. "I cannot wait until the stitches are removed. I look horrible."

"Nonsense. You don't look horrible. Besides, mended dolls are the favorites, don't you think? They were in my *haus*."

Frannie rolled her eyes. "I'll remember that, *danke*."

"Anytime, friend."

The sweet tone in Beth's voice reminded her of just how much she had to thank Beth for. Not only had she called for the ambulance, but she'd cleaned up after accident, and had even given up a few days of her own job to keep things running at the inn.

"How can I ever thank you enough for all you've done?"

Beth's gaze warmed, then the light dimmed as her gaze darted away. "That's the good thing about us, Frannie. You don't need to thank me at all. Friends help each other."

Beth had a point. There was no way Frannie could repay

Beth for her friendship, and it would hurt them both to try.

"Instead of me thanking you nonstop, how about you finally fill me in on everything that's been going on here instead?"

Once again, a shadow felt around Beth's eyes. "Don't you want to rest first?"

"I just woke up."

Beth blinked, making Frannie realize that she'd been in such a state that she'd already forgotten her nap. "I know . . . but maybe you still need to take it easy?"

Now she was truly getting worried. "I've done nothing except sit on a small bed in a beige room. I definitely do not want to rest right now."

"But the detective said you were supposed to rest."

"And I will. But come now, Beth. Don't be stingy. This inn is like my child. Give me some news. What food did you make?" She paused, remembering how much Beth was ill at ease in the kitchen. "Were you able to cook anything?"

"You don't need to sound so skeptical. Yes, I cooked." After a pause, she added, "Lydia came over to help, too."

"That's *gut*. Did everything turn out all right?"

A slow smile lit her lips. "I baked the best cinnamon rolls this side of the Mississippi."

"Did you, now?"

"I found your cookbook and followed the directions exactly."

"Cookbook?"

"Yes, the cookbook. You do have them, you know."

"I know, I'm just trying to imagine where you found one."

Beth's eyebrows rose. "There were several on the back bookshelves. And one in particular that looked well used. It was black and red and had a torn cover."

Frannie had almost forgotten about that. Now the memories flooded back . . . of her Aunt Penny pushing it her way with a sad smile when she'd been so sick with cancer. "The book was Aunt Penny's."

"You didn't mind me using it, did you? It was full of recipes for foods you seem to make often."

"You know, I'd forgotten about that book. It's been years since I followed a recipe. Those family recipes are all in my head."

"Since nothing was in my head—of the cooking nature—I was very glad for it. I made those rolls and some more quiches, and a fruit salad, too. Oh, and some apricot scones."

"Scones?"

"They're in the cookbook, Frannie. You really should read it."

Rather than debate the cookbook some more, Frannie attempted once again to discover the source of Beth's uneasiness.

And that's when she realized that not once had Beth mentioned their newest guest. "Hey, Beth, is Chris Ellis still staying here?"

To her surprise, Beth's expression stilled. "I think so."

"Think?"

"Well, he left yesterday and I haven't seen him since. But his things are still in his room, so I don't think he's gone for good."

Beth's report was very peculiar. Frannie didn't understand how she could be so unaware of one of the guests' comings and goings. Frustrated, her head was starting to pound. "I could have sworn that he booked a room for a whole week. Did he say what he was doing?" Maybe he'd decided to go explore another town for a day?

Beth shook her head with a quick jerk. "He . . . he didn't have a chance. But I hope he'll be coming back."

Beth was speaking in so many riddles that Frannie was becoming annoyed. "I don't understand what you're talking about, Beth."

"All right. Yesterday, some men came and he left with them."

Some men? Beth made it sound like she didn't trust them. Playing detective, Frannie sought more information. "All right. Did he give you any clues about what they were doing?" Sometimes guests asked for maps of the area.

"He wasn't able to." Tears began to fall down Beth's cheeks. "It was so awful. And what's worse, I don't think he wanted to go with them."

Her mouth went dry. "How do you know that?"

"He looked really worried when he got into the truck with them. He looked like he wanted to escape but couldn't." Her voice lowered. "Actually, I think he was protecting me."

What was Beth talking about? Perhaps she was becoming way too involved in the goings on of the guests?

"Look, a lot of things happen between people that you may not agree with," she said as patiently as she could, "but that doesn't mean we spy on them. Everyone has the right to their privacy."

"I didn't spy on him. All I did was stand at the window and watch them leave."

"People don't like that. Maybe he got upset with you about that, and now he's never coming back." There was a good chance that Beth's curiosity had made him feel uncomfortable. Remembering how upset Luke had been when she'd been too interested in his comings and goings, she frowned.

Full of indignation, Beth said, "It wasn't like that, Frannie.

I had started to talk a little with Chris. We had a connection, of sorts."

"What was it like, then?"

"Chris is different. I think he was keeping secrets from me."

"Just because he was staying here didn't mean he had to become your friend, Beth."

"Stop. You're not listening to me." Looking very agitated now, she glared at Frannie. "I am not as silly or naïve as you think I am. I may only watch children for a living, but I know when someone is evading the truth, and that's what Chris was doing."

Now she felt horrible. "I am sorry, Beth. I didn't mean to make you upset. Please go on, and I'll be quiet."

After taking a fortifying deep breath, Beth continued. "When I asked him things, like where was he working or what was he doing here, he never gave me a straight answer."

"That does sound strange."

"And these men who came to see him, they didn't look like they were friends of his, either." Her voice rose. "And now he's gone and I don't know what to do."

Stunned, Frannie stared hard at Beth. "I don't know what to do either . . ."

"But wait, it gets worse."

"What else happened?"

"I . . . I got your master keys and went into his room."

Frannie closed her eyes. Oh, but this was not good. "Beth—"

"I only went inside to try to figure out who he was, what he was." She rushed forward. "I found a gun, Frannie."

"A gun?"

"He had a gun and it's sitting upstairs, and he might have needed it to fight those men who took him away." She breathed in and out deeply. "Oh, Frannie. I don't think I've ever been so scared in my life."

"*Nee*," she said weakly. "I don't imagine so."

A chill passed through Frannie. She'd thought coming home would be wonderful. She'd thought all of her worries that she'd harbored in the hospital would disappear and she'd feel the sense of peace that always infused her when she stepped through the front door of her little inn.

But now, instead of feeling better, she felt only more confused and stressed.

Suddenly she longed for her hospital roommate and her chatty laughter and playful comments.

But all she had now was a missing guest and a distraught best friend. And no earthly idea of how to make any of it better.

Chapter 18

"Perry had the kind of smile that could light up the world. He had the same type of temper, I'm afraid."

Luke pulled into an empty space at the end of small parking lot. As the car idled, he kept his foot on the brake and seriously contemplated putting the car back into gear and driving away.

It had been just hours since he'd last seen Frannie. He didn't want to question her now, but he didn't have a choice. The latest update from Mose had made avoidance impossible.

Besides, he'd come to Crittenden County to solve a crime, not to make friends. Certainly not to begin a romantic relationship!

He grimaced as every word from his conversation with Mose echoed in his head.

"I got some news for ya, Luke," he'd said. "I'm afraid it concerns Frannie."

"What happened? Did she get an infection at the hospital?"

"No . . . it ain't nothing like that. I heard from the ballistics lab. They identified two sets of fingerprints on those sunglasses you found, Luke."

Finally the lead he'd been waiting for! "And?"

"Perry's are on them . . . but Frannie's are, too."

"Frannie?" He ached to ask if Mose was sure, but he didn't dare question his friend's information. Mose wouldn't have told him about the fingerprints if he wasn't sure.

"You'll have to get her side of the story, Luke, but if I had to take a stab at it, I'd say Perry probably tried to give them to Frannie, she held them, then for some reason gave them back." Continuing slowly, he said, "Who knows? Maybe she even tossed them on the ground."

They'd talked for a few more minutes, Luke feeling more angry and betrayed with every second. He'd been a fool to not question Frannie more attentively . He'd been questioning Mose's abilities, when all the time he'd been slowly letting himself be so charmed by Frannie that he'd accepted her story far too easily. Just like some rookie cop with a chip on his shoulder.

Still stewing on it, Luke drummed his fingers on his steering wheel and prepared to steel himself against her injuries. And from her blue eyes.

When his phone chirped, he put the car into park, and picked up his cell in relief. Any excuse to procrastinate was welcome. "Hey, Mose. Great to hear from you."

"I haven't been greeted like that since my grandmother was still living," Mose quipped.

Embarrassed that Mose was right—he'd answered the line like his buddy was his long-lost cousin—Luke asked, "Most people aren't that happy to hear from you? Not even your mom?"

Mose chuckled. "Luke, most folks start worrying about parking tickets and speed traps when I call them out of the blue. But my *mamm?* Well, she always focuses on my bachelor status."

Luke smiled. "My mom only pointed out my flaws when she was trying to make me feel guilty so she could get me to do something I didn't want to do."

"My *mamm's* good at that, too. She can name my failings quicker than most folks can say *jackrabbit.* So . . . care to tell me what brought on your happy greeting?"

"Our earlier conversation."

Immediately, Mose's tone turned businesslike. "You still thinking about the sunglasses?"

"Yeah." He ran his fingers through his hair, wishing time would slow down so he wouldn't feel like he had no choice about what to do next. "I'm getting ready to question Frannie about those Oakleys."

Mose sighed. "I'm not sure what those sunglasses have to do with Perry's death, but her not telling us the whole story has wasted quite a bit of precious time."

Luke frowned. The whole scenario was bizarre. The expensive designer sunglasses had been a strange item to find, strange for Perry to own, and strange for Frannie to lie about. It made something that might have been a peculiar quirk into something of importance. "I hope she has a good reason for not telling you about them."

"Think she'll tell you the whole story now?"

"I hope so." But what did it mean when a woman he was starting to have feelings for lied to him during an investigation?

It was a good warning to himself. He had to stop thinking that any relationships he made here could be long-lasting. If he let himself believe such things, he was only going to get hurt. Solemnly, he said, "I'm still trying to come to terms with the fact that she lied to me, Mose."

"She didn't lie to you. She lied to me," he corrected. "There's a difference."

"It's the same thing."

"Think so?" Mose said slowly. "For me, I'm not so sure about . . ." There was a noise in the background, followed by some angry chattering and a door clanging. "Uh-oh. I gotta go, Luke," Mose blurted before he disconnected with a click.

For a moment, Luke imagined what his friend was dealing with. Any altercation—no matter how small—could always be a danger. He took a moment to pray for Mose's safety. He'd made the mistake when he'd first arrived to think that nothing dangerous happened in this small area of western Kentucky. Now he was coming to find out he couldn't have been more full of himself. Or more wrong.

A job in law enforcement wasn't easy, whether one was patrolling the highways and interstates, working in the housing projects in Cincinnati, or being a sheriff in a rural spot like Crittenden County.

Mose had cases other than just Perry's murder. And Luke had a whole career to get back to in Cincinnati. He definitely needed to remember that.

He needed to solve this case, stop letting his feelings about acceptance get in the way of his job, and go talk to Frannie. And he intended to stop treating her like some lovesick pup and to start viewing her like the suspect she was.

Finally accepting the inevitable, he jumped out of his truck and strode to the Yellow Bird Inn's front door. What had to be done had to be done. He needed to ignore his feelings for her and force Frannie to be completely forthcoming about the last time she saw Perry Borntrager.

Even if it ruined their relationship.

When Frannie opened the door, all of Luke's intentions were immediately forgotten. Her face—what wasn't bruised and bandaged and sewn together—was white as a sheet. "Frannie, what's wrong?"

"So much," she said as she reached out for him, tears bright in her eyes. "Oh, Luke, please. You've got to come in and help us."

Pushing aside his new resolve, he pulled her to him. Wrapping his arms around her, he held her close. Her body trembled against his and she felt as cold as ice. Seeking to calm her, he rubbed her shoulders and pressed his lips to her forehead. Little by little, she relaxed against him.

Only then did he realize they were still standing in an open doorway. And that what they were doing was probably not a good idea.

"Let's go inside," he murmured, pulling away from her.

Frannie blinked. "Oh! Yes, yes of course." Abruptly, she turned away and led him into the living room. There he saw her friend standing to one side, looking even more agitated than Frannie.

"This is Beth," Frannie said. "Beth Byler. She is my friend."

"Good to meet you. Now, what's going on?" he asked.

After a wary nod from Frannie, Beth spoke. "A guest was taken away, I think against his will yesterday. He still hasn't returned and I am *verra* worried."

"Say again?" he asked. Surely they weren't talking about a kidnapping happening right here in Crittenden County?

Frannie grabbed his hand and gave it a little shake. "Luke, listen!"

He kept his mouth shut as she directed him to the couch because she was still holding his hand, and still looking like she was shaken three ways to Sunday.

But he still needed some information. "Frannie, maybe you and Beth could backtrack a bit?"

Stepping away, Frannie took a deep breath. "All right. Well, first off, I have a guest staying here named Chris."

Opening up his notebook, he flipped to a clean page. "Chris what?" he asked, his pen hovering over the notepaper.

"Chris Ellis," Frannie said impatiently. "He had just arrived before I went into the hospital."

"Okay . . ."

"But, see, Beth thought he was shifty. He wouldn't tell Beth where he was working and left for long hours at a time."

Folding her arms across her chest, Beth nodded. "I didn't trust him. He worried me."

Before Luke could dig for more information, Frannie continued in a rush. "Then, yesterday three men came here to talk to Chris."

"But he didn't want to see them at all," Beth said. "I didn't blame him. They were scary."

"But he still went, because he was upset that they came here to the inn," Frannie said. "He got into their car and drove away."

"And he hasn't returned yet," Beth said. "I'm afraid something very bad has happened to him."

Luke wrote more notes quickly. "Any idea where they went? Did they mention anything?"

Beth shook her head. "*Nee!* Last night, I was so worried, I

went into his guest room, even though I shouldn't have . . .
and found papers having to do with Perry . . . and a gun."

Luke blinked as all the assurances he was about to utter
flew out the window.

Frannie placed a slim hand on his forearm. "Luke, I know
Beth shouldn't have gone in his room. We both know that it
was wrong. But the gun worries me."

"It worries me, too," he said honestly. "After you finish
telling me what you know, I'll talk to Mose about obtaining
a search warrant." Since they were already knee-deep in the
mess, he said, "Do you remember anything on the papers
you read, Beth?"

"They were letters. With lots of initials. Places with initials."

Initial places? "I'm sorry. I don't understand."

"I don't know what they mean, either." Her eyes widened.
"But perhaps they stand for something?"

"Do you remember any of the letters?"

With a pleased expression, she nodded. "The papers had
the letters ATF and DEA." She bit her lip. "Do those mean
anything to you?"

"Yep. The letters stand for Alcohol, Tobacco, and Firearms
and the Drug Enforcement Agency."

The women looked more confused than ever, but things
were starting to make sense to Luke. Both of those agencies
could have a lot to do with Perry, and a lot to do with why
Chris had left.

But what he didn't know was which side Chris was on—or
what to tell the two women sitting across from him who
were scared to death.

Chapter 19

*"Perry used to say it wasn't a crime to want something differ-
ent. I agreed with him for a time."*

LYDIA PLANK

The tension in the room was terrible. Beth backed away from
Luke and Frannie, sensing that more was going on between
them than either wanted to let on. Yet again, she wished that
she could close her eyes and make the past few days disappear.

Until she'd come to the Yellow Bird Inn, Beth had been
happy, almost content with her life. She'd found great joy
in being around children. And she'd always felt well appreciated and respected by the mothers of the children she
cared for.

If, by chance, she sometimes wished for a life of more
excitement, she brushed it off quickly. When her mother
reminded her that she'd made no time for courting or sweet-
hearts, or even the opportunity to meet men, she'd made
excuses.

But then she met Chris. With one look . . . that man, so different from her, had ignited every nerve. With one smile . . .

she'd begun to think that maybe she was more than who she'd thought.

And now he was gone—in company of men she didn't trust.

What if he never returned? She would always feel guilty that she hadn't done more to help him.

As the silence continued and Frannie and Luke eyed each other warily, Beth knew she would go out of her mind if she didn't say anything.

And so she did. "Would you two like some coffee or tea?"

Both looked at her blankly. Like she'd just offered them funnel cakes, or some other strange food.

Luke was about to answer when he turned abruptly and strode toward the window. "A black Suburban just pulled up. Does this look like the same vehicle, Beth?"

She scurried to the window. Feeling like she was a spy, or worse, Beth peeked around him. Though she couldn't be absolutely sure, it definitely looked enough like the vehicle she'd seen Chris leave in the evening before for her to nod.

Her breath caught as one of the doors opened. Then she saw a boot, a jean-covered leg. And finally Chris himself.

He wore sunglasses and walked with an easy stride toward the inn's front door. He didn't look back toward the car behind him. Not even when it slowly moved forward, gathered speed, then drove out of sight.

She was just wondering why he'd never looked back when the door handle turned.

Darting around Luke, she raced to the door.

"No. Stay quiet, Beth," Luke warned.

"But—"

"I mean it."

"Please listen to him," Frannie pleaded. "He could be dangerous."

Only for Frannie did she keep silent as Chris entered the room. The moment the door closed behind him, his whole posture changed. Almost as if he was pulling off a costume, he looked less cocky and sure. More exhausted.

No, completely exhausted. And maybe in pain, too?

When he saw them standing in a line, all staring at him, he stopped abruptly and scowled. "What's going on?"

"I want to know who you are," Luke said.

Still wearing his sunglasses, Beth felt rather than saw his gaze move from Luke's to hers to Frannie. "Name's Chris Ellis."

"Who do you work for?" Luke's voice was clipped and full of authority, and it was evident to Beth that Chris didn't care for that tone one bit.

His chin rose. "Who I work for is none of your business."

"Actually, it is. I'm with the police."

"You're with the Cincinnati Police," Chris pointed out as he crossed his arms across his chest. "We're here in Kentucky. And unless you say I've done something wrong in Cincinnati, I don't owe you anything."

To her amazement, Luke backed off. If he was surprised that Chris knew who he was and where he was from, he didn't let on. But his body seemed to change, too.

Before her eyes, his shoulders relaxed, as did the muscle jumping in his jaw. Little by little, he became less territorial and abrasive and more friendly. Almost easygoing. "You're right," he said. "You don't owe me a thing. But I'd appreciate some candor. Professionally speaking."

Chris sighed. "Fine, but not here. Not in front of the women."

"No, I think we should be able to hear," Beth said. Surprising even herself.

Everyone in the room turned her way.

"And why is that?" Chris asked.

Now she felt a little embarrassed about her gumption. But not enough to backtrack. "I want to hear what you have to say. Because . . . because I saw the gun in your room. And because I'm involved now, too."

All at once, Frannie gasped, Luke rested his head against the wall in frustration, and Chris pulled off his sunglasses and glared at her. "You searched my room?" he nearly shouted.

But she didn't care about what tone of voice he used. She wasn't afraid of him. Because all she could do was stare at his face. His once smooth, tan skin . . . was now cut and bruised.

One of his eyes was swollen shut.

Without thinking, she rushed to him and pressed her palm lightly on his cheek. "Oh my heavens, Chris! Someone has hurt you."

"I'm okay," he murmured. "Right now, I'm okay." As he reached up and lightly pressed his fingers on top of hers. Just as if her touch was the very thing he needed.

For a moment, right then and there . . . Beth was sure there wasn't another person in the room.

Not one who mattered, anyway.

Funny how life was like a bramble bush, Deborah Borntrager thought. Their lives were all so muddled together, linked and pulled, that one person's decision affected so many other people's.

When Frannie Eicher got hurt and had to go to the hospital, Beth Bylar made the choice to step in and help run the Yellow Bird Inn.

And when Beth made the choice to do Frannie's job, that meant that she couldn't watch the children she usually did. Which was how Deborah had come to be holding a baby.

The sweet baby was an angel for sure. Only four months old, she reminded Deborah of a doll, she was so tiny and perfect. She was a good baby, too. During the four hours she'd watched her, all little Pippa had wanted to do was be held and rocked.

Deborah figured she could do that all day long.

"Ah, Pippa," she whispered when the baby squirmed a bit and shifted closer to her chest. "You are a miracle, now, aren't you?"

Baby Pippa responded by kicking her feet a little, then curling back toward Deborah, claiming her heart.

"You better be careful, Deborah," her mother teased from the door. "You've got such a look of love and affection on your face, you're going to change your mind about children."

"That's not likely. Pippa is definitely not like most babies in the world."

One afternoon when Deborah was seven, after sitting through hours of church in a muggy barn, next to two squirming three-year-olds, Deborah had claimed that she would never have children.

Though, of course, she'd said that as a child, privately Deborah had never felt her mind would change. She'd never been one to ache for motherhood like so many of the other women in their community.

Maybe she'd feel differently when she was married and had her own house. She hoped so. But for now, she was thankful to only be watching another woman's baby for a short amount of time.

With a dreamy expression on her face, her mother spoke. "I think little Pippa here is like most babies. She reminds me of you, as a matter of fact. You were a wonderful-*gut* baby."

Deborah chuckled. "That's not what you used to say about Perry!" she teased. "You said he was a real handful."

"That's different. Perry was a boy. Besides, he was always stubborn and restless. Even before—" Her voice quavered, then with a jerk, she turned and rushed away.

Deborah sighed.

Living with Perry's memory and all of the assorted mixed-up emotions that came with it was becoming harder and harder to do. Never did her parents want to hear even the slightest criticism of his character.

Not even, it seemed, when he was a baby.

As Pippa squirmed in her arms again, Deborah found herself praying that Sheriff Kramer and his city detective friend would never uncover the truth about Perry's death.

If it simply remained a mystery, she could pretend that she didn't know more than she did. And that would be a very good thing.

Chapter 20

"Finding Perry Borntrager's body wasn't the worst thing to happen to me. Dreaming about it every single night is."

ABBY ANDERSON

When Frannie spied the pain etched in Chris Ellis's face, she rushed to his side to be of help. "Come sit down, Chris," she said gently. "I'll bring you a glass of water and a cold compress for your eye."

"He needs a steak or something for that shiner," Luke said. "But I'll take care of that in a little bit." As his gaze rested on her, he frowned. "Frannie, you should sit down, too."

There was no way she was going to have other people wait on her in her own home. "I'm perfectly fine. Beth's been waiting on me hand and foot from the moment I got home."

"No, I've been *trying* to do that," Beth corrected. "And you still aren't taking it easy. If you're not careful, I'm going to tell the doctor that you should've stayed in the hospital longer."

Ignoring Beth's jibe and Luke's watchful eye, she walked toward the kitchen. "I'll be right back with that water, Chris."

Just as she was at the sink, filling a mason jar with ice and water, she heard Luke begin his questioning.

"I'd guess you got that black eye recently?" Luke asked.

"No wonder you're a big city detective," Chris replied sarcastically. "You obviously don't miss a thing."

"Watch your mouth," Luke warned. "Just tell me what happened."

"I don't answer to you, Reynolds." A chair scraped the wood floor.

"Chris, have a care, now. Don't stand up!" Beth called out.

"Beth, I'm fine."

"Yeah, right," Luke scoffed.

Frannie grimaced. Uh-oh. It was becoming obvious that the conversation wasn't going to get much smoother. Putting aside her intention to wrap up some ice in a dishtowel for Chris's face, Frannie hurried back and attempted to ease the tension in the room.

"Luke, perhaps you could wait a bit to ask your questions? He is hurt, you know."

"I don't think so."

Fixing a glare on Luke, she took her guest's arm and guided him across the room. Of course he didn't need any help, but his expression looked so guarded, she didn't want him to think he was all alone. "Here, Chris. Please sit, wouldja?"

But to her surprise, he glanced at Beth. For the first time, his eyes turned tender.

"Please," she whispered.

"Fine." Chris sat down gingerly.

Worried, Frannie turned Beth's way. Had Chris been injured in all sorts of other places besides his face? "Do you need to go see the doctor? We could take you. I mean, Luke could."

"I don't need the doctor."

"Chris, what happened?" Luke asked, this time obviously tempering his voice.

As Chris sipped the water, Frannie felt the tension in the room rise. All of them wanted to know the truth, but it didn't seem as if Chris felt his pains were any of their business.

After draining almost half the glass, he set it down carefully on one of the coasters and then straightened up with a sigh. "I guess I'm not going to get out of telling you all my story, am I?"

"Nope," said Luke.

"We are only trying to help you, Chris," Beth added.

Chris's jaw tightened. "All right. Here's the deal. I work for the DEA."

That meant nothing to Frannie. She'd heard Luke explain the letters, but she'd already forgotten what they stood for. Warily, she met Beth's eye. Beth shrugged, too. Only Luke seemed to find the statement interesting.

"Do you have any identification?"

"It's up in my room. You're welcome to go through my papers. But do you really think I'd make that up?"

"Probably not."

"I'm sorry, but I don't remember what a DEA is," Frannie said.

"Drug Enforcement Agency," Chris explained. "I was asked to go undercover here in Crittenden County."

"You came here, looking for drugs?"

"For drug dealers." Chris exhaled. "There's a lot that's going on, but suffice it to say that Perry Borntrager's death has caused quite a disturbance in a lot of circles. We've got some informants who say he was the middleman between St. Louis and this area. When he died, the people above him on the food chain got desperate."

"So that's where you come in?" Luke prodded.

Chris nodded. "We were hoping his suppliers would be so desperate that they'd accept me fairly easily." Fingering the sunglasses in his hands, Chris added, "I even said the reason sales were slow was because there were more police in the area than usual."

Luke grimaced. "So let me guess—they picked you up to show you just how unhappy they were with you."

Chris nodded as he shifted, then winced. "Pretty much."

Gesturing around the cozy living room with the over-stuffed floral couch, Luke said, "I don't understand why you would stay here and not someplace more private."

"I thought it might be a good place to start out. Everyone knows that the Yellow Bird Inn doesn't get a lot of customers. I thought I could pretty much come and go as I wanted, unobserved." With a sardonic direction Beth's way, he said, "I thought I was pretty much under the radar, too . . . until Beth here showed up."

Across from Frannie, Beth gulped. "Me?"

Chris smiled wryly. "Yep. You asked more questions about my business than Frannie did."

"I don't know whether I should be embarrassed about that or not," Frannie said. "After Luke said I was too nosy, I decided to give my guests more privacy."

"I shouldn't have been so rude," Luke murmured. "You were fine."

Frannie gazed at Luke and felt her heart skip a beat. It seemed to her like there was much more meaning in his words than what he was saying out loud.

Oblivious to the new tension rising between her and Luke, Beth spoke again. "Now I'm embarrassed. Oh, Chris. My questioning didn't cause the men to come find you, did they?"

Right before their eyes, Chris's gaze softened. "Not at all. You reached out to me when I needed a friend. I'm grateful for that."

Frannie looked from Chris to Beth to Chris again. Beth looked like it was taking everything she had not to jump from her chair and perch at Chris's side. And Chris? Well, he truly looked ready to shield her from the worst news about his abduction.

With a heap of satisfaction, Frannie realized that her earlier suspicions had definitely been on the mark. A connection had sprung up between these two while she'd been sitting in her beige room at the hospital.

Luke looked even more alert. "What are your plans now?"

"Now that I've been beaten up?" he asked wryly. "Now I need to check out of here and report in to my supervisors in Chicago. We'll wait a few days to see if I can continue what I'm doing, or if I need to head out." He stood up with a wince. "But first I better go lie down."

Just as Frannie was about to volunteer Luke to take him to the doctor or offer some more bags of ice, Beth rushed forward. "I'll help you up the stairs."

"Thanks."

Luke stood up, too. "I'll leave my card with Frannie. I'd love to talk more with you. Maybe some of your leads could be the break in my case."

"Will do," Chris said, then turned and walked slowly upstairs with Beth by his side.

When the two of them were out of sight, Frannie turned to Luke. "Wonders never cease! Never would I have imagined I would be housing such a man. I feel like I'm in the middle of a spy novel."

Luke ran a hand through his hair. "You shouldn't be more

shocked than me. I thought I knew a lot about Perry's case but Chris just showed me I know next to nothing. I'm going to have to talk to Mose again. I thought he was keeping me informed about everything, but that obviously isn't the case."

"Maybe he didn't know about Chris and his DEA job, either?"

Staring at the empty stairway, Luke's expression darkened. "Mose knew. He must have. He knew and he decided not to tell me."

"Try not to be so upset. Maybe there's a good reason?"

Turning to her, his posture relaxed. "Yet again, I'm finding that there's more going on under the surface of Crittenden County than appears at first glance."

The small smile he sent her way made the rest of the day's aches and pains fade away to something manageable. She felt her heartbeat quicken as a new awareness passed between them.

Nothing about her and Luke made sense. But perhaps there was a reason they'd been thrown together for such a dark time?

As the silence between them grew heavy, Frannie gathered her courage and touched his hand again. "So, Luke, did you come over to make sure I was resting? "

He blinked, looking taken off guard by her question. For a moment, she felt sure he was going to turn his hand and enfold hers in his own.

But then, with a small shake of his head, he replied. "No. Actually, I came over here to speak to you."

"Oh?" Perhaps he, too, had realized that there was something special between them! If he took a chance and told her his feelings, Frannie felt sure that she could gain the courage to share her feelings, too. "Did you want to speak about anything special? We're alone now, so we have some privacy."

"Frannie, I . . . I feel a lot of the same things you do. I do care for you. But now isn't the time to talk about that."

"It can be." Oh, she couldn't believe she was being so bold!

With a look of real regret, he shook his head. "Frannie, I want to know about the sunglasses."

Once again, his voice was hard and cool. All business.

Frannie was struck dumb. She had completely misread the signals and let her dreamy nature get the best of her.

In spite of his handsomeness and the way he'd seemed to care for her in the hospital, he really was *Detective Luke Reynolds*. The police officer visiting with only one goal in mind—to catch Perry's killer.

Attempting to cover up her disappointment, she tried to play dumb. "Sunglasses?"

"The ones in the field. The sunglasses that Perry wore. The ones that have your fingerprints on them." With his voice cold and clipped, he said, "Frannie, I cannot even believe you've been keeping those sunglasses a secret."

He couldn't believe? Her temper flared. "You make it sound like I didn't tell you about them on purpose. As if I was trying to stop you from solving Perry's murder. But it wasn't like that at all."

"Then how was it?"

"I didn't mention them because I didn't think they were important." But of course that wasn't the whole truth. She hadn't told him because she'd feared they had meant something important to the investigation.

"You were wrong."

She bit her bottom lip. Didn't know what to say. Because, well, there really wasn't anything to say.

"You shouldn't have kept information from me, Frannie. It really was a mistake to do that." His look was solemn, his words laced with disappointment.

Her mouth went dry. And that was when she realized that nothing she imagined was ever going to happen between her and Luke.

Because no matter how hard she tried, everything in her life always came back to Perry.

Glad to be of help, Beth wrapped an arm around Chris's waist and helped him walk up the stairs to his room.

"You don't have to do this," he said.

"Nonsense. I'm stronger than I look. Now, come take a few more steps, if you will."

Looking weak and sore, and like he was hiding a hundred hurts, he continued. With each step he climbed, his pace had become slower and more hesitant.

After another six or seven steps, he stopped to catch his breath. "Beth, this probably isn't a good idea . . ."

"Don't make this into something it isn't. All I'm doing is helping you to your room."

He frowned at her logic, but didn't say another word. Instead, he continued his journey, taking a full five minutes to do something that usually only took a minute or two.

By the time he unlocked his door and reached his bed, the skin around his mouth had whitened with the strain. So much so, he hardly did more than bat a hand at her when she knelt down and unlaced his boots, then pulled them off.

Yet again, he tried to push her away. "I'm fine."

"Shush. Now sit still and let me help you with your boots." As she placed her hands on his boot and pulled hard, he almost smiled. "Careful. These boots are smelly. Feet are, too."

"I imagine I'll survive." She tugged off one, then with a grunt, tugged off the other steel-toed Timberland.

He gave a noise that sounded like a half-grimace, half-chuckle. "Looks like you have plenty of experience pulling off boots."

"You have no idea how squirrely four-year-olds are in the winter," she said as she carefully placed his boots in the corner of his room. "I've helped put on and take off more boots than you can ever imagine."

"That's to my benefit." He lay down with a sigh.

He looked so pained, she stepped to his side.

"Don't worry." He turned his cheek to the down pillow. "You need to get out of here, Beth. It's not right for you to be alone in here with me."

Though she'd been aware of that, she flushed, not liking his tone. It sounded as if he was talking to a silly teenager. She was definitely not that. "I'm not some innocent young girl, Chris. Just because I'm Amish, it don't mean I'm skittish."

His ice blue eyes warmed on her before flickering away. "No one would ever accuse you of being skittish. You're a brave woman."

At the moment, she felt as far away from being brave as she did from the moon. "Don't tease."

"I'm not teasing. Actually, I'm pretty darn impressed with your breaking and entering abilities. If you weren't a sweet Amish girl, why, there's no telling what kind of cop you could make."

Secretly, Beth thought the same thing. Oh, not about being a police officer, but oftentimes she, too, thought she could have done a great many things in the outside world.

If that had been her calling.

His eyes were at half-mast now. "You better go. I'm about to fall asleep. I didn't get much rest last night."

"They didn't let you sleep?"

One side of his mouth turned up. "I'm afraid not, Beth. I wasn't there as their guest."

Embarrassed by her naïveté, she straightened and moved away from him. Though she ached to ask him exactly what happened, ached to discover how hurt he truly was, she knew he would never tell her. It was none of her business.

Realizing she'd stood too long at his side simply gazing at him and wishing that things were different, she clasped her hands together. "All right, then. I'll go now and let you rest. I'll see you when you wake up. Perhaps then you would like some soup? I can keep it warm for you."

That half-smile appeared again. "Look at you, Beth. You really are turning into quite the innkeeper."

"All I'm doing is offering soup, and anyone can open up a jar. Frannie canned at least two dozen jars of chicken noodle soup this past summer. It's good, I promise, and it will be sure to make you feel better."

For a moment, something soft and sweet appeared in his eyes. Then he shook his head. "I won't be able to stay for soup, Beth."

"Pardon me?" Surely she'd heard him wrong?

With a wince, he moved and pulled himself up to a sitting position. Looked at her directly. "Beth, in a few hours, I'll be gone. The only reason I haven't left yet is because my partner wants to pick me up. There's a lot that needs to be done and I'm going to need some support."

"You're not going to stop and rest? Chris, you're hurt."

"I can't, Beth. It's important that I do my job."

She could understand that. Though it wasn't quite the same, she'd watched children even when she was tired or under the weather.

He winked. "And before you give me any advice, you should know my partner doesn't put up with much foolishness. If she doesn't think I can work by her side, she'll let me know."

Her? "Your partner? She is a girl?"

"A woman, not a girl," he replied with a wry grin. "Taylor would have my head if she heard I was referring to her as a girl."

Beth couldn't begin to understand the innuendo. "But you are hurt, Chris."

"Not too bad." He sobered. "But even if I was, it's clear that I can't stay here in Crittenden County any longer."

"Why not? Surely a day or two won't make a difference."

"It's going to make all the difference. It's not safe for me or anyone here. I got the names of the men Perry reported to, and some of the details about their base of operations. But doing so cost a lot to the investigation." His eyes turned haunted when he exhaled, then spoke again. "It's almost a certainty that my cover is blown."

"But where will you go?" At the moment, she didn't care about her safety, only about his.

And perhaps about something else, too. There was something about him that had her heart and she wasn't ready to either analyze it or to let him go. All she wanted was to enjoy his company just a little bit longer.

"I'll head on home for a little bit. Then I'll get reassigned." Lying back down, he added, "That's the usual thing that happens."

"Where is your home? I don't even know."

Instead of answering her, he merely stared at her. Silently begging her not to ask anything else.

Though she knew he was only doing what his job required of him. Though she knew he was keeping a careful distance between them, as was proper, she felt betrayed. Just yesterday, she'd thought there had been something special between them. "But Chris—"

"It's what has to happen, Beth." He paused, then said, almost grudgingly, "You had to know that there could never be anything between us. It wasn't possible."

Instead of making her feel worse—knowing he, too, had felt their curious connection—his words made her feel braver. "Where is home? You never told me."

"I know."

After a moment, she realized he wasn't going to tell her. He wasn't going to tell her more about himself, or about his past. He wasn't going to let her get to know him better.

Carefully, she gazed at him, trying to catalog every scar and mark and detail of him into her memory. "Is Chris even your real name?"

He swallowed. "Yeah. *Chris* is."

But he didn't say that his last name really was Ellis.

"I'm sorry, Beth. I know you don't understand any of this. But I promise I didn't intend to hurt you. I tried to stay away from you."

"Is that what you usually do? Stay to yourself? Stay private?"

"It's easier that way." He lay back down with a wince. And Beth knew he wasn't going to be able to continue their conversation much longer. He was in pain and exhausted.

And her questions and worry weren't helping him. If anything, she was making things worse.

But sometimes a woman's heart and brain didn't work in sync. "Chris, do you think I'll ever see you again? Do you think we'll ever talk again?" Even as she heard the whine, the desperation in her voice, she felt a true despair. She hated sounding so weak.

But even more than that, she hated feeling . . . abandoned. And at a loss of what to do.

He took a breath. Seemed to hold it. Then exhaled with another direct stare. "No."

He paused, then, seeming to have lost a battle with himself. "Listen, for what it's worth . . . you matter to me. I'm not going to lie and say I didn't feel anything for you. I do. I think you're just about the prettiest thing I've ever seen. And I admire your loyalty to your friend. But . . ."

"But I'm Amish and you're not?"

"Partly. But it's also because of who I am. I'm not a suitable boyfriend for any woman right now, no matter what her religion is or how her life is. I've come to accept it. I live my life undercover. I carry a gun . . . and I've used it, Beth. I'm not all that good of a man. I'm definitely not the kind of man you deserve."

"That's not true. Those men, they hurt you because you are trying to do something good."

"I'm trying to do a good thing in a very bad business," he corrected. "Believe me, there's a difference."

"Chris—"

He cut her off. "You take care, okay, Beth? Take care of yourself and find a decent man who will appreciate you. Find a guy who will let you be spunky and order him around a little bit."

She was so hurt, she spoke without thinking. "But . . . but I don't want that guy."

Mirth and a warmth that she'd never spied before lit his expression. "I'm really going to miss you." And then, right before her eyes, he lay back down and closed his eyes.

Effectively removing himself.

Even though she still stood there, stunned.

When she realized he wasn't going to speak to her again . . . or even look her way, she turned and walked out. Closing a door had never felt so hard.

But she didn't get very far. Only two steps. Her mind was spinning and her feet felt like lead. She stood against the wall and tried not to cry.

Tried not to care.

But when she heard Chris walk to the door and lock it, she knew that everything he said was right.

Everything that had been between them was over. Over before it had ever begun.

Chapter 21

"Perry knew about my crush from the very beginning. More than once, he threatened to tell Jacob Schrock about my foolishness. Funny, I'm still surprised he never said a word."

DEBORAH BORNTRAGER

Luke had out a tape recorder and his usual pen and tablet. His expression was solemn. And for once, he didn't look harried around her, or distracted by the pain in his leg. Or eager to trade barbs with her. Instead, he was all business when he turned on the tape recorder and faced her across the kitchen table.

"All right. Let's begin. Tell me what really happened with those sunglasses, Frannie. Tell me exactly what Perry said when he tried to give them to you. And exactly how you replied."

It was hard to imagine how one small incident could possibly change her life. Though Luke would be disappointed with her, the things that she remembered had little to do with the actual conversation about the sunglasses and more with her feelings of being betrayed by Perry.

Across from her, Luke snapped at the end of his ballpoint

pen. The spring made a little sharp click with each hammer of his thumb.

The recorder was on and Luke was waiting.

She cleared her throat. "Perry gave me the sunglasses as a gift." Going back to that day, she tried to think about the mixture of emotions she'd been feeling. It wasn't hard to remember that. She'd been anxious to get away from him. Perry had been suspicious, argumentative, and mean.

"Things between us had been rocky." She looked at Luke. "I don't exactly know why I thought they wouldn't be. For most of our lives, he and Lydia Plank had been courting."

"And you?"

"Me? Me, I'd been especially close with Micah." She shrugged. "But there had been something about Perry that was special. Maybe I liked that he felt a little dangerous?" Opening herself up a little more, she said, "To be honest, I thought I could change Perry."

"Change how?"

"I thought if he had me, I could guide him back to our ways. I thought if he loved me and if I loved him enough, he would forget about the drugs and the *Englischers*, and the outside world." She cleared her throat, fighting back the thick feeling that always came when she remembered just how naïve she'd been. "Anyway, when were in that field, he'd tried to give the sunglasses to me. He acted like the gift was something special."

He circled back to the original topic. "Tell me about the sunglasses."

"Well, Perry said a friend of his had given him two pairs, but I didn't understand why he was giving one pair to me. The glasses were expensive and men's. I felt like him handing me that pair was a true sign that I was merely an afterthought in his life."

She continued after swallowing down her disappointment. "After we talked for a little bit, and after he said he wanted to leave, both Crittenden County and our lifestyle, I was eager to put some distance between us."

"Were you afraid he was going to hurt you?"

"No."

"Sure about that?" He looked down at his notes. "You've said more than once that you had worried about his behavior . . ."

"I didn't fear him, didn't fear for my safety. But I was wary and uneasy around him. I don't know what I was feeling, if you want to know the whole truth. I was frightened of him because I didn't understand how he was acting. But I was also frightened of myself." She paused, struggling to find the right words. "You have to know how I was feeling back in December."

"How were you feeling?"

Tears of betrayal stung her eyes. She was so tired of reliving those moments, and so tired of feeling like she was failing in spite of her best intentions. "When Perry and I first started courting, I had hope, Luke," she blurted. "That is what was different. I was still hopeful that everything between Perry and me would somehow work out. That eventually we would fall in love. I couldn't imagine that he had any other path to choose. I wanted to believe that he would stop taking drugs, and stop hanging around the dangerous-looking men. I thought if he really wanted to, he would change. If he'd just had a reason."

"You wanted to be the reason." His voice was softer—soft with understanding. But now, even his understanding didn't ease her hurts.

"Yes," she said, though even saying that one word was a

painful thing. "I hoped I mattered enough to make a difference with him. But I didn't."

After a moment, he said, "Let me be sure I understand this. He wanted you to have the sunglasses . . ."

"He offered them to me, but I didn't want them." Her cheeks burned as she remembered how shocked she'd been. She held up a hand. "And before you go about asking me why yet again, I'll tell you. Those sunglasses didn't seem like a gift to me. They were a symbol of everything that he'd become and I was not. They were an afterthought, turned and twisted around in order for him to get me to do something."

Luke's head popped up, his eyes piercing. "He wanted you to leave the Amish," he said softly.

Satisfied that she had his complete attention, Frannie continued. "Yes. But the thing of it is, he knew I wouldn't have left the order."

"You'd never leave?"

"I would never leave . . . unless I knew, deep in my heart, that it was the right choice." But Perry hadn't been the right person. At the end of the day, she knew that Perry had had no idea what would have made him happy.

Softly, she added, "I didn't want to change for him, Detective. I didn't want to be the kind of woman who would change herself for a man." And though it was almost physically painful, she finished her thought. "I didn't want to be the kind of woman to change herself for a man like that."

She sighed. "I ended up throwing those sunglasses into the woods. Then I turned and ran back through the Millers' farm."

"Where did you go?"

"Home, of course. I was crying terribly." Remembering

how she'd passed Schrock's Variety through a haze of tears, she said, "I was so distraught, why I almost ran over poor Jacob Schrock."

His eyes narrowed. "What?"

"Oh, it was nothing. He was sweeping the front walk of the store when I ran by." Smiling at the memory she'd almost forgotten, she said, "He was worried about my tears. Angry at Perry for causing me pain. He even offered to walk me home, but I didn't want any company. I only wanted to be alone." Bitterly, she smiled. "And I've been alone ever since."

Her words seemed to echo in the room. They sounded sharp and bitter and sad. And maybe they were. She still had a lot of hurt inside her that she couldn't seem to come to grips with. And here she was, practically shaking with tension, she was trying so hard to keep a tight grip on herself.

And Luke was looking at her with new insight, as if he was suddenly seeing her for the first time. And maybe he was? Perhaps he was finally now seeing her for what she was. Not just an innkeeper. Not just a woman who'd dated a man for a brief amount of time.

Not just a faceless Amish woman, blending into the other women the tourists saw when they came to visit—making the mistake of imagining that all people of the Amish faith act the same way, or believe in the same exact things.

Or love the same way.

Perhaps now Luke saw her through clear eyes, and saw her for what she was. Just Frannie Eicher. No better and no worse. She was strong, but perhaps not strong enough to accomplish what was most important—to help Perry find his way back.

And because of that, no matter in how many ways she would succeed over the years, she was also a failure.

And now Luke knew it, too.

As he stared and her breathing slowed, and the lump in her throat grew, he stood up.

"Frannie, I need to go."

She stood up, too, and approached him. Figuring she no longer had anything to lose, she said, "Am I the most naïve woman in the world, Luke? Did I simply imagine Perry and I could ever be happy?" She took a breath and continued. "Did I just imagine that there was something between us as well?"

He hadn't moved. His expression was frozen, as if it was taking everything he had not to show emotion.

"I don't know about you and Perry. As for us?" He shook his head. "You didn't imagine it," he murmured. Reaching out, he clasped one of her hands. Tugged her a little closer. "There's something about you that draws me close, Frannie. Something that I can't seem to stay away from."

"Then don't stay away."

There. She'd said it. She'd put her feelings out in the open, just waiting for him to take them to his heart and hold them close.

Something dark flickered in his eyes. And to her surprise, he bent slightly and brushed his lips against hers.

Happiness coursed through her. Everything was going to work out. Somehow, someway, she was going to have Luke. No, they were going to have each other.

"Frannie, I'm a cop. I'm still investigating this murder. Even though there's something special between us, I don't think anything can ever become of it. Before long, I'll be back in Cincinnati . . . and all of this between us will just be a memory."

She didn't bother to say a word as he looked at her one last time with regret, then turned and walked out the door.

When she was alone, she lay down on the couch and cried. As usual, she'd misread the man she was interested in. Yet again, she'd begun to have feelings for a man who didn't deserve them. She'd thought that a man's smiles meant more; that his desire to visit with her meant that he liked her. She'd imagined that holding hands and exchanging flirty glances were signs of tender feelings. But she'd been wrong. To Luke, she was only a suspect. Her feelings only mattered if they gave him clues.

And now that he had gotten the whole story?

He, like Perry, was gone.

Pippa's parents had picked her up early, giving Deborah an unexpected few hours of freedom.

Well, freedom of a sort. True freedom would mean she could relax at home and read or do some needlework. Maybe work in the garden a little bit. But being home meant that she would be in her mother's company—and, like always, that was anything but relaxing.

Her mother was spiraling downward, deeper into depression. Though she tried her best to make a meal or to spend an hour or two with Deborah, more often than not she had taken to bed. Preferring the dark silence instead of the glaring reality of daylight. When she did engage with her family, her mother could only speak of one thing—darling Perry and how upset she was that everyone was saying such hateful things about him. As the days passed, her mother seemed to enjoy reinventing Perry. No longer had he been slightly lazy as a child. No, he'd always been a hard worker.

No longer had he been a picky eater or had a penchant for sneaking Hershey bars.

No, he had been perfect. He certainly hadn't had a drug problem. And he never, ever would have encouraged others to take drugs.

It didn't matter that Sheriff Kramer had proof. It didn't matter if other people came forward with stories about Perry. As far as they were concerned, people were being disrespectful because Perry had passed away and couldn't offer excuses.

And besides, no one should ever speak poorly of the dead. Especially if the dead was a beloved son.

Deborah was finding it increasingly difficult to talk about Perry with her parents. The more stories that surfaced about his behavior, the deeper they went into denial. To even attempt to correct their delusions was an invitation to punishment from her father.

And their anger about Mose and Detective Reynolds was reaching epic proportions. They firmly placed all blame on those two men's shoulders, imagining that somehow Mose should have known what Perry had been sneaking around doing. And that they should have solved the crime in a matter of hours, not days or weeks.

Deborah wasn't sure what the right answers were. But she did know that everything with Perry had been complicated. Complicated enough not to be untangled without a lot of cooperation from everyone who had been involved in Perry's life.

So she escaped. The day was lovely and the fresh air invigorating. She walked to the park, and was just about to head over to the library when she spied Lydia Plank and Walker Anderson sitting on the swings together.

Lydia spied her and smiled, then waved her over.

After a brief hesitation, Deborah joined them. The community's newest couple seemed perfect for each other in many ways . . . except for their very different lifestyles. Most folks Deborah knew were keeping their guesses about their religious differences—and their concerns about what would happen to them in the future—to themselves. At the moment, Deborah had heard that Walker was still going to the Congregational Church with his family while Lydia continued to go to church with her family.

"Welcome back," Lydia said when Deborah got closer. "Walker, you know Deborah, don't you?"

"Yep." He smiled. "I saw her in the store the other day, as a matter of fact."

The reminder of being around Jacob caused Deborah to clear her throat. "How are those puppies?"

He laughed. "Mr. Schrock has already sold two! I never would have imagined that he'd have much luck selling those dogs."

"They're really more like small horses," Deborah said.

"Perhaps that's why they're selling?"

"Who knows? At least they're penned up and cute. I don't always care for some of Mr. Schrock's ideas."

Lydia spoke up. "How are you, Deborah?" she asked kindly. "It's been quite a time since our paths have crossed. Is your family all right?"

"Yes. They are fine." But as she met Lydia's gaze, Deborah knew her lie had been caught. She flushed, knowing she was behaving like her mother. "I mean, we are doing our best." She shrugged.

"Be sure and tell your parents hello from me."

"You can tell them yourself on Sunday."

Lydia stilled. "Perhaps."

"Is something wrong?"

Lydia and Walker exchanged glances. "No, it's just that we might be pretty busy for the next few months."

Deborah raised her eyebrows but tried to keep the promise to herself of not badgering them about their relationship.

"There's a group of Amish in the next county over who are New."

"New?"

"New Order," Lydia explained, coloring slightly. "Walker and I decided to go visit with them for a few Sundays. And I'm going to attend Walker's church. And we might also visit the Mennonite one, too."

"We want to be a part of each others' lives . . . but we're having a bit of difficulty about making a decision."

Lydia bit her lip. "Meshing our faiths and interests is a difficult thing."

Resting a hand over Lydia's, Walker continued. "I want to be part of Lydia's life and world. But I'm not quite sure if I can embrace everything your order does," Walker said slowly. "I talked to my grandparents about it. They're the ones who suggested that we try out different churches."

Deborah was shocked. "Is this allowed?"

Lydia shrugged. "I don't know. No one is real happy about the idea, but after Perry . . ." Her voice drifted off. "I think there's a part of my parents that understands each person has to go on their own walk with God."

"Just because someone is different from you, it doesn't mean he or she is wrong," Deborah murmured, thinking about her parents' unyielding views for everyone but Perry.

"Exactly," Walker said. "I don't know if belonging to this 'new order' is the right step for us. Or if we should become Mennonite."

"Or if I should become more of a part of Walker's English world," Lydia murmured.

"Luckily, our families are being pretty understanding. They seem to understand that it is something we need to investigate."

"You're lucky, Lydia," Deborah blurted. Deborah could never imagine her parents ever being so open.

"My parents like Walker very much," Lydia said with a quick smile.

"I'm happy for the both of you," she said, meaning every word.

"Danke," Lydia said. "Now, where were you off to?"

"Oh, nowhere, just going out for a walk."

"You should stop by the store and see the pups," Walker said. "They're worth a long walk."

For a moment, she considered lying and telling Walker that she'd stop over soon. But she was tired of lies, and at the moment, very tired of pretending to be happier than she was. "I'm afraid Jacob doesn't want me to be there," she said lightly.

"He doesn't want you at the store?" Walker asked.

"Definitely not at the store."

"Oh, surely you misunderstood," Lydia said quickly.

Walker nodded. "Yeah. I bet you just—"

"I didn't misunderstand. He told me, Walker." She held up a hand when it looked like Walker was going to argue the point. "But that's okay with me." Of course it wasn't, but what could she say?

"Even if it's okay, I'll talk to him," Walker said. "I know Mr. and Mrs. Schrock would be really upset if they heard about this."

"Please don't tell them!"

"Oh, I won't. I just meant, I bet he didn't realize how you'd take it. Or how it would sound. I mean, no one blames you for Perry's actions, Deborah."

"Are you sure?"

"As sure as I can be. Jacob, well, he's having a really hard time. That's all."

What none of them said was that they'd all been going through a very hard time. Everyone who'd ever known Perry had been affected by his life and his death.

"I know. Like I said, I'm fine. And, goodness . . . I had better get on home. I'm sure my *mamm* will be wondering why I haven't shown up to help her with supper."

After saying goodbye, she turned and walked back toward home . . . thinking about the changes both Walker and Lydia seemed willing to make for their relationship—thinking about the note she'd removed from Perry's bedside table in order to protect Jacob.

She wondered if Jacob would still hate her if he ever found out what she'd done for him.

Chapter 22

"The first time I took Perry hunting, he was nine years old. Three hours in, he raised his rifle and shot an eight-point buck. He never wanted to hunt again—don't know why."

ABRAHAM BORNTRAGER

Mose's criticism was sharp and to the point. "Wow, Reynolds. Just when you think you can't make things worse, you do. In spades."

They were sitting in Mose's cluttered kitchen eating Trail bologna sandwiches and canned vegetable soup. "Thanks. So glad you had time to tell me what you really think."

After taking another bite of a sandwich liberally slathered with mustard, and hastily swallowing it with a gulp of chocolate milk, Mose replied with a dry look, "Can't help it. Someone had to say it. You really put your foot in it this time. I thought you would have been a bit more smooth with the women."

He didn't even attempt to temper his sarcasm. "Obviously, I'm not smooth."

"At all."

It was on the tip of Luke's tongue to argue. But he didn't

have the energy or the inclination. Mose was right. He could have handled his conversation with Frannie a dozen better ways than he had.

Though, if he were honest, he would have to admit that he didn't know if it would have ended any differently. "I know I hurt her feelings. I get that. But I had no choice. I had to ask her about the sunglasses. And she had been lying to us about her last conversation with Perry."

"That is all true," he said around a spoonful of soup. "For sure."

"Those sunglasses might be a lead. I had to know." Luke took a bite of his sandwich, wishing that he could settle down and approach things as calmly as Mose seemed to do. "Hey, what did you find out from the DEA?"

Mose stretched his arms like they were sitting at the park, watching a ball game. "Well, when I talked to Chris Ellis, you know, the man in Frannie's house from the Drug Enforcement Agency?"

"I remember him," Luke said sarcastically. "You're talking about the guy who just got the stuffing beat out of him by a mysterious group of men in a blacked-out Suburban, right? The guy you never told me was working undercover?"

Mose shifted uncomfortably. "I wasn't supposed to share the news, Luke."

"Not even with me?"

"Not even with you." After a moment, Mose shrugged. "Anyway, when I was visiting with Chris, he told me that the dealers had recently taken to needing a new signal to meet."

Everything fell into place. "You think that's what the sunglasses were?"

"Un-huh. In some places, sunglasses like those would be a dime a dozen. Here in Crittenden County? Not so much."

He cleared his throat. "I happened to look them up on the Internet, on eBay and Amazon.com. Those glasses can go for over four or five hundred dollars, Luke."

Mose said the amount like he could never have imagined such a thing, but after living in Cincinnati and not only dealing with the wealthy folks in the city but also some of the well-off drug lords in the area, five-hundred-dollar sunglasses weren't shocking. Luke had seen some at the Oakley store at Kenwood Mall priced at over a grand. "That makes sense."

"Shame that Perry wanted Frannie to have a pair, though." Mose scratched his closely trimmed beard. "What do you think Perry's motivation was? Give a gift to his girl for cheap . . . or that he wanted her to start carrying drugs for him?"

"I couldn't tell you. I never met the kid." Luke's voice hardened. "But I do know that Frannie never would have done such a thing."

"My money is on the business aspect of it," Mose said after another two bites of sandwich and a slurp of soup. "Perry might have still had feelings for Frannie, but those men he was dealing with aren't easy or flexible."

"If Chris's body is any indication, they aren't shy about using pressure, either."

After pushing his plate to the center of the table, Mose stretched out his legs. "So, we now know who Perry was working for. We know that the men who beat up Chris had been his contacts. So is our murder solved? Did one of those men who beat up our DEA officer decide Perry Borntrager wasn't worth the trouble to beat and decide just to put him out of his misery?"

Remembering Chris's bruises, Luke pursed his lips. "I'm just not sure. Perry was hit on the back of the head, then his body was hidden. I could see these guys beating him to death, then laying him out so everyone could see." Holding out a finger, he made another point. "And, Chris had been beaten up pretty good. With Perry, if they were going to prove a point, they wouldn't have only hit his head with a brick or a rock. Perry would have had a heck of a lot more bruising."

"Maybe they just wanted to kill him?"

"But if they wanted him dead right away, why not simply shoot him?"

"So if it wasn't them, who could it be?"

"Between you and me, Mose . . ."

"Yeah?"

"I still have no idea."

Mose closed his eyes. "I was afraid you would say that."

Frannie was keeping company with a pot of hot tea when Chris Ellis trudged down the stairs, looking as if his whole body was in pain.

It probably was.

"May I get you something to eat or drink before you go?" she asked when he set his duffle bag down by the door.

"You're not going to try to keep me here?"

"I've given up forcing my guests to stay where they don't want to be."

"It's not that I don't want to be here. It's nothing personal."

"I know that, Chris. Giving you something to eat before you leave is the least I can do."

"All right. I've got to wait for my ride, anyway."

She looked at him curiously. "I thought you had a car."

"I did, but I can't take it with me. By now the guys who picked me up earlier have probably marked it."

"What are you going to do with it? It isn't going to stay here, is it?" She hoped not, the last thing she wanted was to see any of those scary men lurking around the inn late at night.

"When I get picked up, another pair of officers are going to dispose of the vehicle." He placed a hand on her arm. "Please don't worry. Yet another man is going to stay here with you for the next forty-eight hours. Just to make sure you are safe."

She sighed and shook her head. "I never thought I'd have to worry about such things in Crittenden County."

"I know it's hard. Chin up, though, 'kay? You're not alone in this."

She appreciated that. "If you can promise that you won't go away, I will keep my chin up," she called over her shoulder as she led the way into the kitchen.

"I can promise that the agency will be by your side even if I won't be here."

After motioning him to a chair, she opened up her oven and pulled out a surprise for him. "Look what I've got—cinnamon rolls!"

Chris visibly blanched. "Did you make those?"

"Beth did."

"Ah."

Feeling a little awkward, but not sure why, she said, "Are you upset that these weren't made by me . . . or that Beth made them?"

"I'm not upset."

"Chin up, yes?" She said the words on purpose, hoping to create a bit of recognition in his eyes.

He exhaled deeply. "You're not going to give up, are you?"

"I'm a woman who owns my own business. I can't give up

easily. If I did, I think I would fall apart. I surely wouldn't have an inn."

"All right. You got me. I was in here when Beth made those rolls. I . . . cleaned up the kitchen for her. That's all."

"Beth is a good woman. She's my friend."

"She said you two were close."

Frannie pulled out a spatula and carefully cut out a generous portion for him.

When she put the plate in front of him, he half smiled. "These smell great."

"I think so, too. I was so thankful to have them to come home to. I don't know if you realized this, but Beth is a terrible cook. Usually."

"Believe me, I know she doesn't cook much."

Frannie looked at him encouragingly. More than ready to hear a fun story about their time together. But Chris didn't expand on his statement. Instead, he seemed intent on eating his treat as quickly as possible.

She took an exploratory bite and almost groaned. Not only were the rolls delicious, but they were better than hers.

Or maybe they just tasted better because she hadn't had to go to all the trouble to knead and roll out the dough?

"So, do you have a message you'd like me to tell Beth? If you do, I'll be glad to pass it on . . ."

"There is no message."

She was a little surprised by his harsh tone. "Okay . . ."

"Sorry. I am what I am, Frannie."

"You're a good man."

"I didn't say I wasn't. It's just that I have no place in my life for a woman like Beth."

"Like Beth?"

"Not only is she Amish, but she's sheltered. And sweet.

My life wouldn't mesh with hers. Ever." He raised his chin and met her gaze. "You know I'm right."

She knew. This man was in a terribly dangerous line of work, and seemed to live his life pretending to be other people, too. Living with such a man would be a difficult thing. A scary thing.

"You are right."

Chris looked like he was about to explain himself some more when there was a knock at the door. A hard rap. She froze.

Without hesitation, Chris pulled a gun out from the small of his back.

She gasped.

He spun to face her. "Stay here," he ordered, his expression dark and fierce. "Don't move."

He turned and walked toward the front of the house before she even had time to nod.

A cold sweat trickled down her back, matching the tears slowly running down her cheeks. She wanted to be brave, but she was afraid. Afraid for Chris and afraid for her beloved inn.

But selfishly, she was also very afraid for herself. What if the men overpowered Chris? What if they hurt him again, and then found her and hurt her, too?

Her hands were shaking now. With a grimace, she folded her arms over her chest. What she needed to do was relax and trust Chris to do his job and keep her safe.

And to trust in God, of course!

Feeling hopeful for the very first time, she walked over to the back door of the kitchen. The one that led to her little vegetable and herb garden. Though Chris had asked that she not move, surely he wouldn't mind if she stood by the door?

The moment she looked out the window that made up the top of the door, she felt her spirit lift. The sun was shining brightly. Casting a warm, optimistic glow over the whole property.

Reminding her to always have hope, because tomorrow was a brand new day—a day when anything could happen.

Closing her eyes, she said a fervent prayer. "Thank you, Lord, for giving me protection, and for helping me during each day. Thank you for giving me strength. And please be with Chris, too."

There. It was a clumsy, hasty prayer. Not the kind of prayer she liked to say at all. But what could she do?

Opening her eyes, she sighed happily. Yes, everything was surely going to be all right.

Jah. Just fine. Her heartbeat slowed and she started breathing more evenly.

Until she spied a man's face looking right back at her, on the other side of the glass.

Chapter 23

"There's no strength where there's no struggle. My Mamm taught me that."

More frightened than he'd ever been, even more scared than the first time he'd made an arrest by himself in the middle of a drug bust in a dark alley in Cincinnati, Luke prayed that Frannie was all right.

Seeing her through the window, he pounded on the door. "Frannie! Let me in!"

But she seemed frozen to her spot. Staring at him like he was a stranger, and a scary one at that.

"Frannie, it's me. Luke. Come on. I need to talk to you."

Two blinks and a mental shake later, she had refocused. With precise movements, she unlocked the door and opened it for him. "Chris is meeting with someone. He had out his gun. Did you see him?"

"Yeah. His buddies from the DEA are here. I was pulling up when they arrived. When I realized he was going to need some time to brief them, I told Chris I'd come back here to see you."

"You scared me something terrible."

"I know. I'm glad you opened the door." He smiled softly at her, hoping against hope that she'd be still so shaken up by his visit that she'd practically leap into his arms so he could comfort her again.

She didn't look like she was in a hurry do any such thing. No, right before his eyes, she began to distance herself from him.

"Why did you come over, Luke? Did you have more questions for me?"

"I suppose I deserve that. I came over to make sure you were okay." Of course, the minute he said that, he felt like the biggest fool in the world. She had a team of armed DEA agents in her front parlor, and last time he'd seen her, he'd practically called her a liar and a suspect in his case. He'd also told her that they didn't have a future.

After he'd kissed her.

And—oh yeah—she was still recovering from her surgery.

"I am fine. You may go now."

Though he tried to tamp his expression, he felt his eyes widening. No doubt showing Frannie how surprised he was. "I don't want to leave you yet. How about I stay here with you until the agents get organized? You don't want to do all of this alone."

"That is not necessary." Her voice was a little snippy. Curt. "Chris said he would protect me. One of his coworkers is going to come here so I wouldn't be alone."

Chris would? A bolt of jealousy that was completely ridiculous came out of nowhere. "I'm staying."

"No, Detective, you will not. It is not necessary." And with that, she turned her back on him and traipsed out to the front room.

Luke stayed in the back as he heard Chris greet her, then introduce the other men on his team to her. As Chris began to explain what would happen next, Luke edged into the back of the room, nodding at the other men when they took note of his appearance.

Then Frannie looked his way once more. And right in front of everyone, she said, "Detective, if you have no other questions for me, I'd appreciate it if you would be on your way. It's been a long day."

Conversation stopped. The three other men looked his way, all of them wearing expressions of varying degrees of amusement.

Yes, Frannie Eicher had effectively managed to put him in his place. With witnesses. There was nothing to do but leave, as she asked. "All right, Miss Eicher," he replied, speaking just as formally as she had. "Thank you for your time." They both knew he was saying goodbye.

Frannie nodded.

That was it.

One of the men a few feet away coughed—a not-too-subtle attempt to remind Luke to move on.

Looking neither right nor left, he walked to the door and let himself out. And noticed that the conversation resumed once he was out of the way.

Just as if Frannie had hardly noticed he was gone.

Only by thinking about bugs and snakes did Frannie keep her posture straight and her bearings tight.

Thirty minutes later, she met Jack, the man chosen to stay with her at the inn. "I'll do my best to keep you safe, ma'am," he said.

"*Danke*," she said, before turning to Chris, who was standing at the door. "You're leaving now?"

"Yep. Thanks for everything, Frannie," he said. "I am sorry about all the scares. I promise, if I could have prevented them, I would have."

"I understand. You take care, Chris. May the Lord watch you and take care of you."

Chris looked genuinely touched. "Thank you for that."

"I will pray for you, Chris."

The expression on his face—a mixture of gratitude and surprise—would have made her weep if she hadn't been able to relate to it so well. "Even if—" He stopped talking.

She knew why. Sometimes it was too hard to come to terms that an almost-stranger could care so much. She did the speaking for both of them. "Chris, I will pray for you even if I never see you again. You matter to me."

"Thank you." Carefully, he reached out and squeezed her hand for a second before dropping it. As if he was embarrassed—but why a man who was so tough would ever be embarrassed by such emotions was hard to fathom. "I won't forget you," he said. "Or Beth. Please tell her that—even though I doubt she'll care. Would you?"

She smiled slightly. "I will." Privately, Frannie knew that Beth would care very much that Chris planned to keep her in his thoughts. But it was likely that she would never confide in Frannie about that.

After he left, Jack stepped forward. "Ma'am, just tell me where you want me and I'll get out of your hair."

Frannie blinked. For a moment, she'd forgotten that the other man had been in the room, watching and observing and listening. But as she noticed the same pent-up emotion that had surrounded Chris, she rubbed her palms—still tender from the cuts—along her sides. Then got to business. "Nonsense. I just took some fresh cinnamon rolls out of the oven. Why don't you have a few?"

"Oh, I couldn't. I mean, I don't want to take advantage of your hospitality." But his eyes had lit up with anticipation.

"Sure you could, *jah?*" she said briskly, thickening her Amish accent a tiny bit. "I mean, you need to eat, so you might as well eat in my kitchen as long as you're here with me, right?"

"Right."

She turned on her heel and was gratified he followed her into the sunny kitchen. Later, after Jack had eaten not one but four cinnamon rolls and then had taken himself up to Room 3C, Frannie sat down in her favorite chair with a sigh. Oh, but she was so tired.

So, this was how it was, she realized. She was destined to be an innkeeper. A woman who excelled at taking care of others, but had little luck taking care of herself.

She seemed to pick the absolute worst sort of man to fall in love with. First there had been Perry, who she'd hoped would change, if she'd only loved him enough.

But then it had become obvious that he hadn't loved her at all.

Now, of course, she'd practically thrown herself at Luke, an English detective, no less! She'd fooled herself into thinking that he had found something pleasing about her that had nothing to do with Perry or detective work. She'd imagined that when he'd looked at her cut-up face, he'd ignore the ugliness and remember how she looked when she was at her best.

But he'd let her know that his only reason for seeing her had nothing to do with friendship or love, but everything to do with his job.

He hadn't left her bed-and-breakfast because he'd thought staying there would be complicated for a couple that was inclined to flirt a bit. No, he'd moved because he had considered her a suspect in a murder.

Frannie only hoped and prayed no one else would ever find out how silly and juvenile she'd acted around the man. If they had, she'd be the cause of gossip and rumors for years to come . . . and she would have no recourse but to realize that she deserved every sly look and whispered comment.

She was deep in thought when she spied a shadow at the door. For a split second, her heart leapt to her throat. Then she recognized the slightly slumped posture.

And the black hat that was always slightly skewed.

Her father had come to visit.

Chapter 24

"Perhaps Perry and I could have come to an agreement after a time. Perhaps I could have learned to adjust to his restlessness and Perry could have learned to like who he was."

FRANNIE EICHER

Just as the door slowly opened, Jack bounded down the stairs like an overeager Doberman. "Hold it right there!" he barked.

Her father practically jumped out of his skin.

And Frannie felt as if she was about to both laugh and cry all at the same time. "Thank you for your diligence, Jack, but this man is okay, I think. He's my father."

Jack backed down, but his expression still looked like he was ready to do harm. "All right, but remember, I need to check everyone who enters, Frannie."

"I won't forget."

Her father glared at Jack. "Who are you? Frannie's doorman?"

"I'm just a guest."

"Harrumph. More like yet another fancy detective, I'd say."

"Daed, this is Jack. He'll be staying here for a few days, to make sure everything here is safe and *gut*."

"Hard to imagine that you need such a person, Frannie."

"We can't be too careful," Jack said.

"Perhaps." To Jack's credit, he stood tall and proud as her father looked him over like he was an awkward suitor who didn't stand a chance.

Frannie looped her hand around her father's elbow and tugged. "Come on, Daed, I have cinnamon rolls fresh from the oven on the counter. Come have one."

As she'd expected, her father's interest peaked. "Any good?"

"They're terrific, the best I've ever had," Jack said.

"That's probably not saying much," her father retorted.

Frannie hid a smile as she once again led an uneasy man into her kitchen for sustenance.

This was turning into a mighty interesting day.

After serving him both a treat and a cup of coffee, she joined her father at the kitchen table and got to business.

"Why did you come over, Daed?"

"I wanted to check on you, of course."

That would make sense if he'd done that before. But he never was one to pay her visits. Well, not unless she was in the hospital, she amended to herself. "I'm feeling better."

"You still look a mess, daughter. You look tired, too. Have you been sleeping?"

Of course not. "Some."

More gently, he asked, "When do you get your stitches out and the rest of the bandages off?"

Self-consciously, she touched the bandages still covering her brow. "In a week or two. I'll look at my checkout sheet. There are follow-up appointments."

"Still can't believe one glass bowl did so much damage to ya."

Frannie knew that rather quiet comment was her father's way of worrying. "God makes everything happen for a reason," she soothed, hoping to calm his fears. "Perhaps one day I'll understand why I had to go through this."

"I've never understood why the Lord plans things like he does," he said, each word coming out slowly. Almost haltingly. "I've accepted His will, but I have to say I never understood why He took your mother so many years before me. It ain't been easy, living in that house without her."

Frannie noticed that he was disappointed about being left behind more than her mother leaving earth early. The wording hurt a little, though she'd always known in her heart that her father truly resented making due without her mother's calm nature by his side. "I guess you'll have to ask when you get to heaven," she said lightly.

Almost as soon as she said the quip, though, she wished she could take it back. That was just the type of comment her father hated. He took his faith seriously. And he took her mother's death to heart, too.

But to Frannie's surprise, he smiled slightly. "You can bet your last dollar that I'll do that. I've got quite a few questions for Saint Peter when I get to heaven."

Thinking about her father's surprising comments, she was happy to sit quietly as he contentedly ate two cinnamon rolls and leisurely sipped his cup of coffee. As always, sitting with her father brought a sense of calm to her soul. She loved him without reservation, and knew that he felt the same way. Even though she didn't always do what he wished or wanted.

And even if he didn't always say the words of love or praise that she would like to hear.

"Kind of surprised to see that *Englischer* here," he said when his plate was empty. "I would've thought you'd be ready for some peace and quiet."

Briefly, she told him about Chris and the men they were afraid would be returning.

"Do you want to come back with me, child?"

"No, I am not going to let those men drive me from my home."

He leaned back. "You're calling this place home now?"

"I think so."

Looking her over, he commented, "I had thought that city detective would have been here instead. He certainly liked visiting you in the hospital."

"Luke?"

"*Jah*, Luke. I may be old, but I got the feeling you cared for him."

She wanted to lie, but she was too worn out for more dishonesty. "I did. But that doesn't matter. I don't think he felt the same way. And besides, nothing could have ever become of us."

"Did you like him that much? To even think about a future together?"

"I did imagine that there would have been something between us. Even though it wasn't proper," she said grudgingly. There was no need for her father to know that Luke had thought about it, too . . . but had cast their chance of a future together away.

"Who said your relationship wasn't proper?"

She looked at him in surprise. "Father, we are too different."

"Are you sure about that? People change. I mean, look at you. Here you are, living with a policeman who is worried about a band of drug dealers coming to storm your house and business. If I had told you that this was in your future, you would have been mighty surprised."

With a laugh he added, "And never would I have imagined that you and I would calmly discuss it."

She couldn't argue with that. "You're right." She sighed. "I think all this was God's way of talking to me, Daed. I mean, I need to get my feet firmly on the ground and begin to look at the man who is right near me."

"Me?" He grinned. Making her giggle softly.

"No. Micah."

He scratched his graying beard. "Micah has certainly been in your life for some time. That is true."

"He's a very loyal man. And he did come see me at the hospital twice."

"Yes, for sure, he has always been around." With a sideways glance, he added, "Remember how he used to hover around you at singings?"

"I didn't know you knew about that." Frannie was surprised. Never had her parents seemed to be too aware of who she'd kept company with at those singings. Even so, she wouldn't have thought of her father having any interest in her social life at all.

"Oh, daughter. Believe me, both your mother and I were well aware of what you did back in those days." The skin around his eyes crinkled as he grinned. "And I have to say that watching young Micah hover around you like a sluggish hummingbird was a great source of amusement for many of us."

Frannie knew it wasn't very nice, but she did enjoy that analogy. "Sometimes I simply wished he would land in a chair next to me and say what was on his mind."

Her father's eyebrows rose. "Or, perhaps, fly to another woman?"

She tucked her chin. "*Jah*. Sometimes I did wish that." Even back when she was a young teenager and Micah had first shown his preference for her, she'd felt awkward around him. She'd been torn between feeling lucky that a boy had singled her out and guilty for not being able to return his feelings with more enthusiasm.

"But your feelings have changed?"

They hadn't in many ways. But did romantic feelings even matter all that much? "They have to change. I have to learn from my mistakes."

"Not liking or loving a person ain't a mistake, Frannie. God made sure that we'd all have a mate in life. If you don't feel love, then it's not meant to be."

But obviously she didn't have good judgment when it came to love. "Daed, Perry was a bad mistake. And Luke . . . Luke was a terrible dream."

"Perry was a good boy until he wasn't. It wasn't your fault you thought you could help him back to the right path."

Her father's simple statement couldn't have been more true. She had liked a lot of things about Perry until he'd embraced a whole set of new ideas and changed. "That is true. God rest his soul, he wasn't all bad. He just made bad choices and his life was taken from him before he could repent."

"Well said." He cracked his knuckles. "And as for Luke . . . I'm not so sure what to think about him."

"I didn't say he wasn't a good man. He is. But he is different than me."

"Luke is different, that is true. However, he said a lot of nice things about you, Frannie. But more important than that, I think he understood you. And he liked you for you."

He cleared his throat. "That can't be underestimated, you know."

Somehow Frannie was getting the feeling that her father felt like Luke was special because he had been willing to take her on. And she was starting to feel a little awkward, knowing that she'd shared so much with her father, the one person in her life who'd never seemed interested in sharing his feelings.

Well, at least until about an hour ago.

"Daed, I'm embarrassed that you spoke to him about me." After debating whether to complete her thought, she added, "I wish you wouldn't have said a word about me."

"I don't regret a thing."

What? "Daed—"

"Listen, child. I know how I can be perceived." He looked away, the words coming in chunks. "Sometimes my shyness, my awkward way with people . . . well, I know I can seem a little unconcerned. Distant."

"I never thought you were indifferent."

"Fact is, I admired the man for being unafraid of me."

"Luke isn't afraid of anything—" She stopped herself in the nick of time, feeling embarrassed all over again. For a moment, she'd been ready to talk about Luke in a personal way. As if he was special to her. Like she meant something to him, which of course was not the case.

Would she never learn?

Annoyed with herself, she scooted closer to her father and curved her hand around his elbow. As always, his elbow felt bony under the washed cotton. He'd always been a little on the skinny side, not thick with heavy muscles like Perry. Or fit and lean like Luke. "Daed, you need to tell me what to do."

"Child, you are too old for that. You need to decide for yourself."

She loved how only her father could speak of her as his child, but being grown up, too . . . all in one sentence. She loved his trust in her. And because of that, perversely, she ached to lean on him even more. Even though for the last year or so, all she'd been doing was reminding him that she was too old to need him.

"Please, Daed?" she asked. "You need to tell me that I'll be happy with Micah. That he's the right choice for my future."

"I can't do that. You will be the woman living by his side, Frannie."

"But it was like this with Mamm, right? Didn't you have doubts about Mamm and you?"

"You sound like you want that to be the case!"

"Well, no. But maybe . . . yes."

"I was anxious to marry your mother. I wasn't torn between two women."

His voice was so gruff and stiff, Frannie felt her cheeks flush. Put that way, her actions were shameful. She should know what was in her heart .

As he watched her sort through her confusing thoughts, her father laughed. "Oh, Frannie. You'll always make me smile, that is a fact."

"Daed—"

"The fact is, you don't need me to tell you a thing. You and God will make your choice soon enough."

"It doesn't feel like it's going to happen soon." She knew she sounded petulant, but she couldn't help herself. She was so tired of fumbling with her emotions. "I'm not very close to making up my mind, either."

"I disagree. I, for one, would guess that you've already made your choice."

"But . . ."

"I am not the detective or the sheriff, daughter. You don't need to conceal the truth with me."

She hung her head. "See how confused I am? At least tell me what you're thinking."

He stared at her hard. For a moment, she was afraid that she'd been too flighty, that he was simply going to get up and leave and wash his hands of her. But finally, he spoke. "Micah is Amish. Micah admires you. He is a good man and hard worker. He will be a good father. A good companion."

All of that was true. All of those reasons were accurate and correct. Her heart sank. Her father was leaning toward Micah, and she needed to wrap her mind around that and realize that he was exactly right. "So Micah is the one?"

Holding up a hand warning her to be quiet, her father continued. "Though Micah has many mighty fine qualities . . . I do not feel that he is the man for you, Frannie. And once more, I believe you know that."

Her heart stopped for a second, then started beating again as pure adrenaline coursed through her. "Daed? Truly?"

He nodded. "Take it from me, daughter. Mourning a spouse ain't easy. But it would be far harder if I didn't feel that my marriage to your *mamm* was one of the best things that had ever happened to me. I have mountains of memories to hold close and keep me warm on frosty nights." He paused. "Frannie, you do not want to marry a man who doesn't make you think that. And I don't believe that Micah makes you feel that way. Perhaps Luke isn't the man for you, right now, either. But one day he might be. Or, one day you will meet someone new who is your perfect fit."

While she sat, stunned by his sudden willingness to reminisce, he continued. "Don't give in just because you are anxious to be in love. You have to let things happen in their own time."

"What should I do?"

"I've said enough, child. Now it's your turn to make decisions." With a grunt, he got to his feet and stretched. "I think I'll head on home now. You have your hands full here, and I have a need for some peace and quiet."

She couldn't help but smile. "You mean you want to sit somewhere without a girl asking you to figure out her love life?"

"Oh, I didn't say that now, did I?" Tenderly, he ran a hand down her jaw. "You are not doing as poorly as you seem to think, Frannie. Believe in yourself and God will take care of the rest."

As she watched her *daed* walk out to his buggy, she realized the challenge of the last few days had taken its toll. Even though it wasn't much past eight o'clock, she walked up the stairs and knocked softly on Jack's door.

He opened immediately. "Anything wrong?"

"Not at all. I just wanted to tell you that I am going to go to sleep now. But I know it's early. There's some turkey and ham in the icebox, and fruit and other things on the counter. Please feel free to eat whatever you'd like."

"I'll do that. Thanks."

She smiled over her shoulder, then made her way to her room. She barely remembered closing and locking her door before lying down on the bed and shutting her eyes.

Chapter 25

"A good aim in life isn't enough. You have to pull the trigger."
SHERIFF MOSE KRAMER

The buzz in the police station was both grating and completely familiar.

Luke walked through the maze of desks and cubicles slowly, stopping often to shake hands and catch up on news.

"Hey, Detective Reynolds!" Teresa in records called out. "Long time, no see. How's your bum leg?"

"Better."

"Good to hear. It's been quiet without you."

As he smiled his thanks, Scotty, one of the sergeants who'd been with the CPD forever, clapped him on the back.

"So, you back for good now?"

"I don't know. I've got to go check in with the captain." He glanced at Captain Sullivan's closed door and wished he could delay the inevitable. Within the hour, Sullivan would be handing over his orders and Luke would be back in the thick of things.

His trip to Crittenden County would turn into just a memory.

Scotty turned his head to one side, looking him over like he was a suspicious dish at a potluck. "You seem different."

He felt different, too. "Must be because I've been used to just sitting around all day."

"In front of the soaps again, huh, Reynolds?" another co-worker said with a smirk.

Luke waved off the jab, as well as most of the trash talk that was happening around him as he continued his way to the captain's office. It felt good to be back. The energy in the room invigorated him, made him feel more alive, like all of his senses were now on high alert.

It struck him that while he was enjoying seeing all the guys, he really hadn't missed the frenetic grind that was the heart and soul of a big city police force.

When he got to his captain's office, he knocked once and stuck his head in.

Greg Sullivan saw him and grunted. Putting his hand over the phone's receiver, he said, "Wait outside a couple. Would you, Luke? Something just came up."

"Sure, Cap."

Luke sat down in one of the crummy plastic chairs outside the office, the ones that he and the boys had always half taken bets on, wondering who was going to finally break one. They were that rickety.

As one minute rolled into five and then ten, he let his mind drift to the last conversation with Mose.

"I need to leave," he'd said. "Now that we know the DEA is involved in the investigation, you don't need me involved as well."

"I wouldn't have called you if I didn't need you, Luke. Besides, the Feds are here to follow the drug money, not to solve Perry's murder."

"It seems to me they're linked."

Mose narrowed his eyes. "Maybe. Maybe not. But we still don't know who killed Perry."

Luke had felt that failing all the way to his toes. He'd been in Crittenden County for almost a month, and he should've been able to solve the murder by now. Lord knew, he'd handled far more crimes in Cincinnati at one time.

Self-recrimination dug deep into his gut. He should have been smarter. He should have kept his mind on his job and what was right.

He shouldn't have been so full of himself when he'd arrived, thinking that he could solve everything because he had experience in the big city.

On a personal note, he'd managed to ruin Frannie's life, too. He'd become too attached. Made her believe that they could have a relationship . . . when all the time he'd been planning on being right back here. Shoot, even if she'd been willing to leave her faith, she'd never be happy in a place like Cincinnati. Or being married to a guy who was a cop, working long hours, being frustrated, on edge, and stressed out most of the time.

But instead of being a man and putting his feelings aside, he'd given in to them and had hurt her in the process. All in all, his visit to Kentucky had been a huge mistake.

"Luke? Come on in," Captain Sullivan called out.

Luke entered and stood in front of the man he'd worked for for the past five years.

The captain looked him over with a slow smile, then waved him to a seat. "How ya doing?"

Sullivan's Irish accent was alive and well. He'd grown up in the East and hadn't completely gotten rid of either the fast clipped way New Englanders spoke or his mother's family's Irish lilt. "I'm fine, sir."

"Seen the doc yet? Has she given you clearance?"

"No. I thought I'd check in with you before I went downstairs."

"All right."

Luke braced himself, ready to be told to go down and get examined, then to hook up with his partner. But instead of giving those orders, his captain leaned back in his chair. "So, we had a real flurry of phone calls and emails regarding you last night."

"Sir?"

"A DEA agent filled us in on your moonlighting job down in Kentucky." Sullivan glanced at Luke over the wire rims of his glasses. "Real shame you didn't feel the need to call in and tell us what you were doing."

"I was on leave . . ." He rubbed his leg. "Recovering."

"That's what I thought you were doing. But it didn't sound that way, Reynolds. The agent I spoke to said you've been busy." Steepling his hands on his scratched, regulation metal desk, he said, "Care to tell me your version of it?"

The request wasn't a request at all. It was actually a direct order wrapped in congenial language. With that in mind, Luke attempted to arrange it concisely in his mind. "It all started when I got a call from Mose Kramer. He's the sheriff down in Crittenden County. We went to the police academy together. He called me up and told me about a body they'd just discovered in an abandoned well."

"Tough, huh?"

"Yes, sir." Slowly, Luke outlined the case and the roadblocks Mose had been against. He told him about interviewing kids, Perry's parents, and all those he spoke to but never came out with the complete story. Finally, he mentioned Frannie and her inn, the sunglasses, the DEA agent, Chris, and the drug connection his unit was following.

"So has this Kramer made an arrest?"

"No, sir."

The Captain frowned. "You still don't know who killed that boy, do you?"

"Most likely it had something to do with the drugs."

"But that hasn't been proven."

"No, sir," he bit out, feeling like an even worse failure.

Captain Sullivan stared hard at him, then at the papers in front of him. Sighed. "I can't believe I'm saying this, but I think you need to go on back down there."

"Sir?"

"The agent I spoke to said real good things about you. But he also talked about the community. Amish, right?" When Luke nodded, he continued. "The agent said you've done real well integrating yourself into the community. You've built trust."

"That's Mose's doing, not mine."

"Maybe. Or maybe it's your doing, too, Luke." He drummed his fingers. "This is no surprise, but the reason you're a darn good detective is that you don't give up. You inhale information like it's a cigarette and you're a nicotine addict."

Luke grinned. His captain certainly had a unique way of describing things.

The captain grinned, too. "I know, poor analogy. But you know what I mean. You've got a gift for finding the truth, Reynolds," he said, his accent turning thicker. "And for whatever reason, you were finding out more than your buddy.

You need to stay there and see this through. Both for them and for you."

"Me? But I'm fine. I don't need—"

"You don't want you to start giving up on things because they are too hard, Luke."

Luke tensed. "I've never given up on a case because it was difficult."

"Okay. Let's be honest then. I also happened to talk to Sheriff Kramer. He seemed to think you got involved with an Amish woman and you're scared and running."

He was going to kill Mose. Slowly. Feeling his neck turning red, Luke scrambled to regain his pride. "Sir—"

"And now you're back here. Hoping to put it all behind you. But you can't do that. You can't go searching for clues or love or the truth and not see it to the end." He smiled softly. "That's the thing about searching, Luke. Sometimes you don't like what you find. But you still have to deal with it."

Everything his captain said made sense. "I'm sorry. I don't know what's wrong with me."

The captain stood up and grinned broadly. "I know. You're in love. You're in love and you're running scared."

"I hope not."

"Look, you may be healed, but you still have some medical leave days available. You're still limping, too, so I don't think you're completely ready to give us a hundred percent."

Sullivan slapped his desktop lightly, the sound reverberating around the room. "Go on back to Crittenden County and go find what you've been searching for. When you find it, give me a call. We'll still be here." He frowned. "And I promise you this, we'll still have cases on file. Murder and mayhem don't stop, Luke. Not even for you."

Luke shook his hand before turning on his heel and walking out. The moment he opened the door, the constant drumming of voices slammed him hard.

This was what he'd been used to. This constant noise and pressure and energy had been his life. He'd thought it was going to be what he always loved, and what he was always going to need. But then an old friend and the haunting beauty of western Kentucky had made him realize that everything he'd always known wasn't everything that his future could be.

That new awareness had been a surprise and humbling, too. It wasn't easy for a city detective to realize he'd been naïve.

Now, as Luke heard the voices and watched the constant macho interplay, the ribald joking back and forth that came from living on the edge for twelve hours at time, he realized that it wasn't for him.

Not any longer.

There were two ways to leave the floor. Out through the main doors or down the back stairs. He'd always chosen the first. He'd enjoyed the camaraderie and conversations. Loved getting in everyone else's business as he passed them.

But instead of going that route, he turned around, opened the worn, slightly warped door that led to the back stairwell, and slid into the dimly lit passage. It seemed there was always at least one halogen bulb burnt out. The thick walls insulated him, the silence they brought felt right.

Thinking about how he'd changed while everything else had stayed the same . . . he slowly took the stairs down to the parking garage.

Less than five minutes later, he was pulling onto the highway, heading south on 71 toward Kentucky, then crossing the bridge over the Ohio River, and realizing . . . his captain had only ordered that he go find what he'd been searching for . . .

Not that he solve the case and apprehend the murderer.

Until this very moment, he'd been sure that they were one and the same thing.

Chapter 26

"I wish I had tried harder to understand my son. But that don't count for much now, does it?"

ABRAHAM BORNTRAGER

The Schrock Variety Store loomed in front of her like an imposing city skyscraper made of glass. Staring at it made Deborah sweat. She truly wished she was anywhere else in the world.

Though she'd been happy to accept Abby Anderson's invitation to run errands together, Deborah had never imagined that Schrock's Variety Store was Abby's destination.

Through the partly open doorway, she heard a few voices chattering. Children's laughter. She spied the store's vast array of merchandise. Until recently, just seeing all the bright items made her feel like an excited child in a candy store.

Now it only made her uncomfortable. Somewhere inside was Jacob Schrock. "Abby, I'll wait here while you go inside," she said. "Take your time."

Abby rolled her eyes. "I was afraid you were going to do this."

"I'm not doing anything."

"Oh yes, you are. We both know that." Grabbing her hand, Abby tugged. "Come on, Deborah. There is no way you are going to stand out here on the porch."

But just like an ornery mule, Deborah didn't want to be budged. "Abby, don't push so. I'm perfectly fine sitting on one of these rocking chairs."

"Like the old people do on Saturday afternoons?" Abby shook her head. "No way are you doing that." Lowering her voice, she said, "You've got to face him sometime, Deborah. It's not like you can avoid people you don't want to see. It's impossible to do that in Crittenden."

Abby had a point. But still, there was no need to be in a hurry to be scowled at. "I'll see him soon. Maybe at church we'll talk."

"If you're going to see each other during church services, you might as well talk to each other now." Obviously trying to hold on to her patience, Abby tugged again. "Come on, Deborah. You know as well as I do that you'll feel better after you see Jacob again. It's always the waiting and wondering that's the hardest."

"When did you get so full of wisdom?"

"Since I've been hanging around my Amish grandmother," she said with a smile. "And since I learned to . . . you know . . . like myself."

Abby's words were heartfelt and simply said. Since Deborah knew how hard it must have been for her to admit such a thing, she let herself be pulled into Schrock's.

When the door partially closed behind them, Abby darted a concerned look her way. "Okay?"

"I am fine." With a shooing motion, she presented a fake smile. "Now go do what you need to do. I'm going to look at these things here."

"Sure?"

"Positive." She smiled more brightly until Abby turned away. Then, as Abby darted down the aisles looking for her brother, Deborah hovered around the front display of garden tools.

For once, Mr. Schrock wasn't manning the front counter. She couldn't find a stray animal or snake, either. Instead, it was fairly quiet—the only voices she heard were mumbled conversations in the back near the dairy and some children giggling by a candy display.

Little by little, she relaxed. Yes, all she was going to have to do was stay in the front of the store. Out of the way. Hope and pray that the one man she wanted to avoid at all costs was working in the back storage room.

And if she was really lucky, Abby would decide that she didn't need to spend much time talking to Walker and would want to leave. Soon.

Resigned to her fate, she picked up a metal gnome and looked at it. Turned it on one side then the other. Noticed the spout was from the top of the red hat. A handle arched out from his back. The gnome's expression was of perpetual surprise, as she would be if she'd become a watering can, Deborah supposed.

Who would buy such a thing? she wondered.

And if it was purchased, what did the owner do with it? Trying out the handle, she knew she, for one, would feel terribly silly fetching water in such a thing. Though, well, it certainly did seem to be a trusty sort of object.

"See something you like?"

Jacob! Deborah almost dropped the gnome. "*Nee*." When his eye followed the length of her arm, she felt obligated to explain herself. "I was just examining this . . . ah . . ."

"Gnome?"

"Jah. This gnome."

"It's a watering can."

"*Jah*, I figured that out. It is mighty uncommon, you know."

He walked around the other side of the counter; his steps slow and slightly stilted—as though he was coming to her side against his will. "Some people collect them."

With effort, she met his gaze. "You've sold these?"

"We've sold quite a few. The gnomes with the green caps went first." To her surprise, his voice had a thread of humor in it. Just as if he, too, thought the watering cans were silly.

"Ah." She had no idea why he was being friendlier, but she was grateful for his change in attitude.

Jacob's eyes lit up. "You know how my father is. People are used to his whimsical ideas."

"Yes." She flashed a smile. "Yes, I suppose so." When he continued to stare, she cleared her throat. "I'm only in here to wait for Abby. She had to talk to Walker about something."

His face became a blank wall all over again. "Oh. Sure."

If she didn't know better, Frannie would have guessed that Jacob was disappointed by her statement.

But she did know better. Never would she forget the anger that had emanated from him at their last meeting. "We'll be gone soon." She raised her chin. "I'm sure of that."

"*Gut.*" He looked like he was ready to turn away, but for some reason he didn't. Maybe he, too, was struck by the connection that was felt between them. Even if it was a prickly, painful one.

Feeling like she had nothing else to lose, she asked the question that had been wedged between them like a pebble in a shoe. "Jacob, why do you hate me so much?"

The skin around his lips tightened. "I never said I did."

"You might not have said it, but I know you felt that way. I couldn't help but notice. Why do you hate me?"

"I don't hate you."

She was tired of pussyfooting around. "But? . . ."

He sighed. "Look, just because I don't hate you, it doesn't mean I want to think about Perry. Or everything he did to us. To all of us."

He turned away then, leaving her to stew about their conversation. And to remember once again the sweet, buttery feeling that she'd used to feel every time their paths had crossed.

To remember the way Perry had once been friends with everyone, and how hurt she'd felt when he pulled away and began his dark descent. And how much she still missed him.

Now there was no chance of patching things up between them. No chance that Perry would redirect his life and come back to their family.

When he'd changed, her life had changed, too. And quite honestly, she hadn't been all that happy about the transformations. Fact was, she'd resented Perry for making their parents worried and depressed.

For making members of the community mad.

For the guilt she felt because there hadn't been anything she could do to make things better. For making her be afraid that everything she had always taken for granted could be taken away in an instant.

And now she realized that she wasn't the only one who had felt that way. Not at all.

Quietly, she set the gnome down, then walked out the front door. Took a seat in one of the white rocking chairs that lined the front of the store.

Abby was just going to have to come look for her. Because it was evident that she couldn't be inside with Jacob for another minute.

"Frannie, it is a nice surprise to see you here," Micah said as they walked side by side to bring one of the horses into the barn. "I'd practically stopped hoping you would visit me."

"I've been here before, Micah."

"You've come with your *daed* to attend church," he corrected. "You've never come over just to visit me. I would have remembered."

As always, his kind way of speaking was interspersed by thinly veiled criticisms. "You know I don't have a lot of spare time. The inn is a busy place."

"That is true. The inn is busy. And you have no help."

She flushed. Once again it was what he didn't say that hurt. He didn't mention that she'd been injured. Or that while the inn kept her busy, the fact that she had guests at all was a blessing.

"But though I've been busy, I've also been remiss," she said, giving him what he wanted. "I'm sorry. You've been a good friend to me. Always."

The wrinkle between his brows eased. "You don't need to apologize for anything, Frannie."

Easily, Micah hopped over the fence, then turned and opened the gate for her to walk through. She blinked, realizing she was finally seeing him in his element. Here, he was easy and relaxed, far more so than when he called on her.

The land was made for him, and he was obviously meant to spend his days farming and working on it.

"Not too cold today," she murmured.

"I'm glad of it," he replied as he wrapped an arm around a horse's neck, patting her gently.

The horse stood still, seeming to enjoy his tender attentions, then with what looked like the gentlest of coaxing, Micah pulled on the horse's bridle and started walking back through the field.

"What's her name?"

"Belle." He chuckled. "It's quite a name, ain't so? I didn't name her, though." Idly running a hand down the horse's mane, he looked at Frannie. "Perhaps one day soon I'll hitch her up and take you for a ride. She's a *gut* buggy horse."

This was it. She needed to say something. Before she lost her nerve, she spoke in a rush. "Micah, I came here to tell you that I have fallen in love with Luke. That is, Detective Reynolds."

He paused for the briefest of seconds. "You mean the *Englischer*."

"*Jah*."

"Do you two even have a future together? I thought he left."

"I care for him enough to wait to see if he'll come back." Privately, she resolved to even go visit Luke in Cincinnati, if that's what it took.

"You don't want to try to make things work between us?"

"No. I don't." Frannie looked down at her feet, embarrassed because she knew no words could repair the damage that had been done. She'd hurt Micah by loving someone else.

"So you fancy the police detective now."

Stung by the bitter tone, and by the way he'd emphasized *now*, her chin popped up. "You make it sound like I've always got my eye on someone new."

"Don't you? First me, then Perry. Now the *Englischer.*"

"I'm not like that. I'm not flighty."

"I didn't call you flighty." His voice was noticeably cooler. "Only pointing out that your attentions have turned. Yet again."

As they walked through the ankle-high grass toward the barn, Belle easily clopping along by Micah's side, Frannie did her best to push her feelings to one side and concentrate on Micah's.

But it wasn't an easy thing to do, because it seemed like he had deliberately misunderstood what she was saying.

But her relationship with Luke hadn't occurred the way he was describing it, of course. Not the simple way he was describing it, anyway. Though she shouldn't have been surprised, she was still hurt by the way he was turning the tables on her. She'd known telling him that she didn't return his feelings would be difficult to do. And yet she'd still gone to his house to tell him face-to-face.

As best as she could, she grabbed hold of her pride as she watched him open the gate, guide Belle through it, then close it again.

When they started walking along the path to the barn, she forced herself to speak. "Micah, I came over here to tell you that I hope we can still be friends."

The three of them stopped at the front of the barn door. "Is that what you want now?" he asked derisively. "To be friends with me?"

All she really knew was that she wanted to end the conversation. "Can we still be friends?"

Pale eyes scanned her from top to bottom. For a split second, she saw pain appear in his gaze, followed by unwanted resignation.

Then he blinked and his face became expressionless. "Perhaps. Perhaps one day, Frannie." Squaring his shoulders, he looked at her evenly. "I will not wait for you any longer. I am done waiting."

"I understand." She was relieved, actually. She wouldn't feel so guilty if she knew he was happy with someone else.

"All right, then. I think it is best if you go now."

She felt his deflection as strongly as if he'd pushed her away. Which wasn't fair, of course. The man had his pride and he was trying hard to keep it.

She could understand that.

"Goodbye, Micah," she said softly before turning and walking the short distance to her buggy. By the time she'd untied her horse from the post, she saw that Micah was gone.

Chapter 27

"Back when we were in school, Perry would read a whole book in a day. He was a lot smarter than most gave him credit for. It's a real shame he made so many dumb choices."

BETH BYLER

Still shaken by her conversation with Micah, Frannie stopped by Beth's house on her way home. She hoped to relax for a few hours away from the inn, but Beth had asked if they could spend the time at the inn instead.

An hour later, Beth showed up with a basket of sewing projects, and Lydia Plank.

"As soon as you told me about Micah, I decided reinforcements were in order," Beth said.

"I hope you don't mind?" Lydia asked.

"Definitely not," Frannie said with a smile. "The more the merrier."

Pulling out a pretty tin from her basket, Beth said, "I've got both peanut butter and chocolate chip cookies."

Frannie winked at Lydia. "You've been baking, Beth?"

"Definitely not! My *mamm* made these this morning. Today was one of her better days."

"Praise God," Frannie said with a smile. "Those cookies look *wunderbaar*! I'll brew some coffee."

Soon she, Lydia, and Beth were sitting and eating cookies, moping and pretending to sew. Finally, Frannie looked at her two best friends and grimaced. "We're quite a sight, aren't we? All we're doing is getting fat and creating frown lines."

"Not too fat. I've only eaten three cookies," Lydia said.

"Five. You've eaten five," Beth countered.

Lydia frowned. "Truly?"

"I'm sure," Beth replied. "I know because I've only picked up a new cookie when you have."

Lydia slumped. "Next time, don't count cookies."

"Don't feel bad. I would've eaten more if you two hadn't been here," Frannie admitted.

"I ate two before I saw you both," Beth confessed. "They're good. And no matter what people say, chocolate does help make you feel better."

"I'm not about to argue with that." Frannie sewed a perfect line, then continued. "If we've been in worse moods, I'm not sure when." Afraid to talk about what was really on her mind, she said, "There has been much going on lately. Perhaps we're all exhausted."

"There has been a lot going on," Lydia said around yet another bite of cookie. "Walker and I can't seem to figure out what we are going to do with the rest of our lives . . . and my *mamm* is pressuring me to figure it out quick."

Beth rolled her eyes. "Mothers."

Frannie felt a momentary pinch in her heart—the same thing that always happened whenever she contemplated how much she missed her own mother. "At least you have a man in your life, Lydia."

"Frannie, you and I might as well admit what has us so shaken up," Beth said. "We're grumpy because we're broken-hearted over two men we shouldn't have ever thought twice about." She picked up another cookie, stared at it, and then set it back on the plate. Curving her arms about her stomach, she said, "I never should have eaten so many. Do you two feel sick?"

"Only a little," Lydia admitted.

"I don't," Frannie said. "At least, not yet." She grabbed another cookie. Maybe that's what she should be doing—eating cookies until she only thought about a squeamish stomach . . . not a broken heart. It would hurt far less.

Beth picked up a piece of lint from her fabric. "We are smart girls. We should have known better than to get involved with men we have nothing in common with. No good could have come from it. But maybe we were just tired of all the same prospects . . . Is that what happened with you, Lydia?"

"I don't think so." After a moment, she said quietly, "It just happened that one day I knew Walker was the man who could make me happy."

Lydia made love sound so easy, Frannie thought. But it wasn't easy at all. After all, Micah should have been the perfect man for her—they were part of the same community, and had many of the same values.

But instead of making her feel happy and secure, Micah had only made her feel doubtful and troubled. And sometimes . . . even annoyed!

Now, Luke, on the other hand, he did make her feel excited and happy. But he was a policeman! Furthermore, he left for Cincinnati without even telling her a final goodbye!

How could something so wrong feel so right? It made no

sense. How could falling in love be the wrong choice? She bit the inside of her cheek to distract herself from the burning ache in her chest.

"I tried to fall in love with Micah," Frannie admitted over the lump in her throat. "But I just couldn't do it."

Beth nibbled her bottom lip. Her eyes sparkled with unshed tears, and Frannie suspected she harbored a painful heartache of her own.

Diplomatically, Beth said, "Micah is a good man. That is true. But he wasn't ever the man for you."

"I know." Heaven knew she had tried hard to make it work. But it hadn't been enough. And once she met Luke, she knew it would have never been enough.

She hadn't loved Micah.

But she did love Luke—with all her aching heart.

"Only the Lord knows." Lydia shrugged. "Perhaps one day he'll see fit to tell us why."

Beth pulled the tin closer, then picked up another cookie. "It's probably best they're gone from here. I mean, it's best Chris left and that I have no way to get in touch with him ever again." She shoved the cookie into her mouth and chewed for all it was worth.

"I suppose so," Frannie reluctantly agreed. Because, well, what else could she say? Beth was right. But that didn't mean she had to like it. Where was Beth's happy ending?

Where was hers?

And here, Lydia wasn't all that happy, either.

Maybe, she reflected, happy endings didn't exist. Maybe happy endings were what you made of the pieces left behind, like some sort of crazy quilt.

She grabbed a cookie, popped the whole thing into her mouth, and let the peanut butter melt on her tongue. After a long moment, she said, "Girls, do you think one day we'll look back at all this and laugh? No doubt we'll wonder why we ate ourselves silly!"

"I'll know tonight when I have a stomach ache," Lydia said darkly.

Beth, on the other hand, didn't look as if she'd ever look back on her feelings and feel like laughing. No, at the moment, Beth looked only like she wanted to cry. "I told my *mamm* I don't understand why the Lord brought me and Chris together in the first place, if we were never meant to be."

"What did she say?"

Beth slumped. "She said she'd given up wondering why God made things happen. And then of course I felt terribly guilty for bothering her with my selfish problems."

"Maybe your *mamm* liked being bothered," Lydia ventured as she picked back up her sewing. "I've always thought your mother liked being involved in your life."

"She does. I try to protect her by telling her that I'm always fine. But sometimes we both know I'm not."

Tentatively, Frannie said, "And how do you feel when your *mamm* tries to protect you and not tell you when she's feeling poorly?"

Beth ran her finger over a row of stitches. "I do not like it much." She glanced up and gave a watery smile. "When did you become so wise, Frannie Eicher?"

She grinned and held up a cookie. "It must be the chocolate." She brushed away crumbs and said, "Sometimes it's impossible to pretend you're not upset. Sometimes, it's more important to share your feelings with friends."

She bit into the cookie. When the yummy combination of peanut butter and chocolate settled on her tongue, she smiled in bliss. "These are the best cookies ever."

"I agree," Lydia said. "They are truly *wunderbaar*."

Beth's expression lit up. "I'll tell Mamm that!"

Frannie laughed. It helped ease the hollowness in her chest. She glanced out the window and wondered where Luke was. What he was doing. Then she shook her head. She had no right to be thinking such things.

After a few moments, Beth said, "Frannie, do you think we'll ever truly know what happened with Perry?"

"We might find out, but I doubt we'll ever understand why he got mixed up with so many dangerous people." He'd become such a lost soul—looking to find his way. Only he'd looked in all the wrong places.

"I'm wondering if those men who hurt Chris had anything to do with Perry's death."

She shrugged. "Maybe." Thinking about those sunglasses, Frannie figured Chris's investigation had a lot to do with Perry. "Drug dealers in Marion." Frannie shivered. "I never thought I'd see the day. That is one bit of news I would have been happy to never know."

"I agree." Shifting, Beth wiped her hands, then picked up her needle and thread and focused her attention once again on the sheet she was mending.

Obviously hoping to lighten things up, Lydia said, "Maybe you should think about finding another man?"

Beth stuck her tongue out at Lydia.

Feeling mischievous, Frannie said, "Micah is available now."

Beth raised two hands in mock horror and smiled wide. "No, but *danke*. I'm afraid he'd drive me crazy in a week."

Frannie laughed. "Maybe not that long. You have less in common with him than I do."

Beth grinned, then little by little her smile faded. "Oh,

Frannie, I am just so sad . . . sad, and with a stomachache, too. Ach." Carefully, she clipped her thread, then neatly folded the sheet she'd been mending and put the needle and spool of white thread away. "I think I'm going to head on home now."

"But it's only two o'clock," Lydia protested.

"I'm watching a couple's children tonight."

Frannie shared a knowing look with Lydia. "You're now babysitting in the evening, too, Beth? You need some time for yourself."

"No I don't," she said quickly. "That is what I absolutely don't need. If I think too much, I'll hurt too much."

As Lydia frowned, Frannie nodded. She knew the feeling well.

Lydia stayed a little bit longer, then soon left, too. She had a date with Walker.

When she was alone again, Frannie sat in silence sewing for at least an hour, with Beth's last comment ringing in her ears. She privately felt the same way as Beth, though wasn't brave enough to admit it. At the moment, she was sad that only she and Jack were in the house. She ached for an inn full of people so she wouldn't have time to be alone with her thoughts.

She yawned, and let her eyes drift shut. Her insomnia had returned, and she hadn't been sleeping well at all lately. She supposed it was time to accept that she was now going to sleep whenever her body demanded it—even if it was in the middle of the afternoon.

She'd just drifted off into that first layer of rest when there was a pounding at the door. She sat upright with a start, but now knew enough to wait patiently for Jack to open the door first.

He came down the steps and advanced toward the front door.

She was shaking out the skirt of her dress when she noticed that Jack hadn't checked the safety of his gun. Instead, he was unlocking the door and opening it with a broad smile. Just like he was a doorman!

"How are you doing, Luke?" he asked.

Luke? Was she dreaming?

She peered around the corner. It wasn't a dream at all. Luke Reynolds stood just inside the doorway, murmuring something to Jack when he looked in her direction and paused.

It was as if all time stopped as they stared at each other, neither blinking.

Her heart forgot its pain and was now beating a rapid rhythm that sent her pulse pounding. She didn't know whether to laugh with joy at seeing him—or cry with the knowledge that she would have to say goodbye. Again.

He cleared his throat and stepped forward. "Hey, Frannie."

"Luke." She didn't even try to be formal enough to say *Detective.* Her throat had gone dry as she looked at him with foreboding. "Has . . . has something happened with the case?"

He smiled slowly. "As a matter of fact, yes."

Frannie darted a look in Jack's direction. But instead of taking out a pad of paper or peppering Luke with questions, he was grabbing his coat off the hook by the door.

"If you two don't mind, I'm going to take off for a little while, to, ah, get some air." He handed Luke a card. "Call me when you are ready to leave, and I'll come back."

Frannie stared after Jack in confusion. "Well, that was mighty strange. He's never done that before."

"I guess he thought you were in good hands?"

She caught the flirty tone in his voice and wondered at it. "So I suppose you want to talk to me alone? Want some coffee?"

"I do." He followed her to the kitchen, and sat at the table and watched her pour water into the old percolator just like it was part of their daily routine. She really hoped he couldn't see her hand shaking.

"Luke, I thought we wouldn't see each other again." She really was proud of the way she was keeping her voice even.

Looking sheepish, he said, "To tell you the truth, I wasn't planning on it."

"Yet," she said, "here you are."

"Yes. Here I am."

As she carefully measured out coffee, and wondered why he was here, he said, "Did I ever tell you about Renee?"

Her hand shook, spilling coffee grounds everywhere. "*Nee.*" She grabbed a sponge.

"Renee was a woman I was seeing off and on before I got here. We kind of had a 'thing', an understanding, between us."

She squeezed the sponge extra hard. "I see." So that was why he had returned! To tell her in person about his girlfriend. She now wanted to throw the sponge at his head. There were some things she didn't need to know.

There was a hint of humor in his voice as he said, "No . . . I don't think you do see. With Renee and me, when we were together, we got along fine. We never argued. But when we were apart, I hardly ever thought about her." He laughed softly. "I felt kind of bad about that until I realized she felt the same way."

Carefully, she wiped the coffee grounds off the counter, closed the lid, and put the percolator on the burner.

But still couldn't summon the courage to face him. Absently, she noticed that her heart had begun to ache again.

"Now you," he said softly, "on the other hand . . . I can't help but think about you."

She gripped the edges of her black apron tightly and stared at the coffeepot. "You sound like that's a bad thing."

"I was kind of disturbed about it, if you want to know the truth. And I tried to blame my thoughts of you on the case." He paused. "But it wasn't the case that had me thinking about you. It was you."

Did that even make sense? She sort of thought it did. Her lungs squeezed tight. "What did you think about? That is, when you thought about me?" Mentally, she braced herself for Luke to tell her the many reasons she wasn't right for him. All the reasons she knew she wasn't right for him.

"Us."

"You said we needed to stay apart."

"I was wrong. I was completely, utterly wrong."

She exhaled and blinked. Then, when the silence between them lengthened, Frannie found herself turning and staring at him in wonder.

His eyes were fixed on her and shining. Showing trust and happiness and a sureness. Yet, there was also a mischief lurking in their depths. That same look the boys used to have back in fifth grade when they pulled braids and ran away.

Bracing her hands on the table, she drew in a shaky breath. "Luke, what are you saying?"

His gaze didn't waver. "I'm trying to say that I've fallen in love with you, Frannie."

"You have?" Tears welled in her eyes.

"I have." Slowly, he rose, and then bent down onto one knee.

"Luke?"

"Frannie, I love you, and I hope one day you will love me, too."

Happiness coursed through her like millions of tiny white lights, illuminating her heart. This was why she'd never been able to love Micah.

This was why she'd been sad for Perry's death but not heartbroken for their parting.

She'd never felt this powerful pull of rightness toward another person.

His boyish look returned, tenfold. "Francis, are you ever going to answer me?"

"I'm trying to get my mind around what you are saying."

"It's not too hard to understand. I love you. I want to be with you for the rest of my life."

She knelt down next to him, looking at him eye to eye. "But what about your job? And my inn?" And everything else, too, she wanted to scream. She wanted to believe that love was easy, but she knew it was not. She'd learned that with Micah. Your heart didn't always do what your head needed it to.

He sighed as he swiped a tear from her cheek. "Only you would want things organized when I'm trying to tell you I love you."

"Luke," she began, then abruptly stopped talking. What was she doing? Luke was the man she wanted.

There was nothing more to say! Suddenly something she thought was so wrong felt very right. But there were still issues—problems . . .

He chuckled, showing he wasn't upset. On the contrary,

he looked rather amused. He took her hands in his. "So, I started thinking that maybe I don't have to work in the city any longer."

"What would you do?"

"I thought I'd talk to Mose. Maybe work with him, if he wants help."

After all the waiting and worrying, everything was happening so fast! "You'd do that? You'd work for Mose?"

He shrugged. "Maybe. Maybe I'll go into private practice. I inherited some money from my parents years ago, and invested it well. As long as I don't do anything too crazy, I don't need much as far as paychecks."

The idea of not worrying about an income was foreign to her. But so was what he was suggesting. "But what about us?"

"I want to date you."

"What?" She hopped up.

"You know what I mean . . . right?" He swallowed as he struggled to his feet. "I want to court you." Looking resolved, he said, "Seriously. I mean . . . I want to court you seriously."

"But I'm Amish!"

"Are you? Mose gave me some information about being Amish. He said you don't get baptized and join the church until you're ready to marry." He looked at her searchingly. "Frannie, have you joined the church already? You didn't, did you?"

She shook her head. "I've been waiting for the right time." Actually, she'd been searching for a reason to stop waiting.

"Frannie, I can't be Amish. But I don't mind a wife who embraces a lot of the ways she was brought up. I'm willing to live in your bed-and-breakfast, learn to adjust my way of life to yours."

"You'd do that?"

"I'd do just about anything for you, Frannie. I love you."

He'd said it again. Love.

She leaned closer to him. Dared to believe. "Luke, you truly love me?"

"More than you'll ever know." He drew her hands to his chest.

She felt his heart beating under her palm and wondered if it had been aching like hers had. "What if I told you that I loved you, too?"

He smiled as he tugged her closer, then linked his hands around her waist. "Then I would probably tell you that I'm the happiest man in the world right now."

She couldn't help but loop her hands around his neck. "I must warn you, I don't sleep."

"What?"

"I can't sleep at night. I worry too much."

But instead of being worried by her proclamation, he chuckled. "Frannie Eicher, you need to get married quickly. Because I happen to know that if you weren't sleeping alone, you'd sleep like a baby."

She felt her cheeks heat at that talk. But she wondered if he was right. "What should we do now? Go talk to my *daed*?"

"Frannie, you have a lot to learn," he chided as he leaned closer. "When a man says he loves a woman—and she says she loves him too—they kiss, Frannie."

Their lips were only inches apart. "And then what?"

"And then he holds her close," he murmured after a very lengthy kiss. "And then he holds her close and never lets her go."

The last coherent thing Frannie remembered thinking . . . was that Luke was full of very good ideas.

Epilogue

"Once, when the rains came, the whole community gathered at the Yoders' greenhouse. When the water got high, we all carried furniture to safety. Our clothes were soaked, two men caught pneumonia. When I got up the nerve to ask Perry where he'd been, he'd just shrugged."

JACOB SCHROCK

Luke was walking along the well line again, thinking about the case, about how sure he'd been that the sunglasses were the link to Perry's killer . . . and then how they'd only led him to a whole other investigation.

Pulling out the file he'd brought with him to the Millers' property, he reread the medical examiner's findings—about how there had been traces of meth in Perry's blood, but an overdose hadn't killed him. His death had been caused by the trauma to his head.

"Who killed you, Perry?" he asked and listened as his voice echoed across the empty field.

He wanted to do right by the kid, the kid who'd caused so much trouble to so many people. But who had also been a victim. "Who did this?"

He knew Mose was getting pressure from Perry's parents to drop the investigation. The Borntragers wanted everything to be over. They wanted to move on with their lives. They were willing to accept the idea that a drug dealer from outside the county killed Perry.

Mose hadn't said it, but Luke knew the sheriff was leaning toward that route, too. They weren't finding much, and seemed only to be hurting a lot of local people by continuing to ask questions.

Everyone seemed to be in agreement that some things were better left alone.

But that wasn't the way to do it. Flipping through the pages again, he started skimming interview notes, looking for common phrases, discrepancies that a careful reading didn't always register.

Then he saw it.

Times that didn't match up. A mixed-up alibi. An obvious lie. A person several people happened to notice walking toward the Millers' farm.

And suddenly—to Luke at least—it all made sense.

Finally, after thirty-two days in Crittenden County, the killer had been found.

Now all he had to do was figure out how to prove it.

Dear Reader,

Every so often, a particular character seems to take on a life of his or her own. In *The Search*, that person was Beth. When I began the novel, Beth's whole purpose was to call for help when Frannie got hurt. That was it. She was supposed to be a minor, secondary character who would appear in one scene, maybe two at the most.

But I guess Beth had other ideas! Before I knew it, Beth had a last name, a mother fighting a disease, a job caring for children, and had set up shop in Frannie's kitchen. Then, when Chris Ellis walked in that kitchen, a whole new storyline emerged. I really had no choice but to accept that Beth and Chris needed to be a part of the book!

Discovering a new character or storyline is what I love about writing, and especially what I love about writing these trilogies for Avon Inspire. I so appreciate that I'm given the freedom to include new characters that I hadn't planned for, and I am thankful that I'm given the chance to see where those characters take me.

I hope you've been enjoying this series, and this journey into Kentucky's Crittenden County. As I write this, I'm putting the finishing touches on *Found* and have already started thinking about a new series. I can't wait to research a new setting and develop a whole new plot and cast of characters!

But first, no letter would be complete without me offering my thanks to the many, many people who work so hard to make these books the best they can be. Thank you to my editors Cindy and Julia, to my publicist Joanne, to the art department for the beautiful covers, and to all the folks at Harper who do so much for me. I feel so blessed to work with you all.

And thank you, of course, to all of you who pick up my books and give them a try. Thank you for writing me about them, and for telling your sisters and aunts and neighbors about them, too! Thanks to all of you who've asked your librarians and local booksellers to carry my books as well. It's because of all of you that I get to write every day. And for that, I am so very grateful.

With my blessings,

Shelley Shepard Gray

Please "friend" me on Facebook, visit me at my website, or write to me at:

Shelley Shepard Gray,
10663 Loveland, Madeira Rd. #167,
Loveland, OH 45140

Questions for Discussion

1. All of the characters in *The Search* yearn not only to discover the truth about Perry's murder, but also the truth about themselves. For Frannie, it's that she couldn't really ever love Perry, but that she could love Luke. What was it about Luke that Frannie needed? What do you think would have happened to her if she hadn't met Luke?

2. How does Luke's search for the killer mirror his own search to be accepted? Who do you think was more responsible for Luke's acceptance in Crittenden County—Mose or Frannie?

3. What did you think of Frannie's relationship with her father?

4. We learn a lot more about Deborah Borntrager in *Found*, the final book in the series. Is she responsible for her brother's actions? Are any of us responsible for other

family members' choices in life? Have you ever had a family member who grew hard to love?

5.   Lydia and Walker are learning that while they love each other, sometimes love isn't enough to sustain a relationship. Do you know of anyone in your life who's had the same type of experiences?

6.   There were definite sparks between Beth and Chris, but ultimately neither was ready for a commitment. Was Chris right to leave the way he did? Or would it have been better for them to keep in touch?

7.   Frannie has a good heart, and it's shown in the hospital with her "mystery" roommate, but also in her dealings with her friends and with her father. Who do you know in your life who is a lot like Frannie?

8.   What do you think would happen to the characters in Crittenden County if Luke and Mose never solved Perry's murder? Why is closure such an important part of moving on?

9.   I focused on the verse from Philippians, *"I have learned, in whatsoever state I am, therewith to be content,"* while writing this novel. Learning to accept God's will and "to be content" is a goal of mine. Have you learned to "be content" during all times? When is it the easiest? When is it the hardest for you?

10. I thought the Amish proverb, *"Though no one can go*

back and make a brand new start, anyone can start from now and make a brand new end," was a perfect fit for Frannie and Luke. Both characters are ready to begin a new journey in their lives. What about you? Have you ever taken a chance on a new direction in your life?

Turn the page for an exciting preview of
Shelley Shepard Gray's next book,

Found

On sale September 2012

Jacob Schrock knew how to keep a secret. It was the way he had been raised.

His parents ran Schrock's Variety, which was in a lot of ways the center of their community.

Since he was his parents' only child, he'd always known he would take over the business. Even when he was small, sitting by his parents' side at the front counter, he felt a part of things. He also learned that selling merchandise to most of their friends and neighbors meant being privy to a lot of information they'd just as soon keep private.

"It's not our place to comment on purchases, Jacob," his father had told him all his life. "We offer things for them to buy, not gossip about."

By the time he was six or seven, he had taken that advice to heart. He became adept at going about his business with only half an ear to the private conversations floating around him.

Now, though, he wished he hadn't gotten so good at hiding his emotions.

"You sure you don't want to come over to our house tomorrow night?" Lydia Plank asked. "My *mamm*'s going to make popcorn and hot chocolate."

"And probably another hundred things," Frannie Eicher said. "Your mother is a wonderful-*gut* cook."

As Jacob sat, listening to his friends chatter, he felt the iron grip within which he'd held himself so tightly slowly loosen. He'd missed this. He missed this . . . normality.

He and a group of his friends—Lydia, Walker Anderson, Beth Byler, and Frannie—sitting on the store's porch, some in rockers, some on the porch railing, drinking hot apple cider, eating day-old donuts, and basically doing what people his age did when they could—gossiping about their lives.

This slice of normal life was just what he needed.

He craved it after what had happened during his last argument with Perry.

Still talking food, Lydia grinned. "My mother has a reason for making so many treats for me and my friends. She knows if everyone's there, she'll be able to know what we're doing."

"We are all over eighteen," Beth said. Looking around, she added, "Most of us are over twenty. Your *mamm* shouldn't care what we do anymore."

Frannie grabbed another donut and scoffed. "Parents always care, Beth."

"My *mamm* is interested, but she'll stay out of the way, I promise," Lydia said. "It will be fun."

"Sounds exciting," Walker Anderson said sarcastically, but not in a mean way. Just because he was English didn't mean he was stuck up like that. But he didn't hang out with them much.

Jacob considered accepting Lydia's invitation, but only for a minute. If he went, the conversation inevitably would turn to talk of Perry, of his recent exploits, his new friends, and of how Jacob's father had fired him.

Jacob definitely didn't want to go down that rabbit hole. "I don't think I can make it, but thanks for asking," he said.

Ever since his father had fired Perry Borntrager for stealing money out of the cashbox, Jacob had been feeling more and more out of sorts. Perry was angry and hurt that Jacob hadn't warned him that he was going to be let go.

And though his *daed* had been right, Jacob was mad at Perry about the thefts. It had been so uncomfortable—after all, he and Perry had been friends all their lives.

To make matters worse, everyone in the county seemed to know what had happened. And Jacob, used to keeping others' secrets, had been having a difficult time dealing with how everyone knew one of his.

Now, a few weeks later, things hadn't gotten all that much easier. Perry was lurking around the store with new *Englischers*. Sometimes even wearing fancy sunglasses—of all things—even when it was dark outside.

The two of them, once close friends, had become distant. A lot of anger pulsed between them—misplaced, on Perry's part, thought Jacob. Perry never was one to take responsibility for his actions.

And as Jacob had watched his father struggle with firing a boy he'd practically helped raise, Jacob's resentment grew—so angry that Perry had taken advantage of his family, of their friendship.

And that he'd never even apologized.

Lydia shrugged and Jacob was brought back to the present. "All right, Jacob. But if you change your mind . . ."

"If I change my mind, I'll let you know," he replied. He breathed deep, desperate to push away his dark thoughts. Desperate to concentrate on the friends he still had.

But then, another glance toward Lydia, and then over her shoulder, proved that goal was going to be impossible to achieve. "I can't believe he had the nerve to come around here."

Of course, his barely suppressed anger brought everyone else to their feet, and turning around they all saw that Perry was walking toward the store with his sister Deborah at his side.

As if any of them would want to talk to those two.

Lydia closed her eyes and sighed at the sight of her ex-boyfriend.

"You don't have to talk to him, Lydia," Jacob blurted. He knew breaking up with him had broken her heart. "We should go inside and ignore them both." In two seconds, all of them could be inside and pretend the Borntragers weren't a stone's throw away.

"You want to ignore Deborah?" Frannie asked, her tone horrified. "Jacob, we can't do that. It wouldn't be right. Deborah's never done anything wrong."

Still more concerned with Lydia who had tears in her eyes, and, selfishly, himself, he said, "I still don't want to talk to them."

But Beth—being Beth—couldn't seem to let it go. "But that don't make sense, Jacob. You can't blame Deborah for her brother's actions."

Sure he could. He'd always taken responsibility for his family and their actions. He expected the same of others. Plus, he'd watched enough families in the store to know that most family members were aware of what other people in their homes did.

There was no doubt in his mind that Deborah had known that Perry was stealing from the store. For that matter, she'd probably known all along and had been protecting Perry.

"Don't make a big deal out of nothing, Jacob," Walker said. "It's still a free country. You can't expect Perry to never walk on your store's sidewalk."

Jacob knew Walker was probably right. And when he spied Deborah casting a quick, longing glance their way, he knew Beth was probably right, too. It was wrong to shun Perry's sister for his crimes.

But just because he knew what the right thing to do was,

it didn't mean he had to do it. So instead of relaxing, he rose and stood near the door to the store. Watching and glaring. Waiting for them to walk by. In just a few minutes, they'd be gone. Then they could relax and pretend that they'd never seen Perry and Deborah.

But Frannie ruined everything. She rushed down the steps and along the sidewalk. "Hi, Deborah. Hey, uh . . . Perry."

The siblings stopped and looked at her warily.

Beside Jacob, Walker groaned. "I didn't expect Frannie to run down and greet them," he muttered.

Jacob held his breath, hating that he had no control over the situation.

He felt completely ineffectual as Frannie barreled on. "Deborah, you want to join us?"

Both siblings looked startled by the invitation. "Well, I don't know," Deborah said, looking at Perry.

Jacob gritted his teeth. He ached to tell Frannie to take back the invitation. Or to just leave with Perry and Deborah.

After a split second, Perry turned his head. Met Jacob's gaze. Jacob stared right back, daring Perry to approach him.

"Go ahead, Deb," Perry finally murmured. "I don't care."

After another pause she nodded. "Okay, then, *danke*."

Frannie hooked her arm around Deborah's elbow and guided her onto the porch. Almost immediately, Beth walked over and hugged the girl.

All the while, Perry stood off to the side. Watching. To Jacob's surprise, Walker brushed passed him, walked down the steps, and spoke to Perry for a minute or two. Then, with an annoyed shake of his head, Walker rejoined the others on the porch. More cider was poured, more snacks consumed. Their conversation was inane and forced, not a one of them glancing Perry's way.

Jacob knew they were trying to pretend everything was just fine, but Jacob thought their actions were stupid. Perry was standing right there. On his property. He'd stolen money from his parents, he'd sold drugs to other kids in their community.

He was bad news, and he was trouble and he deserved nothing. Not even to be ignored.

How could his friends look past that?

When another minute passed and Perry still stood on the sidewalk, Jacob walked down the steps. "What are you still doing here? You know you're not wanted, don't you?"

"I know. After all, you've made sure of that, Jacob." Laughing softly, he said, "I don't think I would be welcome to even buy a stick of butter in your store."

"You'd be correct."

A look of pain flashed through Perry's eyes. Surprising Jacob—and, for an instant, making him feel guilty.

Though he sensed his friends behind him were listening—and maybe didn't even completely approve of the way he was acting—Jacob didn't give up. "Nothing's changed. You need to go. I don't want you here."

Perry walked closer. Now barely a few feet separated them. Perry was at least thirty pounds heavier than Jacob, and had a good two inches on him, too. A prickly sense of fear inched up Jacob's spine.

With a hard glare, Perry said, "So is it now against the law to stand here?"

"I don't know if it's against the law or not. It don't matter, though. My father doesn't want to see you ever again," he retorted. Though his father had never said that. "I sure don't."

An expression flew across Perry's face. Perhaps it was disdain? Maybe more like disappointment?

After another second, Jacob added, "If Deborah wants to stay without you, I'll make sure she gets home safely."

Jacob waited for Perry to argue. To refuse to budge. But instead, he just shrugged and walked away, his shoulders drooping slightly.

Almost as if he had been the one with a reason to be hurt.

Again, Jacob felt guilty. Maybe he shouldn't have been so mean? Maybe there could've been a better way to remind Perry had he'd been the one to ruin their friendship, not Jacob?

His mind on that, he turned around and walked back up the steps. But when he looked at Deborah, sitting calmly there on his family's front porch . . . as if her family had done nothing wrong, his anger and frustration got the best of him again.

"Listen, I'm going to start locking up. If you all want to hang out together, that's fine. But do it someplace else."

Walker stood up to him. "Jacob, I know you've got a grudge against Perry, but you need to settle down. I don't understand why you're acting so crazy."

Walker didn't understand. None of them did. And, maybe he was acting a little crazy.

Actually, he probably was. As he grabbed a plate of the donuts and strode into the dark store, he fought to control his temper.

Prayed for guidance.

Because one thing was sure. If he didn't find a way to control his temper very soon . . . he would do something he would regret.

BOOKS BY
SHELLEY SHEPARD GRAY

THE SECRETS OF CRITTENDEN COUNTY

MISSING
978-0-06-208970-0 (paperback)
Can two young people survive the suspicions of their friends and neighbors when tragedy strikes a close-knit Amish community?

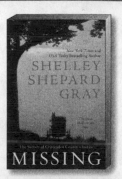

THE SEARCH
978-0-06-208972-4
(paperback)
In the midst of a murder investigation in the heart of Amish country, one young policeman finds his heart led astray.

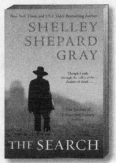

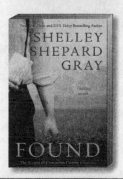

FOUND
Coming Fall 2012
978-0-06-208975-5 (paperback)
Detective Luke Reynolds discovers the identity of Perry Borntrager's killer and the Amish community must come to terms with the revelation.

FAMILIES OF HONOR

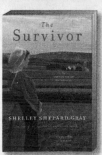

THE CAREGIVER
978-0-06-202061-1
(paperback)

THE PROTECTOR
978-0-06-202062-8
(paperback)

THE SURVIVOR
978-0-06-202063-5
(paperback)